JUN 1 7 2022

W9-DGD-674

Miss Morton
and the
English
House Party
Murder

MR DAVIN

Books by Catherine Lloyd

Kurland St. Mary Mysteries
DEATH COMES TO THE VILLAGE
DEATH COMES TO LONDON
DEATH COMES TO KURLAND HALL
DEATH COMES TO THE FAIR
DEATH COMES TO THE SCHOOL
DEATH COMES TO BATH
DEATH COMES TO THE NURSERY
DEATH COMES TO THE RECTORY

Miss Morton Mysteries
MISS MORTON AND THE ENGLISH HOUSE
PARTY MURDER

Published by Kensington Publishing Corp.

CHARLESTON COUNTY LIBRARY

Miss Morton
and the
English
House Party
Murder

CATHERINE LLOYD

KENSINGTON
PUBLISHING CORP.
www.kensingtonbooks.com

This book is a work of fiction. Names, characters, businesses, organizations, places, events, and incidents either are the product of the author's imagination or are used fictitiously. Any resemblance to actual persons, living or dead, events, or locales is entirely coincidental.

To the extent that the image or images on the cover of this book depict a person or persons, such person or persons are merely models, and are not intended to portray any character or characters featured in the book.

KENSINGTON BOOKS are published by

Kensington Publishing Corp.
119 West 40th Street
New York, NY 10018

Copyright © 2022 by Catherine Lloyd

All rights reserved. No part of this book may be reproduced in any form or by any means without the prior written consent of the Publisher, excepting brief quotes used in reviews.

All Kensington titles, imprints, and distributed lines are available at special quantity discounts for bulk purchases for sales promotion, premiums, fund-raising, educational, or institutional use. Special book excerpts or customized printings can also be created to fit specific needs. For details, write or phone the office of the Kensington Special Sales Manager: Attn. Special Sales Department. Kensington Publishing Corp., 119 West 40th Street, New York, NY 10018. Phone: 1-800-221-2647.

The K with book logo Reg. US Pat. & TM Off.

Library of Congress Card Catalogue Number: 2021953434

ISBN: 978-1-4967-2328-4

First Kensington Hardcover Edition: June 2022

ISBN: 978-1-4967-2330-7 (ebook)

10 9 8 7 6 5 4 3 2 1

Printed in the United States of America

Chapter 1

London 1837

Caroline stiffened as her aunt Lady Eleanor Greenwood cast a dismissive glance around the highly overdecorated drawing room of number eight Half Moon Street. It was well past the usual time for calling, but her aunt had never been one to worry about such niceties when she considered a person socially beneath her.

"Really, Caroline. A *rented* house? Does your employer not have the means to buy something decent for herself?"

"I'm fairly certain she does, ma'am," Caroline said. "But she hasn't decided whether she wishes to stay in London for more than just the current Season."

"And if she doesn't like it, does she intend to drag you back up north with her? I must assume she is a widow, because no husband would allow her to spend so much money on such frivolities." Aunt Eleanor shuddered, making the three tall feathers on her bonnet quiver. She had a sharp face, a pointed nose, and a pinched mouth that currently signaled her disapproval. "Where does her money come from?"

"That's hardly any of our business, ma'am." Caroline

set her jaw. "Mrs. Frogerton has been very kind to me, and—"

"But there was no need for this, Niece." Her aunt interrupted her again. "You demean yourself to accept a wage. You know I would have welcomed you back to Greenwood Hall with open arms."

Caroline curtsied. "You have been more than generous to me and my sister over the years, Aunt, but I fear becoming a burden on your kindness."

"Yet you happily allow me to house your sister."

"I will relieve you of that responsibility as soon as I am able to do so." Caroline held her aunt's derisive gaze.

"On the wages you are currently being paid? I doubt it." Aunt Eleanor sighed. "I suppose you think you might marry at some point and that your husband would be willing to take your sister in." She paused. "Although seeing as your father's unfortunate death has left both of you penniless and homeless, what kind of gentleman would agree to marry *you*?"

"I have not thought of marriage recently, ma'am." Caroline hurried to reassure her aunt. "I merely—"

"Well, I am still determined to change your mind, Niece."

Aunt Eleanor took a short promenade around the room, pausing to stare and shake her head at every garishly fashionable Egyptian object Mrs. Frogerton had hired to furnish the house. The style wasn't to Caroline's taste either, but she'd enjoyed watching Mrs. Frogerton exclaim in wonder over every item she'd ordered from her avid perusal of the furniture illustrations in *Ackermann's Repository*.

Eventually Aunt Eleanor stopped beside the inlaid marble fireplace and turned to Caroline.

"I am holding a seventeenth birthday party for your cousin Mabel next week. I expect you to attend."

"Where is the event to be held?" Caroline asked. "I'm sure I could get the evening off if it is here in London."

"No, Mabel is insisting that everyone must come to Greenwood Hall for a house party."

Caroline braced herself for her aunt's anger. "Then I am afraid I will be unable to attend."

"Don't be silly, dear. I'm sure Mrs. Frogerton won't mind."

"But *I* would mind," Caroline said. "I am employed to be by her side and to help ease her daughter Dorothy's way in society. I cannot abandon my post just as the Season is about to start."

Aunt Eleanor's smile disappeared. "You are being most disobliging." She tapped her gloved fingers against the marble mantelpiece like a mistress testing for dust. "Do you not wish to see your sister?"

Was there a threat behind Eleanor's words? Caroline wouldn't be surprised. Her aunt was more like Caroline's recently deceased father than most people realized and hated not to get her way.

"I would very much like to see Susan, but—"

Again, her aunt cut her off. "What if I invited your employer and her daughter to accompany you?"

"To . . . Greenwood Hall?"

"Yes, I assume the daughter is of a similar age to Mabel. Would it not be in her best interest to be introduced to a select few people who are also about to make their debut in society?"

"I would imagine it would." Caroline's mind worked furiously. "But I will have to consult with Mrs. Frogerton as to whether she wishes to attend."

Aunt Eleanor made a dismissive gesture. "Surely she will be honored by such an invitation. I mean, who else among the *ton* would offer her such an entrance to society?" She picked up her gloves and turned to the door. "I am leaving for Greenwood Hall tomorrow at noon. Please let me know your decision before I depart."

"Do you have the exact dates?" Caroline asked.

Her aunt opened her reticule and drew out a cream card with silver engraved writing on it.

"The details are all here. Do you have a pen?"

"Yes, of course." Caroline rushed over to the desk beneath the window, opened it, and found her aunt a serviceable quill pen and some ink. She waited for the scratch of the pen to finish and for her aunt to blot her script.

"Here you are." Aunt Eleanor held out the card.

"Thank you." Caroline cast a distracted glance at the door. "Are you quite certain that you don't wish to wait while I see if Mrs. Frogerton is awake and willing to answer for herself?"

"I do not have the time, Niece. Your uncle and I are expected at Lord Antwerp's for dinner and I have to change my gown." Eleanor swept toward the door. "I will expect to hear from you before noon tomorrow."

Caroline stared at the closed door for quite some time, her fingers clasped around the deckled edge of the invitation. The thought of seeing her sister after three months was very appealing, but she still doubted her aunt's motives. Did Eleanor think to alienate Mrs. Frogerton during the visit and persuade her to leave Caroline behind when she returned to London? It was all too likely, and her aunt would have no compunction in humiliating a social inferior. She was known to have very rigid standards.

"Who was that calling at such a late hour?"

Caroline looked up as her employer came through the door surrounded by a sea of yapping dogs. Mrs. Frogerton wore a muslin dress in a colorful print and an elaborate lace cap. Her beautiful, fringed silk shawl trailed on the carpet and was being vigorously attacked by one of the dogs.

"Shall I ring for some tea, ma'am?" Caroline inquired as she rushed over to rescue the shawl and guide her employer into her favorite seat by the fire.

"Yes, please, and then sit down and tell me about our visitor."

Mrs. Frogerton had a strong northern accent and, despite her diminutive size and soft roundness, lungs similar to a cavalry officer, making her a somewhat terrifying spectacle. But beneath her loud exterior Caroline had discovered she had a kind heart, a sense of humor, and a sharp intelligence. She always treated Caroline like a person rather than a lowly servant to be ordered around and was willing to listen to an alternate viewpoint. Her daughter, Dorothy, having grown up with a superior sense of her own worth and wealth, was far more demanding and difficult to please.

"My aunt, Lady Eleanor Greenwood, came to call," Caroline said as she took the seat opposite her employer. "She . . . invited us to attend a house party to celebrate the birthday of my cousin Mabel, who will be turning seventeen this month."

She proffered the invitation. Mrs. Frogerton snatched at it with her mittened hand and put on her spectacles.

"Oh, dear Lord above!" She flapped the card like a fan in front of her face and screeched like her parrot, Horace. "What an honor!"

"The party will be held in the countryside," Caroline reminded her. "I know you prefer to be entertained in town."

"Was this your doing, miss? Did you prevail upon your aunt to invite us?" Mrs. Frogerton looked up, her brown eyes sparkling. She often reminded Caroline of an inquisitive sparrow.

"I merely suggested that I wouldn't be able to attend if it didn't suit my employer," Caroline said.

"As if I would stop you from going out and enjoying yourself, my love." Mrs. Frogerton tutted fondly. "You're part of my family now, lass, and don't you forget it."

"Then you think you might wish to attend?" Caroline asked hopefully.

"I wouldn't miss it for the world!" Her employer pointed at the bell. "Now tell Brendan to forget the tea and bring me some sherry to celebrate."

"Celebrate what?" Dorothy Frogerton came into the room, her brow creased with annoyance. "Do you have to be so obnoxiously loud, Mother?"

"We have been invited to Lady Eleanor Greenwood's house party at Greenwood Hall in Norfolk, Dotty!"

"Why would I want to go to a stupid house party in the middle of nowhere when I'm about to have my debut in London?" Dorothy asked.

"It would be an excellent opportunity for you to meet some of the other young ladies who will be making their debuts alongside you," Caroline spoke up. "And I can assure you that my aunt's guests will be of the highest quality."

"Your aunt?" Dorothy swung around to stare at Caroline, making her acutely aware of her plain dress and severe hairstyle. "With all due respect if she can't afford to keep you from having to earn your own living, I doubt she has any standing in society."

"Don't be rude, Dot. Perhaps Caroline prefers it that way," Mrs. Frogerton intervened. "Not everyone wants to be beholden to family."

"My aunt did offer me a home, Miss Frogerton, but I refused." Caroline kept her voice steady as she replied. "I decided to make my own way in the world."

"Then you are stupid," Dorothy said flatly. "Women are not designed to care for themselves. They need a man to do that for them."

"What balderdash!" Mrs. Frogerton snorted. "Who do you think ran your grandfather's business, young lady? Who stayed behind late every night to make sure every order was perfect? Who managed the books? I can tell you that it wasn't my father. He was worse than useless, the drunken old sot."

Caroline still wasn't used to the loud and frank exchange of opinions the Frogertons favored and often wished she could hide under a chair until each storm had blown over.

"Don't talk about the business, Mother!" Dorothy

scolded. "You will ruin my chances of finding a good match if people think my money comes from trade."

"But it does, my love. I'm not ashamed of that, and neither should you be."

For once Caroline had to agree with Dorothy. Even though the young Miss Frogerton was beautiful and very well dowered, she was only one generation removed from the stink of new money, and that would influence the young gentleman who decided to consider her as a potential bride.

Brendan, the young Irish footman, appeared in the doorway with the drinks tray and hesitated as the mother and daughter faced each other like two prizefighters in a ring.

"You can set the tray down here," Caroline murmured to him. "Thank you."

"Thank you, miss."

Brendan departed with some alacrity, and for a moment Caroline wished she could join him. Surely neither of the Frogertons would notice if she went to check on the timing of dinner? Sometimes in this new and uncertain world she now inhabited she felt as if the ground were crazed ice beneath her feet.

Just as she turned toward the door, Dorothy marched over to her. "Mother said I must apologize for calling you stupid."

"Thank you," Caroline said.

"I still think you're foolish, though." Dorothy curled one of her golden ringlets around her finger and pouted. She was a remarkably pretty girl with a large fortune who should take well with the *ton*, as long as she kept her origins and opinions to herself. "But I suppose at your age, the chances of capturing a husband are fairly slim anyway."

"True," Caroline acknowledged. She had no intention of reminiscing with Dorothy about her very successful first Season, when she had attracted the attention of not only a viscount, but the son of an earl. That life was behind her now and she refused to continue to miss it.

"Although you are remarkably elegant looking with your dark hair and blue eyes." Dorothy was still talking. "Mother said I would do well to learn from you about how to comport myself properly."

"I believe that is one of the reasons she hired me," Caroline agreed, although in the last six months, Dorothy hadn't listened to a single word of advice from her. "I have lived in high society since I was born and understand the way of it."

She also knew how quickly such a society would offer you the cut direct if they deemed you or your family unacceptable. Her father's suicide and financial ruin had brought that home to her all too forcibly.

"You think it would be a good idea to go to this house party, then?" Dorothy half turned to include her mother in the conversation.

Caroline retrieved the drinks tray and brought it to the table beside Mrs. Frogerton.

"Yes, indeed. My aunt is an excellent hostess. There will be many opportunities for riding, taking the air, visiting the village, and of course, the ball to celebrate my cousin Mabel's birthday will be magnificent."

"There is to be a ball?" Dorothy immediately perked up.

"Yes, they have an excellent-sized ballroom at Greenwood Hall." Caroline remembered dancing there very well—the excitement of new partners, a new ballgown, the whisper of promise that one night—maybe that night—she would meet the man of her dreams. . . . "You could wear the dress Madame Julie delivered today."

"Or I could get a new one." Dorothy looked at her mother. "Something more suitable to wear to her ladyship's party."

"I would not worry about being too formal," Caroline hastened to say. "Balls are usually less . . . showy in the countryside, and one would not wish to stand out."

"Why ever not?" Dorothy frowned. "I would much prefer to be noticed than ignored."

Caroline turned desperately to her employer, who was listening intently, a smile lingering on her face as she regarded her daughter. She was still quite young, having married and produced her two children before the age of twenty.

"The ball gown that was just delivered will be more than adequate for your daughter's needs, ma'am, and, in truth, we do not have time for the dressmaker to sew a completely new outfit. The invitation is for the upcoming weekend."

"So it is!" Mrs. Frogerton rose to her feet and hurried over to her desk. "I must reply to it at once and get a footman to take our acceptance to Lady Eleanor immediately!"

"I will take the letter for you if you wish, ma'am," Caroline offered. "I haven't been out today, and I'm sure some of the dogs would relish an evening walk."

"I have no objection to you taking the note yourself, dearie," Mrs. Frogerton said. "As long as you eat your dinner before you go."

"Yes, of course, ma'am." Caroline curtsied and turned back to the door, leaving the two women excitedly planning for the trip ahead.

Later as she walked down Half Moon Street with four reluctant dogs trailing at her heels, she had something of a headache. Attempting to curb Dorothy's excesses without offending her or her mother took a set of skills only acquired by years of diplomacy—skills Caroline had not yet acquired, or even realized she might ever need. There was also the matter that Dorothy clearly viewed her as inferior and her lowering suspicion that even when her advice was excellent, it would still be ignored.

Caroline sighed as she mounted the steps of her aunt's town house and rang the bell. It took quite a while for the elderly butler to answer the door. His smile when he saw her was something of a balm to her fractured sensibilities.

"Good evening, Mr. Woodford."

"Lady Caroline! What a nice surprise." He held open the door. "Are you coming in, miss? Her ladyship didn't mention you would be traveling back with us."

"I'm not." Caroline indicated the dogs and proffered the sealed note. "I just came to drop this off before she leaves."

"Oh, that's a shame, miss." The butler's face fell. "We all miss you at the hall."

"I miss you, too." Caroline found a smile somewhere. "Please tell my sister that I will be attending Mabel's birthday celebrations."

"We will all look forward to that." Mr. Woodford took the letter. "Miss Susan will be thrilled."

Caroline walked down the steps and paused to look back at the house she had so recently inhabited. The windows were lit up and she could see her aunt upstairs in her bedchamber getting ready to go out. Her uncle was probably in his study reading and smoking his pipe.

If she ran back up the steps, hammered on the door, and begged her aunt to let her stay, she was fairly certain her wish would be granted, but where would that leave her? Forever trapped in a mesh of family obligation and gratitude that she might never escape, her opinions, her opportunities, her very sense of *self* gone forever.

The shock of her father's death and the ghastly reveal of his lack of fortune and mountain of debts had ripped away any sense of security and safety Caroline had ever had. Her father had even managed to get around the legal implications and plundered the funds left to her and Susan by their mother for their dowries, leaving them penniless and at the mercy of their relatives.

Her aunt expected eternal gratitude for her benevolence, but all Caroline had left was a slow-burning anger that seemed impossible to extinguish. She bent to untangle the dogs' leads and turned her back on the house. She had lost everything and everyone she cared for except Susan, and she would do anything in her power to make certain that her sister never suffered a similar fate.

Just before she turned the corner of the square a carriage arrived at the door. She paused to watch her aunt and uncle leave for their dinner with Lord Antwerp, a man whose eldest son had once courted her rather assiduously. If he saw her now in her drab plain cloak, gray gown, and respectable bonnet, he wouldn't even acknowledge her existence. She increasingly felt that the girl she had once been was disappearing in front of her and being replaced by— what?

That was the question she was still unable to answer even to herself. She started walking again as the carriage with its oblivious occupants swept past her. All she knew was that the forgiveness that she was supposed to feel for those who had wronged her was far from occurring and that the only thing sustaining her through her current existence was that cold, hard store of pride buried deep in her soul.

She relished it, she fed it, and until something happened to show her that the world was not the unforgiving place it had turned out to be, she would bank those fires within her without shame.

Chapter 2

"Well, I never!" Mrs. Frogerton exclaimed as their rented carriage drew up at the entrance to Greenwood Hall. "What a very grand residence!"

Caroline had spent so much time at Greenwood Hall after her mother's death and her father's attempts to foist his two children off on various relatives that she almost considered the place home. Seeing it through the eyes of the Frogerton ladies was both entertaining and instructional.

The flint-fronted house was set on a level plain between several water channels both natural and man-made in a landscape that contained few trees and no visible hills. The immense gray sky hugged the low scrubby marshland where a constant breeze blew in off the cold North Sea to surround and enfold the house.

"It's huge," Dorothy whispered, for once more silent than her mother.

"The original house was built in Tudor times and the two additional brick wings were added about a hundred years ago," Caroline explained as she waited for a footman to emerge from the house, open the door, and let the step down. "My aunt often laments the complexities of the layout, but my uncle will not hear of changing it. His family have lived here since the civil war."

"When was that?" Dorothy asked.

"The sixteen hundreds, I believe." Caroline rolled down the window and stared inquiringly at the still-closed door. "It is most unlike my aunt's staff to be so tardy."

She reached down and released the exterior door handle of the carriage herself. "Perhaps they have been overwhelmed by too many guests arriving at the same time."

She raised the massive brass knocker shaped like a stag that adorned the oak-studded front door and knocked twice before she detected the sound of approaching footsteps. One of the maids opened the door and stood there panting.

"Oh! It's you, miss. I thought it was someone important."

"Good afternoon, Peggy." Caroline concealed a smile and indicated the occupants of the carriage behind her. "Can you get one of the footmen to bring in Mrs. Frogerton's baggage? And where is Mr. Woodford?"

"He's rather busy, miss, what with the party guests arriving, and her ladyship not having come down yet, and two of the footmen being ill . . ."

"Then we will just have to manage by ourselves, won't we?" Caroline offered the girl a bright smile. "Do you know which rooms have been allocated for Mrs. Frogerton and her daughter?"

"Oh, yes, miss. I cleaned out the grates and put some nice fresh flowers in them this morning." Peggy lowered her voice. "Her ladyship wasn't sure if your lady had a maid or not, and told me I should be ready to step in if necessary."

"Excellent." Caroline turned back to the carriage where Dorothy was already beginning to pout. "Do you need help, Miss Frogerton, or shall I just aid your mother?"

Dorothy emerged with a frown and straightened her bonnet. "I knew this was a mistake."

Caroline helped Mrs. Frogerton descend from the carriage and supported her into the house.

"This is Peggy. She will accompany us to your rooms."

Mrs. Frogerton beamed at the maid. "You're a pretty lass, indeed."

"Thank you, ma'am." Peggy bobbed a curtsy. "Please follow me."

Both Dorothy and her mother paused as they entered the marble entrance hall with the six alcoves containing stone statuary, three on either side of the wide curving staircase that led up to a wide landing.

"Ooh, it's grand," Mrs. Frogerton said approvingly. "Like a palace."

"My aunt and uncle will be delighted to hear that you think so, ma'am." Caroline walked her employer toward the stairs. "Lord Greenwood spent some of his youth traveling the world on his grand tour and brought back many treasures to the family home."

Dorothy was looking up, her mouth open at the interior of the dome that was painted to resemble the Sistine Chapel. She didn't say anything but even Caroline could see she was impressed.

"Her ladyship put Miss Frogerton right next door to Mrs. Frogerton with a connecting door between them," Peggy announced as they reached the landing and she turned to the left.

Caroline was slightly relieved to see that her aunt hadn't relegated her unwanted guests to the attics and had instead given them a perfectly respectable set of rooms on the first floor.

"Here you are, ma'am." Peggy opened the door with a flourish and stepped aside. "Her ladyship calls this the Lilac Suite although it looks more blue to me." She pointed at the interior door. "Miss Frogerton's room is right next door."

"Thank you, Peggy." Caroline did a quick survey of the brightly appointed room and could see nothing to fault.

There was already a fire lit in the grate warming the lofty dimensions of the elaborate plaster ceiling and delicate silk-covered walls.

"Would you like me to stay and help you settle in, ma'am?" Peggy asked Mrs. Frogerton.

"I will help Mrs. Frogerton," Caroline said with a smile. "But perhaps you might bring up a pot of tea? I assume dinner will not be served for at least another two hours."

"Yes, miss. Lady Eleanor likes her guests to assemble in the drawing room at six o'clock."

Caroline waited until Peggy had gone before walking through the dressing room that linked the two rooms and into Dorothy's.

"You have a nice view over the park at the rear of the house, Miss Frogerton." Caroline walked over to the large sash windows and rearranged the thick damask curtains. "When Peggy comes back with the tea, I will send her in to unpack for you."

"Thank you." For once Dorothy forgot to be condescending as she wandered around the room touching the drapery and furniture, her fingers testing the strength and richness of the fabric. "I must confess that I did not expect you to have such grand relatives."

"Life is full of surprises, is it not?" Caroline said lightly. "Perhaps that is why one should try not to judge a book by its cover."

She returned to Mrs. Frogerton, who had already established herself in a chair by the fire and was loudly lamenting the absence of her dogs. A knock on the door heralded Peggy with the tea tray.

After pouring the tea and consulting with Peggy about unpacking for both ladies, Caroline turned to her employer.

"Ma'am, would you be so good as to excuse me for an hour? My sister lives here with my aunt, and I would very much like to go and see her."

"Off you go then, my dear, and take your time." Mrs.

Frogerton waved her off. "I'll drink my tea, take a little nap, and be perfectly refreshed in time for dinner."

Peggy winked at Caroline. "I'll keep an eye on her, miss, don't you worry. Miss Susan is dying to see you again. She's been excited all day!"

The moment she left the room, Caroline picked up her skirts and hurried up the two flights of stairs that would take her to the extensive nursery suite just below the attics. She opened the door quietly and was able to observe the tranquil scene in front of her without being noticed.

Lady Eleanor had always been a gatherer of waifs and strays, having a firm Christian belief that charity begins at home. When Caroline's father had been widowed at Susan's birth, Eleanor had taken in her brother's children without complaint and brought them up with her own. They had lived sporadically with their father up until the time of his death, but it had not been a secure existence. At one point Caroline had written a desperate letter to her aunt after her father had left them at an inn somewhere near Calais and failed to return and collect them.

Despite her currently strained relationship with Eleanor, Caroline reminded herself she had a lot to be grateful for. She returned her attention to the game of building blocks that was currently engaging all the occupants of the nursery, whose ages ranged from around five to sixteen. Her sister, Susan, was right in the middle of the group, her expression intent as she watched a young boy place another wooden piece on the already swaying pile.

It collapsed with a satisfying crash and all the children cheered.

"Well done, William!" Susan called out. "That was the highest we have ever managed to go."

A low chuckle behind her made Caroline turn to see her aunt's youngest son, George, had also arrived in time to watch the fun. He wore a conservatively cut coat paired with a brown waistcoat and a rather high shirt collar that made it difficult for him to turn his head.

"George." She smiled up at him.

"Caroline! I was looking for Harry and Mabel. Did you know Mabel insisted Mother invite all her favorite 'waifs and strays' back for her birthday party?"

"I didn't, but it sounds like a very Mabel-like thing to do."

"Mabel was always the heart of the family," George said, and looked over at the children who were busy hunting for the fallen blocks under the watchful eye of Mrs. Whittle and the nursemaids. "She said it wouldn't feel like the celebration was complete unless everyone whom she cared about was here."

"And your mother agreed?"

Her aunt's decision to invite the Frogertons made a lot more sense now. She probably classed them just above Mabel's undesirables.

"I think she is so delighted to be delivering her last daughter into society that she would've done anything if it persuaded Mabel to engage in the process." George chuckled heartily. "And Mabel has always been able to wind Father around her little finger, so he went along with it too."

"How is Cambridge?" Caroline asked.

"Awful." He grimaced. "Don't tell Mother, but the only reason I was able to attend the party was because I've been sent down." He smirked. "She'll never make a vicar of me."

"She'll certainly keep trying unless you come up with an alternative occupation for yourself," Caroline said.

In her opinion, George, who was remarkably easygoing and rather indolent, would crumble into dust if his mother threatened to withdraw his generous allowance. He fancied himself as a man about town but had neither the finances nor the expectations to support himself. He would either need to marry well or accept his lot and become the family vicar.

Even as she considered his prospects, Caroline chided herself for her harsh perspective of his character and future. Was she envious that whatever he did he would still

18 *Catherine Lloyd*

live a generous and full life? George had always been kind to her and was a good soul at heart. Had her current situation turned her into an unfeeling shrew?

"It is good to see you, Coz." George beamed at her. "Mother says you've found employment with a rich northern widow. You should introduce me to her."

"You'd be better off meeting her only daughter, Miss Dorothy Frogerton, who is about to enter the marriage mart," Caroline answered. "She is . . . quite an original."

George frowned and lowered his voice. "Does she know how to comport herself in good society?"

"You will be able to find out for yourself this evening, George, as both she and her mother were invited here to celebrate Mabel's birthday."

"They're here?" George's eyebrows shot up. "I must say that I am somewhat surprised as Mother has frequently expressed the opinion that they are not worthy of your service."

"She has mentioned that," Caroline said. "Is Nick attending the party?"

Her uncle's eldest son and heir rarely bothered to come home, preferring to spend his time carousing and gambling in London with his favorite cronies.

"He said he'd be here, but you know Nick. He's not reliable at all. He and Father are arguing over his 'feckless and rakish ways,' which is rich coming from a man who had a somewhat spotty reputation with the female sex in his past." He paused. "Don't mention that in front of Mother, obviously." George's attention wandered as he looked past her and smiled. "And now I must allow your sister to monopolize your attention. I will see you at dinner."

Susan flung herself into Caroline's arms.

"Peggy said you were here, but I didn't quite believe her!"

Caroline looked down at the smiling face of her much younger sister, who with her blond hair and brown eyes greatly resembled their deceased mother, Jane, and hugged her hard.

"I am here, in the flesh so to speak, and I am delighted to see you again." She took her sister's hand and drew her away to the quieter end of the nursery. "Have you been well?"

She sat on one of the low chairs and Susan joined her. At sixteen, her sister was almost ten years her junior and had been a surprise to their parents, who barely spent enough time together to produce a child. There had been rumors that her mother had been unfaithful, but nothing was proven. Her father hadn't cared either way and had only complained about paying for his own children's upkeep.

"Yes, indeed, Sister. Aunt Eleanor has been allowing me to help with the younger children. She says I have the necessary energy and enthusiasm to become a governess if I wish."

Even as she smiled politely Caroline promised herself that by the time Susan came of age, she would not have to do any such thing.

"You certainly have enough patience." Caroline lowered her voice. "How have things really been? Has my aunt expressed any annoyance with you about my decision to take employment outside her house?"

Susan's smile faded. "I think she was expecting you to stay and look after the remaining children for her. She finds it difficult to deal with them these days and gets quite angry when they do not listen to her."

"I thought as much, which is why she is grooming you to take on the position, probably with no pay or future prospects." Caroline shook her head. "That is exactly why I chose not to stay."

"Aunt Eleanor has been very kind to us, Sister."

Caroline couldn't miss the note of apprehension in Susan's voice. With the uncertainties of their childhood, she had to forgive Susan for never feeling safe in any environment. Unlike Caroline, Susan had always craved security and Greenwood Hall had been her primary home since birth.

"I was surprised that Mabel decided to have a birthday party here." Caroline changed the subject and was relieved to see her sister's expression brighten. "She has never struck me as someone who wishes to draw attention to herself in such a manner."

"She only agreed when Aunt Eleanor said she could invite whomsoever she wished." Susan smiled. "And you know Mabel. She corresponds with everyone who has ever set foot in this house let alone lived in the nursery for any period of time. She said that if she had to have a party then she would make it as memorable and personal as she could manage."

"Good for her," Caroline said as the nursery clock chimed the hour and one of the nursemaids started gathering her charges. "Will you be coming down to dinner this evening?"

"No, I promised Mabel I'd take her place and read everyone a bedtime story." Susan stood up. "It might take some time."

Caroline's amused gaze went to the other end of the nursery where she counted at least six heads. "So I see. If you have time, please present yourself in the drawing room after everyone is satisfactorily asleep so that I can introduce you to my employer."

"Mrs. Frogerton is here as well?" Susan asked as they walked toward the lively group. "I wasn't sure I believed Peggy when she told me that, either."

"Mrs. Frogerton is here with her daughter, Dorothy," Caroline said. "And now I need to go and seek out our aunt. I was surprised that she wasn't downstairs greeting her guests earlier. It is most unlike her."

"She had a headache this morning. She might still be in bed." Susan grimaced. "She hasn't been at all well recently."

Caroline didn't disagree even though her aunt had looked

perfectly healthy when she'd appeared in Half Moon Street less than a week ago to command Caroline's presence at the party.

"Then I will go and see if she has recovered enough to have visitors." Caroline turned toward the door. "And don't forget to come and find me later this evening."

"I won't." Susan's attention was already on the children who were assembling at the table for their afternoon glass of milk. "I must go. Hetty isn't very good at getting the little ones to drink up."

Caroline let herself out of the nursery and went down a flight of back stairs. She wasn't sure if it was because she'd become used to everything being brand-new in Mrs. Frogerton's house, but Greenwood Hall looked drab and in dire need of decorating. The wallpaper was peeling, the skirting boards were scuffed, and most of the drapery needed a good dusting. The yellowish light coming in off the fens and waterways through the salt-encrusted windows didn't help much either.

She emerged on the landing opposite her uncle and aunt's suite of rooms. Even as she approached the door, she detected the sound of raised voices, which made her pause. After the shouting ended, she counted to one hundred and knocked.

"Come in?"

She went in to find her aunt sitting in a chair beside the fire by herself. There was no sign of the person Eleanor had been arguing with although Caroline assumed it was her uncle. Their marriage had always been one of duty and convenience rather than love and they were both rather stubborn. The curtains were half drawn against the light and Eleanor was not yet dressed, which was most unlike her.

"Caroline."

"Aunt." Caroline closed the door and went over to drop a kiss on Eleanor's averted cheek. "I understand you have been feeling unwell."

"I have something of a headache, which is unfortunate

as our guests are arriving today and tomorrow." She reached for Caroline's hand. "I expect you to stand in for me if necessary."

"What about Eliza?" Caroline asked cautiously. "As your oldest and married daughter, she is your natural successor in all things related to the family."

"She's breeding," Eleanor said bluntly. "And not doing well with it. I told her that it is all an attitude of mind, but she is somewhat weak spirited."

Eliza was anything but weak. She'd made Caroline's childhood miserable with her bullying and domineering ways. If she said she was too ill to act as her mother's hostess, then Caroline tended to believe her. Eliza had always relished an opportunity to lord it over everyone and would certainly not enjoy watching Caroline take her place.

"Maybe you should postpone the party?" Caroline suggested. "I could write a letter to each invited guest, and—"

"No," Eleanor said forcefully. "I will feel more the thing by tomorrow and I am not canceling anything. Mabel would never forgive me."

"Then perhaps I should leave you to recuperate," Caroline said. "I'll consult with Mr. Woodford and make sure all your guests are present and accounted for."

"Thank you." Eleanor offered her a stiff nod. "I was unsure about having such an unusual gathering at the hall for Mabel's birthday, but Mabel went to her father, and he insisted that I followed her wishes including the ridiculous guest list. How I'm supposed to tolerate stable boys and peers sharing a dinner table I do not know."

"Perhaps they will enjoy the informality," Caroline suggested. From what she'd heard earlier, it seemed clear that her aunt and uncle were still arguing about the matter.

"I sincerely doubt it." Eleanor sniffed. "What on earth will our guests have in common?"

"A sincere regard for Mabel?"

Eleanor looked pained. "I suppose so."

"I am surprised at my uncle agreeing to hold such a

ball," Caroline said as she picked up the tray beside her aunt. "But I am quite certain that a notable hostess such as yourself will pull it off admirably. Shall I send up some fresh chamomile tea for you?"

"That would be most kind of you, Niece."

Caroline hesitated at the door. "You do realize that I am here with my employer, Aunt?"

"What of it?"

"Any assistance I am able to offer you will have to be approved by her first."

"Don't be ridiculous," Aunt Eleanor snapped. "Surely she will understand that the needs of this family come before her own petty concerns?"

Mrs. Frogerton would probably be the first to agree with her aunt, but Caroline certainly wasn't going to mention it. She gained some perverse pleasure in reminding Eleanor that her time was no longer her aunt's to command.

"I will certainly bring the matter to her attention."

Caroline curtsied and left the room. She went down into the kitchen carrying the tray and spent some time greeting the staff, most of whom had known her since childhood. To her secret relief they made no attempt to treat her differently because of her altered status in life. She was certain that was something she would have to reckon with on her return to London. Hired companions and spinster aunts were rarely accorded any respect or even noticed.

"Where is Mr. Woodford?" Caroline asked as her aunt's maid assembled a new tray of chamomile tea for her mistress.

"I don't know, miss." Ruth Maddox, the cook, frowned. "Come to think of it, I haven't seen him all morning."

"Is he unwell?" Caroline looked over at the two footmen seated at the table. "Has anyone checked on him?"

"He's not in his rooms, miss," Joshua, the senior of the two, spoke up.

"Then, where is he?" Caroline frowned. "Did he appear for breakfast?"

"Yes, miss." Ruth nodded. "I served him myself. He did say his gout was troubling him, but I didn't think much of it because he does like to complain."

"Did he go down to the village or the Home Farm?"

"I hope not because it looks like it's going to rain," Ruth said. "His sister still lives in the village, though. I believe he intends to reside with her when he retires."

Joshua cleared his throat. "He did get a message this morning just after breakfast, miss. Maybe she asked him to call on her?"

"That's possible," Caroline said thoughtfully. "Miss Woodford is quite frail. I wonder if I have time to walk down there and see if everything is all right?"

"Not in this weather, miss, and with guests still arriving for the party." Ruth returned to her breadmaking. "I reckon that with Lady Eleanor sick in bed she'll be depending on you."

"So I understand," Caroline sighed. "Even though I am no longer a member of her household, she still expects me to represent the family. I cannot think it is a good idea to hold a party when both the butler and the lady of the house are incapacitated."

None of the staff answered her, which was understandable seeing as they were currently employed in the house and would not wish to criticize the people who paid their wages. Caroline turned to the door.

"If you have time, Mrs. Maddox, can you send someone to the village anyway?"

"I doubt I will have a moment, miss, what with this dinner to get ready. But when Nathaniel turns up to help keep the ranges fueled and if the rain stops, I'll certainly send him down."

"Thank you."

Caroline already knew she was asking a lot. Her aunt had never been the kind of employer who kept a full staff.

She had often relied on her family members and charity children to supplement their efforts. With Mr. Woodford not at the helm the success of the party looked increasingly precarious.

She went up the stairs and into Mrs. Frogerton's room to find her employer sleeping peacefully in her bed, her lace cap askew over one eye. There was no sign of movement from Dorothy's room either. Caroline left them both to their dreams and went to find her uncle Nicholas in his study.

After knocking on the door and being admitted into his inner sanctum she found him at his desk making some annotations on his game-breeding record book. He was a fanatical hunter and paid his gamekeeper very well to maintain the stock of grouse and partridge, as well as the woodlands needed for his shooting parties. Caroline was fairly certain that the stables and kennels were in much better condition than the house.

"Ah! Caroline, my dear. Have you given up your foolish notion of earning your own living and come home for good?" He laughed heartily. "Eleanor will be vindicated!"

"I am only here for Mabel's birthday party, Uncle. It was kind of you to allow her to have a somewhat unorthodox celebration."

"She's my youngest child. I didn't want to disappoint her." He fidgeted with the pens on his desk. "I also reminded Eleanor that a ball held here is much cheaper than a grand one in town."

"You don't intend to hold one in London?"

"In return for us hosting this one, Mabel agreed to a much smaller occasion when we arrive in town."

"Which is very wise and much more suited to her tastes," Caroline agreed. "I still intend to return to London with Mrs. Frogerton after the ball, sir. Perhaps I will be able to attend Mabel's party there." Caroline curtsied. "It is good to see you, Uncle."

"I'd forgotten that parvenue your aunt mentioned decided to accompany you." He frowned. "She's hardly our kind of person, Caroline."

"She has been very kind to me, sir," Caroline said steadily. "Perhaps you will change your mind when you meet her at dinner this evening."

"I doubt it. She's from the north, isn't she?"

"Yes, from the Bradford area. Her family have several business interests there including textile mills and at least two potteries."

"So, she's wealthy but has no class." He nodded as if he'd already made up his mind to dislike her. "And she's trying to push her daughter off onto some poor gentleman of the *ton*."

"Miss Frogerton is very pretty and has a large dowry."

"Shop money." He wrinkled his nose. "Wouldn't want it in my family."

"With all due respect, I doubt Miss Frogerton would be interested in Nicholas or George. She's aiming for at least a duke if not a royal prince."

"The royal family could certainly do with the money," her uncle said. "They are a disgraceful example to the whole country."

"Hopefully, our new queen will rectify that, Uncle."

"That slip of a girl? I doubt it. She's surrounded by foreigners and listens to that fool Lord Melbourne."

Knowing her uncle was inclined to go on at length about his distaste for the Hanoverians, Caroline curtsied again and retreated for the door. She'd done her duty, made certain that everyone in her family had been greeted and acknowledged, and could now turn her attention to her employer.

"Caroline?"

She halted at the door and looked over her shoulder. "Yes?"

"I am glad to see you, my dear. Your aunt has not been well." He hesitated. "She was somewhat reluctant to hold this gathering here and might appreciate your assistance."

"I will do my best to aid her, Uncle," Caroline said and she wondered whether that was what her uncle and aunt had been arguing about earlier. "I have already promised her that."

"Good girl." He offered her a brisk nod. "Now, be off with you."

As Caroline made her way across the main hall toward the stairs, one of the footmen came through the front door carrying a trunk and was swiftly followed by another. It had obviously started to rain as the footmen's blue livery was covered in dark spots. Aware of her aunt's absence, Caroline decided to stay where she was and welcome the late arrivals.

"Come along, my dear. Let's get you in out of this dire weather."

Caroline stepped forward with a smile and advanced toward the two women who were sheltering under a large umbrella.

"Good afternoon and welcome to Greenwood Hall." Caroline's breath caught in her throat as a third figure stepped in behind the women and closed the door behind him with a bang.

He looked straight at her and then deliberately averted his gaze to his female companions.

"Do you have all your bags, Nora? Perhaps I should return to the carriage and make sure."

"I'm fairly certain I didn't leave anything behind, Uncle Francis." The young woman spoke in a slightly breathy voice. "Did I, Mama?"

"I doubt it. You are usually very organized." The older woman raised her veil, advanced toward Caroline, and then stopped, her expression horrified. "Good Lord."

"Good morning, Lady Helen. My aunt is currently indisposed but asked me to welcome her guests in her stead." Caroline curtsied. "And this must be Nora, who has come to celebrate with Mabel."

"I . . . did not expect to see you here."

Nor I you, Caroline thought even as she tried desperately to keep her composure. She and Helen had once been as close as sisters. "Would you like me to show you up to your rooms so that you can rest before dinner?"

She turned toward the stairs, ignoring the man who was standing by the door and treating her as if she didn't exist. But why would he acknowledge her now? He'd made his decision and she was as nothing to him—possibly even less as she'd fallen so low.

"Lady Helen?" She gestured toward the landing. "If you follow me, I'll arrange for your bags to be brought up immediately."

To her relief, the visitors finally started moving and she went ahead of them, mentally reviewing the list of rooms Peggy had supplied as to where each guest would be located. Why hadn't she noticed Helen was amongst the guests? Because she hadn't connected her daughter's name with her uncle's, nor had Caroline ever expected him to accompany his niece to a party such as this.

She opened the door into the suite and was glad to see that the fire was already blazing and that there were fresh flowers from the glasshouse on the dresser. Her aunt might be unwell, but her servants were still obeying her precise and detailed instructions.

"Dinner will be served at six." Caroline stepped back to allow the ladies into the room. "I'll send your maid up as soon as she arrives."

"Thank you," Lady Helen said distantly, and turned her back on Caroline. "Come on, my dear. Let's get you out of that wet cloak."

Caroline shut the door behind her and almost bumped into Lord Francis Chatham, who had followed them upstairs. She kept her gaze on his highly polished boots.

"You are next door, sir."

"Thank you." He tossed something at her and she instinctively caught it. "Give this to the footman who brings up the bags, will you?"

He'd already walked into his room and closed the door before she thought to unclench her fist to discover the six-pence he'd casually thrown her. She struggled to breathe, anger building inside her. How *dare* he treat her like a servant? She wanted to go into his room and shove the coin right up his nose or somewhere equally painful.

Even as she took a step toward the door her anger died as suddenly as it had risen. She *was* a servant. The fact that she had once been Lord Francis Chatham's affianced bride was apparently something best forgotten.

Chapter 3

Badly shaken by her encounter with Francis, Caroline made her way toward one of the exits into the garden and only stopped short when confronted by a sheet of pouring rain. She took a few deep breaths and was just about to close the door when she heard laughter. Looking out into the gloom she recognized Mabel with two companions running as fast as they could for the door.

"Wait!" Mabel called out. "Let us in!"

Caroline stepped out of the way and held the door open as Mabel came through still laughing and spluttering. Her light brown hair was loose around her shoulders and she wore nothing more substantial than a shawl over her plain muslin dress. She was not as handsome or tall as her older sister and mother but had a sweetness of expression that Caroline had always admired.

"We were in the stable block and the rain came down so hard we thought we might drown." Mabel went to hug Caroline, remembered the state of her dress, and smiled instead. "Cousin Caroline! How delightful."

"Mabel." Caroline smiled back.

"Do you remember Harry Price and his brother, Dan? They used to live with us." Mabel introduced her two companions. "We were just reminiscing about their first jobs in the stables."

Caroline studied the two tall fair-haired men. "I think I remember you both. Welcome back to Greenwood Hall."

They both bowed. "Thank you, miss." Harry was the one who replied. "I seem to remember you trying to teach me my letters."

"That's highly likely," Caroline said. "How good of you both to come back for Mabel's party."

Dan grinned at Mabel. "How could we say no? She was always the best thing about this place. She never made us feel inferior unlike some other folks around here."

Even as a child Caroline had been well aware of the strict lines her aunt had drawn between blood relatives and charity children. Although they were all supposed to be obedient to her rule, she had punished those not related to her far more severely and daily reminded them of their good fortune in being housed and fed in her home rather than in an orphanage.

"Not you, miss," Harry hastened to add. "You were one of the good 'uns."

"Dan found employment with Mr. Wilkes over in New-ley at the dairy, and Harry's been at sea." Mabel beamed at them both. "It was lucky that Harry's ship was in port."

"Lucky indeed," Harry agreed, and turned to his brother. "We should go and get ready for dinner tonight. Pleasure to see you again, miss."

He went off with Dan, leaving a sopping wet Mabel standing next to Caroline.

"I suppose I should change as well." Mabel lifted her damp skirts away from her limbs and grimaced. "I don't want to catch a chill."

"I'll walk up the stairs with you." Caroline turned away from the door. "Are you looking forward to your birthday ball?"

"Yes, indeed." Mabel nodded vigorously. "Mama is already complaining about me inviting the hoi polloi. She says it will make me less 'marriageable,' whatever that means."

"I think that if you enjoy your own birthday then she will be well satisfied," Caroline said diplomatically, and was amused when Mabel snorted.

"She will not, but I don't care. This is the only way she could persuade me to go along with all this nonsense. It will be far more entertaining than enduring the stuffy guests she and Father would prefer."

"I can't argue with that." Caroline paused on the top landing of the stairs. "Do you need any assistance to change out of your wet clothes?"

"No, thank you. I'll just ring for my maid." Mabel grabbed hold of Caroline's hands. "I'm so glad you came and I'm so sorry for everything that has recently befallen you."

"Thank you." Caroline gently released her fingers. "I appreciate that."

"They have all been quite *horrid* to you and I don't think it's fair," Mabel continued. "It's hardly your fault if your father turned out to be a bad man, is it? Yet you and Susan have to pay the price of his wickedness."

Caroline could only nod, her throat too constricted to speak as her cousin passionately enumerated everything that Caroline herself wanted to say and wasn't allowed to.

"Please know that if you are ever in need then you have only to ask, and I will instantly offer my assistance," Mabel said earnestly.

"You are . . . most kind."

"I am not." Mabel started walking again. "I just can't *bear* to see such injustice."

Caroline slowly walked along the other branch of the hall until she reached Mrs. Frogerton's suite. It only occurred to her as she tapped lightly on the door and went in that she had no idea which room her aunt had allocated to her. Perhaps she intended for Caroline to sleep in the maid's room at the rear of the suite to teach her a lesson.

Peggy opened the door and smiled at Caroline. "I've already woken them both up and brought them their tea."

Mrs. Frogerton, who was sitting up in bed, waved at Caroline.

"Good afternoon, dear!"

"Good afternoon." Caroline smiled at her. "Did you enjoy your nap?"

"Yes, indeed. The bed is very comfortable."

"I'm glad to hear it." Caroline turned to Peggy. "Will Mrs. Maddox be able to spare you before dinner to help dress the ladies?"

"Lady Eleanor said I should do so and she's the mistress of the house," Peggy declared. "Mrs. Maddox will have to wait."

"Do you know where I am to sleep?" Caroline inquired as she went around the room tidying up Mrs. Frogerton's things. Her employer had already made herself at home. The only thing missing was a dog sleeping by the fireside.

"In your old room, miss, next to the nursery. Joshua has already put your bags up there." Peggy looked her up and down. "Perhaps you'd best go and get changed for dinner and then come back here. I can cope in the meantime."

All too aware of the state of her traveling gown, Caroline smoothed a hand over her badly creased skirt. No wonder Lady Helen and Lord Francis had looked at her with such horror. "You're probably right. I haven't had a moment to myself since I arrived."

"Then off you pop." Peggy gestured at the door. "I'll be here when you return."

"Thank you."

Caroline left the room and climbed the stairs back up to the nursery level. She only realized how tired she was when her legs started shaking when she reached the top. She opened the door into her old room and noted that nothing had changed. There was a single bed, a chest of drawers, a small cupboard built into the wall that adjoined the nursery, and a rag rug she'd made herself to guard against the cold winter mornings when she had to get out of bed early.

Her trunk sat beside the bed and the window was open at the bottom allowing a fresh breeze to dissipate the general air of disuse. Caroline set her hair brushes out on the chest and hung her four remaining dresses in the cupboard. There wasn't time to press the skirts of any of her gowns, which meant she'd look almost as dowdy in her second-best dress as she currently did now.

There was a jug of cold water, plain pressed soap, and a bowl to wash in which at least revived her. She took a moment to re-braid and pin up her hair in front of the small mirror. Sometimes she longed for curls and ringlets and a maid to make her look her best, but those things were in the past. It wasn't as if she wasn't perfectly capable of looking after herself and Susan if the occasion arose.

She buttoned the bodice of her navy-blue gown, added the single strand of pearls that had once belonged to her mother around her neck, and considered herself presentable. As she left, she paused to listen to the noises coming from the nursery next door. It was suppertime, and the children were obviously enjoying the lack of her aunt Eleanor's supervision. Mrs. Whittle kept good order but she didn't expect the children in her care to be as perfectly behaved as Eleanor did. Caroline hoped Susan would remember to come and meet her in the drawing room later. She had a sense that she might need some support.

Down in the Frogerton suite, her employer was resplendent in green silk, and Dorothy had gone with a beribboned and ruffled concoction in pink that was positively restrained by her standards.

"You both look very nice," Caroline said. "Do you have your fans, kerchiefs, and reticules?"

"We're not children," Dorothy snapped. She was obviously more nervous than she appeared. "We are quite capable of presenting ourselves in society without your assistance."

"Oh! Where did I leave my fan!" Mrs. Frogerton looked distractedly around the room. "That nice girl Peggy put it out for me somewhere."

"Here it is." Caroline retrieved it from the clutter on the dressing table just as the clock struck the quarter hour. "If you are both ready, we can go down."

Dorothy sailed past and Caroline offered Mrs. Frogerton her arm.

"Take your time, ma'am."

"I will. How is your sister?"

"She is very well." Caroline smiled. "It is such a pleasure to see her."

"I'm surprised you didn't choose to stay here," Mrs. Frogerton remarked. "It is a remarkably fine house."

"It is, but it's not mine." Caroline hesitated before continuing. "My aunt is an excellent woman, but I didn't wish to be beholden to her for the rest of my life."

"I think I understand," Mrs. Frogerton said thoughtfully. "Women are often at the mercy of their families, aren't they? When my mother became ill, my father expected me to take on all her responsibilities without complaint. He even ordered me not to consider getting married because I was needed at home."

She chuckled. "I, of course, ignored him and when I met my Septimus I had no intention of staying put. If I had to manage a home and a business, I was determined that it would be for my benefit and not my father's."

"Good for you, ma'am," Caroline said.

She was surprised when her employer patted her hand. "Now, let me deal with Dotty this evening while you enjoy the time with your family."

"I am employed by you, ma'am, and I can assure you that I will be putting you and your interests first."

Mrs. Frogerton smiled broadly. "I admire your dedication, my love. If my daughter has half your determination and stamina, I'm sure she'll be marrying a duke very shortly."

"I wouldn't put it past her." Caroline looked down at Dorothy's bouncing curls as she descended the stairs ahead of them. "If only there was a duke here for her to wed."

"Good evening, Mrs. Frogerton, Miss Frogerton." Aunt Eleanor's voice carried very clearly across the hall. "Do come and join us."

Pleased that her aunt had decided to come down to preside over dinner after all, Caroline approached the open doors of the drawing room with less trepidation than before. Her confidence took a swift dip as she realized Lord Francis, his sister, and his niece were already present and chatting to their host.

After greeting the Frogertons, Eleanor grabbed hold of Caroline's elbow.

"I did not invite Lord Francis Chatham to this gathering, Niece. In truth, I wonder how he dared show his face after his treatment of you."

"I doubt he expected to encounter me, either, Aunt," Caroline replied. "And I was the one who called off the engagement. All he did was accept my decision."

There had been a lot more to it than that, but Caroline wasn't going to share her heartbreak with a woman who would certainly have no sympathy for her.

"I would send him on his way—except the weather has taken a turn for the worst." Eleanor stepped back. "Now, I must speak to my other guests. Please make sure that your employer embarrasses neither herself nor anyone else."

"She is perfectly well behaved, ma'am." Caroline frowned. "Perhaps if you spent a moment speaking to her you would reconsider your opinion."

Eleanor straightened her spine. "No one would ever suggest that I neglect my guests, my dear. I will certainly endeavor to converse with her at some point."

Eleanor had never liked being given advice and Caroline doubted her words had aided her employer at all. She looked around and saw the Frogerton ladies speaking to her uncle and cousin George. As everyone was smiling, she was fairly confident things were going well.

"Good evening, Caroline."

Mabel came dancing up to her. She wore a simple flounced muslin dress in daffodil yellow with a single ruffle of lace around the bodice and one above the hem. Her hair was piled on top of her head and two long curls swung on either side of her face.

"You look lovely, Mabel."

"Thank you." Mabel bobbed a curtsy. "I must confess that it feels very strange to be all dressed up and down here with the adults rather than in the nursery."

"I can hardly believe you are old enough to be here myself," Caroline confessed. "I still think of you as a little girl like Susan."

"She is almost old enough to have her own debut," Mabel said, and looked around the room. "Will you introduce me to your employer? I'd love to meet her."

"Of course."

Caroline led Mabel through to where Mrs. Frogerton and Dorothy were now standing by themselves in front of the roaring fire.

"Mrs. Frogerton? May I introduce you to my cousin, Miss Mabel Greenwood?"

"You're the birthday lass?" Mrs. Frogerton beamed at Mabel. "Thank you for inviting us to your celebrations."

"It was my pleasure," Mabel said, and turned to Dorothy, who was regarding her curiously. "You must be Miss Frogerton. Are you making your curtsy to society as well this Season?"

"Yes, I am." Dorothy managed to nod.

"Then I will introduce you to my friend Miss Baskins, who is also making her debut."

Mabel linked arms with Dorothy. "She is standing over there with her brother, the Earl of Epping. Would you care to meet them?"

Mabel winked at Caroline as she drew Dorothy away with her.

"What a nice girl," Mrs. Frogerton said approvingly.

"She is very sweet. Dorothy is in good hands," Caroline replied, one eye on her ex-betrothed and his family, who were coming far too close for her liking. "My great-aunt Ines is beckoning to me from her chair. Would you care to meet her before dinner? She rarely leaves her room these days and loves company."

"The older lady over there?" Mrs. Frogerton asked. "With the embroidery hoop on her lap?"

"Yes, her hands are rarely idle. She kept all the children in the nursery in scarves, hats, and mittens over the years as well as sewing and embroidering countless baby clothes."

"How very worthy of her," Mrs. Frogerton murmured.

Caroline didn't bother to mention that her great-aunt also had a waspish disposition and a heavy hand when it came to disciplining the children in the nursery. Caroline had learned to be wary of her temper at quite a young age.

"Aunt Ines?" Caroline raised her voice so that she could be heard. "I'd like you to meet Mrs. Frogerton. She was admiring your embroidery."

"Can't see to do it much now." Ines raised her hands. "My hands are crippled with arthritis."

Mrs. Frogerton sat beside her. "Have you tried rubbing them with warm goose fat? I find it very helpful indeed."

As the two ladies started to chat, Caroline automatically checked all the guests now congregated in the drawing room. There were at least two recently married ladies who had once been friends of hers and three older women her aunt and uncle's age. The sprinkling of younger faces spoke to Mabel's influence. Several of them looked rather out of place and were currently being ignored.

"Excuse me, ma'am," Caroline murmured to her employer, who nodded her permission.

She walked over to a small group positioned awkwardly just inside the door and recognized Dan and his brother, Harry, along with a young lady who looked like she was about to bolt.

"Good evening!" Caroline smiled warmly at them. "Mabel is over by the window if you wish to be taken to her?"

"Thanks, miss." Dan bowed. "We were feeling a bit out of place and wondering whether we'd be better off in the servants' hall."

"Mabel would be very upset if you weren't here to celebrate with her." Caroline placed her hand on Dan's arm and maneuvered him and his little party through the guests toward where Mabel was still talking to Dorothy and her other friend.

"May I know your name, miss . . . ?" Caroline looked at the woman, who dropped a curtsy.

"Brownworth, miss, Tina Brownworth."

"Ah! I remember you now. You are two years older than my sister, Susan."

"She's a good 'un, that one." Miss Brownworth ducked her head. "I work at the vicarage now as a parlor maid." Her gaze drifted toward Dan, who grinned. "We're courting."

"How lovely." Caroline touched Mabel's shoulder and whispered in her ear. "Perhaps you might take care of your waifs and strays? It's not as if any of your parents' other guests will make them feel at ease here."

"You're right. I'm sorry." Mabel looked stricken. "It is my responsibility. I just wanted them all to share this moment with me so much."

Caroline nodded and stepped back. She had barely reached Mrs. Frogerton's side before Joshua appeared at the door. Had Mr. Woodford still not returned? Caroline was surprised her aunt hadn't noticed his absence.

"Dinner is served."

Aware that some of the guests might need a little help with precedence, Caroline presented her employer to the

vicar, found that Dorothy had already gone in with the
Earl of Epping, and herded the rest of the attendees into
the dining room.

"Caroline?" Her aunt called out for her. "You will sit
here on my right."

One of her erstwhile friends tittered and whispered
loudly, "Surely, she should be at the bottom of the table,
or not seated at all as she is amongst the employed?"

"She is still my niece and a lady by birth." Eleanor gave
the woman a hard stare. "And always welcome in her
family home."

"Indeed, she is!" George chimed in as he pulled out her
chair for her. "It's a pleasure to be seated next to my dear-
est cousin." He glanced around the table and grinned. "It
appears that my sister Mabel is attempting to set the social
order on fire, and I for one am all for it."

"Thank you, George."

Caroline sat down, only to realize she was directly opposite Lord Francis. The only saving grace was that if they
adhered to current social practices, even the idea of talking
across the table would be frowned upon. Not that he appeared to have any intention of acknowledging her existence let alone actually conversing with her. His gaze
remained fixed on his sister, who sat to his left.

Caroline took a look down the table to see that Mrs.
Frogerton was chatting with the vicar, and that Dorothy
had established herself in the middle of a group of young
people and appeared to be holding her own.

"How nice to see you, Caroline."

She turned to see her cousin Eliza smiling at her. She
bore a great resemblance to her mother and was of a similar autocratic disposition. She'd married a wealthy local
baronet who allowed her to rule his house and his life with
a meekness she obviously appreciated.

"I must say I was very surprised to hear that you agreed
to come to this party."

"Why is that?" Caroline allowed the footman to fill her wineglass and noticed there was still no sign of Mr. Woodford managing the staff. "I am very fond of Mabel."

"Yes, but the shame of coming back here in your current . . . predicament." Eliza's gaze slid to Lord Francis, who luckily appeared oblivious. "It must have been difficult knowing that none of your former friends can acknowledge you."

"If they truly were my friends, I'm quite certain they'd remain so." Caroline helped herself to the soup. "If my change in status affects their judgment that profoundly, then I'm sure I'm better off without them."

Eliza sniffed. "One might have thought that accepting paid employment would have taught you to moderate your tone, Cousin."

"Oh, no." Caroline smiled sweetly. "Mrs. Frogerton is from the north and is a great believer in speaking her mind— something she regularly encourages me to do as well."

"Then perhaps you are well suited after all." Eliza abruptly tossed her head and started chatting to her neighbor.

George patted Caroline's shoulder. "Never you mind her."

"I don't." Caroline only realized she meant it after speaking the words. Eliza, who had often made her childhood a misery, had no power over her anymore, which was curiously refreshing.

The meal proceeded through several courses, and Caroline was relieved to see that all Mabel's misfits appeared to be coping well, as were Dorothy and Mrs. Frogerton. She did wonder if Lord Francis would end the evening with a crick in his neck from studiously avoiding even the most minor eye contact with her. In truth, she almost hoped he would. Once he had meant everything to her and such a betrayal would have crushed her heart. But he had made his choice clear and declined to be associated with her and that was that. She wouldn't give him the satisfaction of knowing how much he'd hurt her.

Just as her aunt gave the signal for the ladies to withdraw and leave the gentlemen to their port, Joshua appeared at Caroline's shoulder.

"Miss, can you come with me?"

"Whatever is wrong?" Caroline followed the young
footman out of the dining room and through the green
baize door into the servants' realm beyond.

"When Bert went down into the cellar to get the port,
he found Mr. Woodford wandering around in one of the
old cellars in a bit of a daze."

"How on earth did that happen? And why didn't anyone notice him there earlier in the day when fetching up
the wine for dinner?" Caroline asked as she hurried along
at his side.

"He was right in the back, miss. Bert heard him calling out."

"Is he all right?"

"Mrs. Maddox has called for the doctor to come up
from the village but it's raining hard, and the roads aren't
fit for driving on."

"Where is Mr. Woodford?"

"In his rooms, miss." Joshua indicated the passage to
the left. "Will you come and see for yourself?"

Chapter 4

"Mr. Woodford."

Caroline sat in the chair Mrs. Maddox had vacated and took the old man's trembling hand in hers. He looked pale and haggard, and most unlike himself.

"Miss Caroline." He gripped her fingers. "Thank God they found me."

"You are quite safe now," Caroline said. "And the doctor has been called."

"I don't remember what happened. One moment I was on my way to the cellars to pick out the wine and spirits Lady Eleanor had requested for the evening's entertainment, the next I woke up with a terrible thirst, and my head was throbbing."

"Did you fall on the stairs?" Caroline asked.

"I don't know." Mr. Woodford grimaced. "I suppose I might have done so, and then wandered around and collapsed."

Caroline patted his hand. "Does your head still hurt?"

"Yes."

"Have you taken anything to relieve the pain?" Caroline looked up at Mrs. Maddox, who had remained in the room with them.

"We thought we should wait to see what the doctor

said, miss," Mrs. Maddox replied. "Head injuries can be funny things, especially at his age."

Caroline couldn't disagree with that. "When did you send for the doctor?"

"Nathaniel set off about half an hour ago on foot. If he was able to get across the stream at the ford, he should've reached the village by now."

Caroline reluctantly stood up. "Perhaps I should tell Lady Eleanor what has happened. Will you let me know when the doctor arrives, and I will come and speak with him?"

"Yes, of course, miss."

Caroline made her way back up the stairs and considered exactly how to frame the matter to her aunt Eleanor. Despite Mr. Woodford's absence, the dinner party had proceeded as planned, and none of the guests would be aware of any problems, which should at least placate her aunt.

She went past the dining room where the loud voices and laughter of the males of the party indicated that they were still enjoying their port and conversation and entered the drawing room. The ladies sat in distinct groups gathered around the fireplace where Eleanor held court over the tea and coffeepots.

"Ah, there you are, Caroline. You may help pass out the tea."

"Of course." Caroline went over to her aunt and lowered her voice. "Mr. Woodford sustained some injuries in the cellar. The doctor is on his way."

"Good Lord, how inconvenient of him. I told Nicholas that he should be forced to retire a year ago. He is far too old to be managing the staff and household." She handed Caroline two filled cups. "Give these to Lady Helen and her daughter, please."

Caroline did as she was asked and received a polite but distant smile as she placed the cups on a small table between the mother and daughter. She didn't attempt to make conversation, having been snubbed enough for one day.

Mrs. Frogerton was still talking to Great-Aunt Ines and the vicar. Dorothy was with Mabel and a crowd of younger people standing beside the pianoforte. Caroline was pleased to see all her charges were coping well with their somewhat snobbish peers. It was hard not to like her employer, who was friendly to everyone, but Dorothy could be quite difficult.

She returned to Eleanor.

"What on earth was Woodford doing in the cellar at his age? Was he *drinking*?" her aunt asked. "That would certainly explain why he injured himself at such an inappropriate time. He should have sent Joshua or Bert down there in his stead." She gave Caroline another two filled cups. "This is for Great-Aunt Ines and Mrs. Frogerton, who has at least proved her worth this evening by keeping my aunt amused."

"She is always good-natured in company," Caroline replied as she carefully took the cups. "She has a gift for making friends."

Ignoring her aunt's disbelieving sniff, she walked over to her employer.

"Would you care for some tea, ma'am?"

"Yes, indeed." Mrs. Frogerton smiled at her. "My throat is quite dry from all this chatting."

Caroline placed her great-aunt's tea on the table beside her. "Here you are, Aunt."

"I don't want it. It's too hot and I can't manage the handle anymore," Aunt Ines grumbled.

"I doubt anyone would mind or notice if you used your whole hand to pick up the cup," Mrs. Frogerton said encouragingly. "I myself find these tiny handles very fiddly. In my pottery we make sure we produce drinking vessels that can be used easily."

"You have a pottery?" Ines was startled into asking a question.

"I own two, ma'am. One for fancy porcelain figurines and the like, and the other for cookware."

"Oh! Indeed. How interesting."

Caroline was amused that her great-aunt had nothing to say to Mrs. Frogerton's frank confession of being in trade.

"Are you enjoying yourself?" Caroline asked her employer while her aunt was occupied with her tea.

"Very much so. Everyone has been very kind and welcoming."

Even though she was surprised to hear that, Caroline smiled in agreement. Mrs. Frogerton did have a way of getting even the stuffiest of people to unbend and had certainly succeeded with the vicar, her rather prickly great-aunt, and surprisingly her uncle.

"Dorothy seems to be settling in well," Caroline remarked as the crowd around Mabel laughed loudly at something George said. "It will be good for her to make some acquaintances here before the Season in London. She will enjoy it more if she has friends."

"I reckon so." Mrs. Frogerton nodded. "And it's all thanks to you and your aunt. I must make an effort and go over there and thank her in person."

She set her cup down and rose to her feet with a determination Caroline was now used to. She linked her arm with Caroline's.

"Come and introduce me to her, lass."

"Of course." Caroline had no intention of thwarting her employer's desires. "I'm sure she'll be delighted."

When she turned, she noticed Joshua waving at her from the door. She escorted Mrs. Frogerton to her aunt and smiled warmly.

"Aunt Eleanor, this is my employer, Mrs. Frogerton. She has been wishing to make your acquaintance all evening."

"Oh!" Eleanor set the teapot down with something of a crash. "I—"

Mrs. Frogerton curtsied. "I just wanted to thank you for inviting me and Dotty to your party. It was very kind of you."

Even as she left her startled aunt being regaled by Mrs.

Frogerton and went to the door, Caroline wished she could stay and listen.

Joshua was waiting for her. "The doctor's here, miss. The young one."

"I didn't know there was a choice." Caroline picked up her skirts and followed him down the servants' stairs to the back of the house where the butler had his rooms. Her swift passage made the stark difference between the luxurious comfort she had left behind and the bottle green paint and echoing tile of the servants' wing even more apparent.

"The old doctor wouldn't have come out in this weather," Joshua confided as he walked alongside her. "Especially for a servant."

Privately, Caroline agreed but decided not to mention it. Even though she was now considered by many to be part of the servant class she still had some loyalty left to her aunt and uncle.

"Dr. Harris is in here, miss." Joshua opened the door and stepped aside. "I'll wait in case you need me."

Caroline paused. "I suggest you go back upstairs and continue your duties as you are already shorthanded. I'll speak to Mrs. Maddox if I require anything."

Joshua nodded and departed.

Caroline went into Mr. Woodford's bedroom to find a dark-haired man standing over the patient. He looked up as she approached and scowled.

"One might ask why you expect a man of his age to climb up and down those dangerous steps into the cellar?"

"Your question is certainly valid, Doctor, but as I'm not his employer, I can't comment. I'm Miss Morton." Caroline raised her chin. "I currently represent Lady Eleanor Greenwood, the mistress of the house."

His frown deepened. "I don't remember seeing you at the hall before."

"That's because I no longer reside here." She looked down at Mr. Woodford's bruised face. He appeared to be sleeping. "Would you care to continue this conversation in the other room?"

"As you wish." He picked up his bag and followed her out. "Now what would Lady Eleanor wish to know about her butler?"

"Everything that is relevant, I suppose," Caroline said. "He has worked here since the age of fourteen and is a valued member of her staff."

"Then tell her he has a concussion and two bruised ribs. I've given him something to help him sleep, attended to the gash on his head, and bound up his ribs."

"Thank you." Caroline inclined her head. She wasn't quite sure why the doctor was being so unpleasant, but she didn't have time to worry about it. "The poor man."

"You almost sound as if you care, Miss Morton."

"I *do* care. He has always been very kind to me. Does he need to stay in bed for a few days, or—"

"Or should he be up and about serving his betters?"

She fixed him with a cool stare. "Dr. Harris, that is both unfair and unkind. My aunt would never expect him to risk his health for her benefit."

Caroline wasn't quite sure that was true, but she wasn't going to allow Dr. Harris to lecture her. Even if her aunt did treat her servants with severity, Caroline certainly would not allow it in this instance.

"Mr. Woodford was absent for most of the day and the staff managed perfectly without him. He is a much loved and respected member of my aunt's staff. She would never wish harm to come to him."

There was a long silence and then the doctor sighed and shoved his hand through his dark hair.

"I probably should apologize, Miss Morton. I was up all night with a dying patient. I am not perhaps at my best."

"It is quite all right." She hesitated. "If you need something to eat or drink, then I'm sure Mrs. Maddox will gladly assist you."

"I can't remember the last time I ate," he confessed. "And my mother always says I become most unpleasant when I'm hungry."

"Then perhaps we should get someone to sit with Mr. Woodford and repair to the kitchen?" Caroline suggested. "I would very much like to know how you wish us to continue to treat your patient."

He turned to the door and held it open for her. "I am more than happy to eat, Miss Morton, but first I would like to see where Mr. Woodford was found. If he really was missing for most of the day, and possibly unconscious, then the injury to his head might be more serious than I assumed. Can you direct me to the cellars?"

"I'll come with you," Caroline offered. "I would not want you to get lost down there. I am quite familiar with the layout."

"Thank you." He cast her a wry look. "You don't intend to push me down the stairs to pay me back for my rudeness, do you?"

"I hadn't thought of it, sir," Caroline said primly. "But I appreciate the suggestion."

His slight chuckle at his own expense made her like him a little more.

She spoke quickly to Mrs. Maddox, who was still busy serving up the dinner, lit an oil lamp, and followed Dr. Harris down the steep stone steps to the cavernous cellars.

"Joshua says he was found toward the rear." Caroline held up her lamp to reveal the carefully curated bottles and barrels of the Greenwoods' generational collection of spirits. The smell of wood, pine, and brandy permeated the cold, musty air. "I am not sure why he would have ventured any farther when everything he needed was right here."

"Perhaps his lordship wanted a particularly ancient bottle of wine?" the doctor suggested.

"I suppose that is possible. My uncle says there are two-hundred-year-old bottles in the vault somewhere." Caroline frowned as she allowed the light to sweep over the dusty stone floor. "There are a lot of footsteps. I wonder if Mr. Woodford fell, hit his head, and became confused?"

"I don't see anything that has been knocked over or signs of blood." Dr. Harris looked around. "But I suppose it is possible that one of the staff cleared up any mess after they found him."

Caroline followed a set of footsteps toward the darker area of the cellar, illuminating her path with the lantern held high over her head.

"Most of the items down here are awaiting repair, out of fashion for the main house, or have simply been left to rot," she commented as she narrowly avoided snagging her gown on a sharp metal spike. "I still don't understand what Mr. Woodford was doing back here."

The light caught on a glint of metal and she moved even farther into the gloom.

"I'd forgotten there were cages here."

"Why on earth are they needed?" Dr. Harris had joined her. He sounded quite unnerved.

"I believe the previous earl used them to house his dogs at night because he couldn't bear to hear them barking even in the kitchen." Caroline's gaze was caught by a swinging door. "When we were children, we used to play in the cages until my aunt decided it was too dangerous and locked them up."

"This one isn't locked." Dr. Harris pointed at the open cage. "And it looks as if someone left a blanket and pillow there on the ground."

"How odd."

Caroline shone the light over the woolen blanket as the doctor crouched down on the earth-packed floor.

He held up his fingers. "There's blood on the blanket."

"Then I wonder if this was where Mr. Woodford fell and hit his head?" Caroline asked. "He might have come to investigate the open cage, tripped over something in the dark, and become confused."

"Except he was found back here, wasn't he?" Dr. Harris stood up, his expression grim. "Maybe someone prepared this cozy corner just for him."

"That's . . . ridiculous." Even as she said the words, Caroline doubted herself. "Why would anyone do that?"

He shrugged. "For a joke perhaps?"

"I cannot think of a single reason why anyone would do that to a man such as Mr. Woodford."

"I can."

Startled, Caroline looked up at her companion, who continued talking.

"A butler commands the whole staff, Miss Morton, and wields much power. His wishes and whims are secondary only to his employers'." He glanced back at the cage. "Perhaps someone on his staff wanted to teach him a lesson or simply play a malicious prank at his expense."

He started walking toward the well-lit part of the cellars. "Shall we go? I must confess that I find this whole place rather oppressive. I'm sure you want to get back to your guests."

"They aren't my guests, but my employer might be looking for me," Caroline countered.

"You are employed by Lady Eleanor?"

"She is my aunt, but I chose to seek employment elsewhere as a lady's companion."

"Interesting," Dr. Harris murmured, even though his manner suggested he found it anything but. "One would've thought it preferable to stay here with your family."

"Well, one would be wrong."

After one last distracted look back at the open cage, Caroline followed Dr. Harris up the stairs and into the main kitchen where Mrs. Maddox and her staff were already cleaning up after the dinner.

"Find anything?" Mrs. Maddox asked as she took a pile of pots through to the scullery.

"I'm not sure." Aware of how quickly gossip spread throughout a house, Caroline decided to be diplomatic.

"Dr. Harris believes Mr. Woodford certainly hit his head at some point and lost consciousness."

"The poor man. And there was us thinking he'd popped off to the village to avoid doing any work." Mrs. Maddox wiped her hands on her apron. "He must have been down there all day."

"It's certainly possible," Caroline agreed. She glanced over at the doctor and decided that now was not the time to ask any awkward questions about the current state of Mr. Woodford's approval amongst the staff. "I wonder if you might provide the good doctor with a meal, Mrs. Maddox? He is quite famished and needs his strength in order to continue caring for Mr. Woodford."

"Of course I can." Mrs. Maddox pointed at a spot at the large table. "Sit yourself down, Dr. Harris, and I'll serve you up something right away."

"Thank you." The doctor did as he was bid and then turned to Caroline. "And thank you for your assistance."

"You are welcome." She hesitated. "If it is acceptable, I will come down later to check on Mr. Woodford."

"Be my guest. I intend to stay here until morning to keep an eye on him." He nodded and picked up the mug of tea Mrs. Maddox had just poured him. "A pleasure, Miss Morton."

"Likewise." Caroline bobbed a polite curtsy.

She headed back up the stairs, aware that things were not right, but unable to decide how to proceed. Should she mention Dr. Harris's theory to her aunt or continue to investigate the matter herself? She no longer lived at Greenwood Hall and had her own life, but the thought that someone had deliberately left Mr. Woodford in a cage didn't sit well with her.

She had barely reentered the drawing room when the gentlemen came in and her sister, Susan, came skipping toward her.

"Caroline!" Susan smiled. "Doesn't Mabel look lovely!"

"She does indeed."

Caroline looked over at the laughing group of Mabel's friends and for the first time felt a little wistful. If she couldn't find a way to repair her family fortunes, Susan would never get to experience the joy of her first Season and would end up in service to her aunt or some other family, with limited prospects and opportunities.

"Caroline?"

She looked down at her sister, who was regarding her rather anxiously, and found a smile. "Would you care to make your curtsy to Mrs. Frogerton? She has been wanting to meet you for months."

"I'd love to." Susan held Caroline's hand as they walked across the large drawing room. "Oh! Francis is here!"

To Caroline's horror, her sister broke free of her grasp and danced over to where Lord Francis stood with his sister and niece. Even as she turned to hurry after Susan her feet refused to obey her. If Francis's family treated Susan as coldly as they had treated her, she didn't know if she would be capable of containing her rage.

Unwilling to watch the encounter and berating herself for her cowardice, Caroline went over to Mrs. Frogerton and Dorothy.

"Is that your sister talking to that handsome gentleman over there?" Mrs. Frogerton asked.

"Yes, indeed. She is looking forward to making your acquaintance."

To Caroline's dismay, Susan was now approaching, but she was hanging on the arm of Lord Francis, who had bent his blond head to listen to her more attentively.

Caroline took up a position directly behind Mrs. Frogerton's chair, her fingers gripping the ornate gold trim as the duo came closer. She kept her gaze on her sister.

Francis bowed as he relinquished Susan's hand. "Lady Caroline."

"May I introduce Lord Francis Chatham to you, Mrs. Frogerton and Miss Frogerton?" Caroline addressed her remarks to his impeccably tied cravat.

"A pleasure indeed," Mrs. Frogerton replied as she patted the seat beside her to encourage Susan to sit down.

"Why did you call her Lady Caroline?" Dorothy asked, her brow creased.

Francis raised a perfect eyebrow. "Because that is her rank, Miss Frogerton. Her father was the Earl of Morton."

"A rank I don't use and don't need," Caroline said firmly. "Miss Morton will do perfectly well."

"As you wish." He bowed again, his expression indifferent, until he smiled down at Susan. "I am glad to see that you are well, miss."

He walked away, leaving silence behind him. Susan glanced anxiously at Caroline.

"I'm so sorry. When I saw him here, I thought that maybe he had changed his mind and that everything would be the same again."

"That is not the case," Caroline said calmly. "But there is no harm done. I am glad that you got to speak to him. You were always good friends."

"Wait." Dorothy insinuated herself into the conversation. "You had a connection with that gentleman?"

"We were engaged to be married," Caroline said. "I released him from the engagement after my father died."

"Oh, you poor love." Mrs. Frogerton patted her hand. "How distressing that must have been."

Caroline focused her attention on her sister's stricken face and took the seat beside her.

"It is all right, Susan. Really."

"Is he an earl, then?" Dorothy was staring after Francis, who had rejoined his sister, who looked quite upset.

"Lord Francis?" Caroline was impressed at how disinterested she sounded. "His father is the Marquess of Ireton. As the oldest son he will inherit the title at some point."

"You would've been a marchioness." Dorothy breathed out hard, and shook her head. "I can't believe it."

"Don't be rude, Dotty," Mrs. Frogerton said. "The last

thing Caroline needs at this moment is you commenting on her ruined hopes."

As Dorothy turned to confront her mother, Caroline drew Susan to her feet and walked away toward the sideboard where the footman had left out a tray of frozen ices in elegant glass bowls. She had no desire to hear either of the Frogertons discuss her broken engagement.

"Would you care for one of these, Susan? I believe Mrs. Maddox said they are rose and violet."

"Yes, please." Susan helped herself and then looked up at her sister. "He didn't seem angry that I talked to him, Caroline, so don't be cross."

"How could I be cross with you?" Caroline instantly replied. "And of course Francis was pleased to see you. He was always very fond of you."

She waited until her sister finished eating her ice and then took her by the hand to go back up to the nursery. It was quiet in the hallway, the house subdued around them as they climbed the endless stairs.

Susan paused outside the nursery door, her expression serious.

"Francis said he missed you."

"That was nice of him," Caroline replied.

"Then perhaps you could be friends again?"

"Unfortunately, society would not allow that, and his future wife would *certainly* not approve." Caroline attempted to lighten her tone, but Susan's face was already crumpling.

"Then society is wrong!"

She wrenched open the nursery door and went inside, leaving Caroline standing alone on the landing. She considered following her sister, but what could she say? There were no comforting words, no happy-ever-afters to give Susan false hope. There was only a future devoid of Francis's presence and Caroline's unremitting quest to provide a home, however lowly, for her sister and herself.

Caroline set off back down the stairs and paused on the

half landing at the top of the wide main staircase to look down at the open door of the drawing room. Within, all was warmth, laughter, and light. She didn't want to rejoin the people who had rejected her—the friends who had ignored her all evening, Helen whom she'd never imagined wouldn't even be able to look her in the eye.

What was the point?

Even as she thought the words, she knew the answer and started down the stairs, her skirt held clear of the steps. As Eliza had suggested, pride might be her downfall, but she would rather face them and be damned than be driven out by people who were no better than she was, and only a hairsbreadth away from the kind of scandal that had engulfed and destroyed her family so easily.

She had nothing to be ashamed of and she refused to be cowed. Raising her chin, she fixed a smile to her face and went through into the drawing room.

Chapter 5

Caroline wasn't sure quite what woke her, but it startled her enough to make her sit bolt upright in bed, eyes wide, and breathing scattered. Somewhere a door or shutter had been slammed either by an inconsiderate person or the gusting wind. Rain slanted against her window in a relentless tattoo and she was glad she'd shut it before retiring to bed.

Something about Mr. Woodford had been niggling at her thoughts and now her sudden wakefulness gave her clarity. Knowing that she wouldn't sleep until she had assured herself that she was mistaken, she put on her dressing gown and slippers and made her way out onto the landing. She paused in front of the nursery, which emitted a soft glow of light from beneath the door.

There was always a maid or nurse stationed at the fireside at night just in case one of the youngest occupants of the house needed anything. Caroline remembered lying in bed as a young girl, watching through her open door as one of the nursery maids knitted in the firelight as she rocked back and forth in her chair.

Anxious to avoid detection, Caroline took the back stairs, pausing at every landing to listen for any voices. She heard nothing but the steady drumming of the rain and the fretful gusting wind. The mist that came off the marshes was impossible to keep out. It curled under the door-frames and down the chimneys and clung to the fabrics, making everything damp.

When she reached the level of the kitchens she went along to the cellars. The door had been propped open, and a lantern sat on the niche in the stone wall. She lit the candle and descended into the depths, surprised that it initially felt warmer than the rest of the house. The smell of brandy and cigars lingered, which probably meant that the servants had decanted the spirits and smoked anything salvageable after finishing clearing up after the gentlemen. Not that she blamed them.

Holding the lantern high, she made her way through to the back of the cavernous cellars to where she and Dr. Harris had speculated about Mr. Woodford's injuries. The cage door still swung open. Caroline made sure it was secure and wouldn't trap her and set her lantern down on an old three-legged chest of drawers wedged into the corner of the space.

She directed the light as best she could toward the locking mechanism of the cage.

"It's been replaced," she murmured as she touched the shiny new lock and chain. "Did someone come down here and deliberately lock Mr. Woodford in?"

Even her whispered words sounded too loud in the cold silence of the ancient stone vaults. She had the horrible sensation that someone was watching her.

"*Why?*"

Her gaze swept over the interior of the cage, the flowered patterned quilt and pillow, the discarded, broken toys, and the odds and ends of furniture that were no longer needed in the house. Was this someone's idea of a joke? Had one of the staff decided to get back at the butler on a day when his services were needed the most by his employer? She considered the staff of Greenwood Hall, most of whom she had known all her life. She couldn't imagine any of them wishing the old butler harm.

Aware that her feet were starting to freeze in her thin slippers, she picked up the lantern and made her way back to the stairs. She climbed to the top, blew out the candle, and left the lantern on the shelf. Somewhere in the house a clock chimed four times. After a glance back at the kitchen where the staff were already stirring, she decided to head for the butler's rooms.

There was a light on in Mr. Woodford's neat parlor and a brisk fire burned in the hearth. Dr. Harris sat in a chair, his spectacles still on his nose, his head back as he snored. The book he'd been reading was propped against his chest. Reluctant to disturb him, especially when she was in a state of undress, Caroline tiptoed past him and went into Mr. Woodford's bedroom. To her surprise he was awake, his anxious gaze trained on the door. The relief in his eyes when he recognized her was unmistakable.

"Lady Caroline."

She went to sit beside him and took his hand.

"Mr. Woodford. Have you recovered from your appalling ordeal?"

"I am much better, miss." He squeezed her fingers. "Dr. Harris says I will make a full recovery, but that I must be mindful of my ribs."

"I'm sure my aunt would agree that you need to take great care of yourself," Caroline said. "Perhaps you could sit in the kitchen and make sure your orders are followed without having to move an inch?"

"I suppose I could manage that." His gaze slid behind her to the door.

"Are you expecting company?" Caroline couldn't help but ask.

"No, miss."

"Have you remembered anything else about what happened to you in the cellar?"

"Nothing at all, miss." He looked away even as his fingers tightened over hers. "It's all a bit of a blur."

Caroline considered her options and decided she had

nothing to lose. "Did you perhaps discover someone where you weren't expecting to see them and receive a fright?"

He shrank against his pillows, his expression aghast. "Why would you say that?"

"Because I have to wonder why you ventured into the depths of the cellar. It is hardly your usual practice to do so when busy with important duties." Caroline paused. "But if you'd seen something out of place, I know you would've gone to investigate."

"I saw nothing, miss. Nothing at all. You are mistaken."

Caroline frowned and leaned toward him. "Please do not upset yourself, Mr. Woodford, I didn't mean—"

"Perhaps you might consider curtailing your visit, Miss Morton?"

She grimaced as Dr. Harris spoke from the doorway.

"You seem to have upset my patient." He went to the other side of Mr. Woodford's bed and took his pulse. "Calm down, sir. I'm sure Miss Morton did not intend to agitate you."

"I certainly did not mean to do so." Caroline shot to her feet and nodded at the patient. "I will come and see you in the morning, Mr. Woodford."

She waited for Dr. Harris to join her in the parlor, her back to the fire, her hands folded together at her waist. When he emerged, he shut the door behind him and leaned against it.

"Whatever did you say to make him so agitated, Miss Morton?"

"I . . . asked him if he had seen anything untoward in the cellar."

"Ah." He nodded. "That would do it. I asked a similar question earlier and he reacted in the same manner."

"I returned to the cellar to look at the dog cages," Caroline admitted.

"And what did you discover?"

"That someone had fitted the open cage with a new lock and chain."

"Which made you think—what exactly?"

She frowned at him. "Isn't it obvious?"

He met her gaze. "That someone deliberately lured Mr. Woodford into the cage, locked him in, and left him there unconscious until they finally decided to relent and release him?"

"Which is completely ridiculous, but—"

"But also likely as he is acting like a man who has been scared out of his wits."

"Yes," she whispered. "He is afraid."

He shrugged. "In truth, Miss Morton, there is very little we can do about that now, except take care of him and ensure he returns to full health."

"If he refuses to confide in anyone, then I suppose you are right." Caroline sighed and gathered her shawl more tightly around her shoulders. "I should go back to bed."

"You should. I certainly don't want to be accused of besmirching your reputation, Miss Morton."

"As if anyone would care about that anymore." She turned to the door. "I earn my living just like you do, and no one would notice if you ravished me on the table."

He frowned as he followed her to the door. "You are Lady Eleanor's niece, and the daughter of an earl."

She glanced up at him as she walked along the corridor toward the stairs. "Have you been gossiping about me, Dr. Harris?"

"*Gossiping*? I'd barely sat down at that kitchen table before half the staff were telling me all about you."

Caroline concealed a smile and was just about to answer him when the clattering of feet on the stairs above alerted her to the imminent appearance of someone in a hurry. Joshua rounded the last corner of the stairwell and halted in front of Dr. Harris.

"Sir! Please come. I think she's dead, but it's horrible, sir. I can't—"

Dr. Harris put a hand on Joshua's arm. "Calm yourself, man. Now, where is the patient?"

"In the front parlor, Doctor, where she likes to do her needlework because the light is better."

Joshua was already turning back up the stairs. Dr. Harris followed him and, after a moment of indecision, Caroline did too. Between the constant rain, dark clouds, and the absence of the morning sun, the house was still full of shadows. Luckily, Caroline knew it well enough to navigate the occasional obstacle. She reached the small parlor just behind the much taller doctor.

"In here, sir. I was just passing the door on my way down to the kitchen when I saw her sitting there in the dark. Gave me quite a turn I can tell you." Joshua stood back, his breathing harsh. "Shall I light a lamp?"

"Yes, please." Dr. Harris had already rounded the first couch and was kneeling beside one of the wing chairs set at right angles to the fire. "Good God."

Caroline found herself moving forward until she abruptly stopped and brought her hand to her cheek. "Great-Aunt Ines."

Even as she whispered the words, Joshua finally managed to set a lamp on the mantelpiece that bathed the chair in light, illuminating the ghastly smile on her aunt's distorted features and the yarn wrapped tightly around her throat. Caroline inhaled the coppery scent of blood. What she'd assumed was a scarf pin was in fact the head of a long knitting needle that had been skewered right through her great-aunt's neck.

She swallowed hurriedly and took an unsteady step backward just as the doctor looked up.

"Joshua? Go and fetch my bag from Mr. Woodford's parlor. Miss Morton? Come here."

"I'm not sure if I can," Caroline said faintly.

"Don't be missish. I need you to help me unwind this wool." He was already acting on his words as he spoke. "I suspect she was strangled, and the knitting needle was an unnecessary flourish, but I could be wrong."

"Who would do this?" Caroline automatically took the

end of the thick yarn he handed her and rolled it back into a ball as the doctor removed it. "It's . . . barbaric."

"Yes." He barely glanced at her as Aunt Ines's neck was slowly revealed. "Can you hold the lantern close to her face please?"

"If I must," Caroline murmured as she fought the urge to swoon. "I refuse to touch her, though."

"Understood." Dr. Harris worked quickly. "She definitely has bruises on either side of her throat, see?"

Caroline suppressed a shudder at the narrow bands of purple bruises that brought to mind splayed fingers and resembled the violet-hued wool all too vividly.

"She is definitely dead?"

"Yes."

"That's horrible."

"It certainly isn't pleasant." Dr. Harris extracted the knitting needle and examined it. "And, as the point of the needle was definitely shoved through the yarn, I stand by my original suspicion that she was strangled and then stabbed." Dr. Harris sat back. "You can put the lantern down now. Do you by any chance know which bedroom belongs to this lady? Joshua and I can take her there to be properly laid out."

Caroline nodded. "Yes, I know where her room is."

Joshua came back in with the doctor's bag, which he relinquished to Caroline as he helped with the body. This time it was she who led the way up the stairs to the modest suite her aunt occupied on the nursery level. It was quite close to Caroline's own room.

"Here we are."

She opened the door and went inside, pausing only to set the doctor's bag on the table next to the bed before she went to open the curtains. Her aunt's room was hung with portraits of people and pets who were long since dead and lengthy embroidered religious scripts expounding on the terror of hell and the devil.

"Let's place her on the bed," Dr. Harris instructed Joshua.

"I'll need to examine her before I can confirm how she died."

"Yes, sir." Joshua looked longingly back at the door. "Can I go now? With Mr. Woodford being unwell I'm needed in the kitchen."

"You can certainly go, but you must promise not to tell anyone what has happened before I have had a chance to inform Lord Greenwood of this tragedy." Dr. Harris looked searchingly at Joshua. "I know the circumstances are peculiar, but we must not jump to conclusions or spread any unnecessary gossip. Do you understand me?"

"Yes, sir. I promise." Joshua nodded. "I'll keep my trap shut until you give the word."

He exited the room with some alacrity, leaving Caroline staring at Dr. Harris.

"The circumstances are *peculiar*? Whatever makes you think that?" Caroline asked. "How often do you encounter an elderly lady with a knitting needle stuck through her neck?"

Dr. Harris frowned. "You seem a little overwrought, Miss Morton."

Caroline pointed a shaking finger at the motionless figure on the bed. "Because it appears that my great-aunt has been murdered!"

"Well, I would agree that it would have been extremely difficult for her to strangle herself." He paused. "Mind you, I have seen my own mother tangled in her wool—"

"Not like that," Caroline stated. "And I doubt your mother managed to stab herself in the throat while untangling herself."

"True." Dr. Harris walked over to the bed. "Will you help me undress her? I just want to make absolutely certain that she hasn't suffered any other injuries that are not yet apparent."

Several hours later, after promising Dr. Harris that she would rejoin him as soon as possible to break the news to her uncle and aunt, Caroline took a breakfast tray through to Mrs. Frogerton. Her employer was already sitting up in bed admiring the somewhat limited view from her window over the park.

"Goodness me, Caroline. You look tired. Did you not sleep well last night?" Mrs. Frogerton exclaimed.

"I . . ." Caroline considered exactly what to say. "Had something of a disturbed night."

"Sit down and tell me all about it." Mrs. Frogerton patted the silk counterpane of her bed. "Did you feel unwell?"

"No, something woke me and then I couldn't get back to sleep again," Caroline explained as she set the tray on her employer's lap and poured her some coffee.

"I'm not surprised your sleep was troubled, my dear. What with those appallingly snobby relatives of yours and your old fiancé turning up and looking down his nose at you." Mrs. Frogerton snorted. "My Septimus always said the aristocracy were a coldhearted lot and having met a whole bunch of them recently I can't say I disagree with him."

"Yet you want Dorothy to marry a peer."

· "I don't want that. Dotty does. I want her to be happy. If it was up to me, she'd marry Fred Guthridge's son and cement the partnership between our two families, but she'll never listen to me even though she's been half in love with Freddy for years. Silly girl got her head turned by too much attention at the local balls and thinks she's better than everyone now."

"She is very pretty," Caroline acknowledged, happy to take the conversation in an all-too-familiar direction. "And I do understand her desire to make the best of her looks and her fortune."

"Be that as it may, I'm more interested in what's wrong with you, my love."

Belatedly, Caroline remembered that Mrs. Frogerton was rarely diverted from her true purpose and tried to decide which parts of the unsavory truth to divulge. Dr. Harris hadn't told *her* not to share with her employer, and it was unlikely Mrs. Frogerton would gossip with anyone.

"When I couldn't sleep, I went down to see Mr. Woodford the butler in his rooms."

"The butler who went missing?" Mrs. Frogerton was always very aware of what was going on in her own household and had obviously noticed the absence of Mr. Woodford in the Greenwood residence. "Peggy mentioned that they were all at sixes and sevens yesterday because he wasn't present to manage the arrival of the guests."

"He went missing yesterday morning," Caroline said. "He was found wandering around in the cellar during the dinner party by one of the staff."

"Good gracious!" Mrs. Frogerton set her cup back down on the tray. "Are the cellars big enough to get lost in?"

"Yes, but Dr. Harris believes Mr. Woodford hit his head and was unconscious for a considerable amount of time."

"And no one found him all day?"

"The general assumption was that he might have gone down to the village to see his invalid sister and been unable to return because of the rain," Caroline said carefully. "But because of the guests arriving, and the grand dinner, no one had time to find out if that was true."

"If my butler wandered off on such an important day, I'd be the first to want to know about it." Mrs. Frogerton frowned. "And then he'd be out the door with a flea in his ear."

"Mr. Woodford has been with the family for over fifty years, ma'am. I doubt Lady Eleanor would dismiss him just for that."

"More fool her." Mrs. Frogerton ate some toast. "Mind, he didn't go anywhere, did he? Although I can't quite imagine how he ended up spending hours in the cellar without anyone noticing."

"I think once the idea was established that he had gone

down to the village, no one had time to question it." Caroline paused. "I wonder who first suggested that?"

"Why does it matter?"

"Because one has to wonder whether someone played a cruel trick on Mr. Woodford and deliberately kept him trapped in the cellar all day."

Caroline glanced over at Mrs. Frogerton, who met her gaze.

"Someone with a grudge against him, perhaps? Not every household exists in harmony, my dear."

"But I just can't imagine any of the current staff having a grudge against Mr. Woodford," Caroline confessed.

"You haven't lived here for almost a year now, lass. Things change, especially when someone like you who used to deal with the servants and their employers leaves and there is no one left in the middle to mediate."

"I suppose that's possible."

Mrs. Frogerton reached over the tray to pat her hand. "I don't wish to be insensitive, but Lady Eleanor's staffing problems are no longer your concern. Turn the matter over to your aunt and let her deal with it."

"I certainly intend to do that, ma'am. I am well aware of my current responsibility to you and Miss Frogerton." Caroline met her employer's gaze.

"There's no need to poker up, lass. I wasn't implying that you'd be derelict in your duty to me or to Dotty." Mrs. Frogerton hesitated. "When I spoke with Lady Eleanor last night, I received the distinct impression that she considers your position with me to be a temporary aberration before you come to your senses and return home."

"She can believe what she likes, but I have no intention of coming back to live here."

"Good." Mrs. Frogerton gave a brisk nod. "She doesn't deserve you."

Surprisingly affected by her employer's frank words, Caroline decided to share the rest of it.

"To be honest, ma'am. Staffing issues are likely to be the least of my aunt's current concerns."

"How so?" Mrs. Frogerton refilled her coffee cup and Caroline added some cream.

"Something else happened last night."

"Goodness me, whatever is wrong with this place?"

"My great-aunt Ines died."

"The lady I was speaking to at dinner? She seemed in robust spirits and good health—if a little quick to complain. Was it her heart?"

Caroline took the coffee cup out of her employer's hand. "Dr. Harris thinks she was murdered."

Mrs. Frogerton gasped loudly and pressed a hand to her bosom. "*Murdered?*" She crossed herself several times and fumbled to find her handkerchief. "Is this house cursed?"

"What on earth are you screeching about now, Mother?" Dorothy appeared in the connecting doorway between the two bedrooms. "Is the toast not to your liking?" She still wore her nightgown and robe and her long fair hair hung down her back.

"Lady Ines, the woman I spoke to at length yesterday evening at dinner, was killed during the night." Mrs. Frogerton shuddered. "We must leave this place as soon as possible."

Dorothy reached over to help herself to a piece of toast from her mother's plate. "I doubt anyone will be going anywhere quite yet. There is a storm raging throughout the fens. From what I've heard from Mabel I would be very surprised if the roads don't flood."

Caroline walked over to the window to look out over the landscaped gardens. Having lived at the hall for many years she was well aware of its susceptibility to be cut off due to flooding. Low sullen clouds were rolling in from the distant sea, obscuring the faint sunlight and cloaking the view in a deadening blanket of fog. She supposed she should be glad Dr. Harris had managed to arrive at the hall. If he hadn't come to attend Mr. Woodford, she doubted he would've been able to get through at all.

"Anyway, I don't want to leave now," Dorothy smirked. "I'm looking forward to the ball."

"You were the one who didn't want to come in the first place!" Mrs. Frogerton said. "Do you really think they'll still have a ball when one of their own has died in such awful circumstances?"

"I don't see why not." Dorothy shrugged. "I mean, it's not as if she was an important person. I'm sure Mabel doesn't give two figs for her."

"You are most unfeeling, Dotty." Mrs. Frogerton set her tray to one side with a thump. "And if there is indeed a murderer amongst us how can you possibly feel safe here? We might be murdered in our beds!"

Caroline moved to stand between the arguing pair. "If you will excuse me, ma'am, Miss Frogerton, I'll ring for Peggy to help you dress. I offered to accompany Dr. Harris to tell my aunt and uncle the bad news."

"They don't yet know?" Mrs. Frogerton shook her head. "Then you must certainly go and inform them." She glanced over at Dorothy. "We will await you here to discover exactly what Lady Eleanor intends to do about it!"

Chapter 6

When Caroline arrived in the main hall Dr. Harris already awaited her with his pocket watch in hand, which chimed as she approached.

"Good. You're punctual, Miss Morton. I asked the Greenwoods to meet me in his Lordship's study. Come along."

She touched his coat sleeve. "Did you discover any other reason why Great-Aunt Ines might have died?"

"Nothing obvious." He paused. "I suppose one might suggest an autopsy, but they are forbidden by religious fools, so I'll have to base my judgment on what I can see."

She gestured toward the right-hand side of the stairs. "My uncle's study is over here."

"Thank you."

He still wore the same clothing as on the previous day and his shirt was creased as was his cravat. His dark hair stuck up on one side as if he'd been sleeping on it. Caroline resolved to ask one of the footmen to find the doctor some clean attire as soon as possible. Her aunt for one would not find his disheveled appearance acceptable.

After knocking briskly on the door, Dr. Harris went in and bowed to Lord Greenwood and Lady Eleanor, who awaited them behind the desk.

"Good morning. I have some sad news to impart." He briefly inclined his head before continuing. "Lady Ines died in suspicious circumstances last night."

"She died?" Lady Eleanor raised an eyebrow. "She was in her seventies, I believe."

"I should imagine so," Dr. Harris said. "But her age was immaterial because I believe she was murdered."

"Don't be ridiculous!" Lady Greenwood snapped, and looked at her husband. "Where is Dr. McGregor? Is this man even qualified to offer such an excessively dramatic opinion?"

Dr. Harris bowed. "I attended the University of Edinburgh, my lady. I can assure you that I am better qualified than your previous physician will ever be. I will be taking over Dr. McGregor's practice in the summer."

"Not if I have anything to say in the matter." Lady Eleanor was not the kind of woman to shrink before an opponent. "And why are you here, Niece?"

"I was with Dr. Harris when he went to administer to Great-Aunt Ines."

"How so?"

"I was visiting Mr. Woodford earlier this morning when Joshua came in to say that he had found Aunt Ines in the small parlor and that the doctor was urgently required. Dr. Harris asked me to accompany him and I complied with his request."

"And was your aunt dead or murdered?" Lord Greenwood asked.

"She was definitely dead, sir." Caroline paused. "And I would have to agree with Dr. Harris that she was murdered."

"Nonsense!" Eleanor snorted. "How pray were the two of you able to make such a decision?"

Dr. Harris raised his eyebrows. "It wasn't exactly difficult, my lady. She'd been strangled with her own yarn and stabbed through the throat with a knitting needle."

Eleanor gasped and pressed her hand to her mouth.

After a long moment Lord Greenwood cleared his throat. "Ah. That would put things in a different light, then."

"We can't let anyone know about this." Eleanor began to pace the room. "There must be some reasonable explanation."

"I doubt it," Dr. Harris said. "Someone in this house made a deliberate decision to end Lady Ines's life."

"So you say, but I still don't wish to alarm my other guests." She stared at the doctor. "Who knows about this?"

"Apart from me? Joshua, Miss Morton, and now yourselves," Dr. Harris replied. "But obviously we will need to alert the authorities as soon as possible."

"I am the local magistrate," Lord Greenwood spoke up.

Dr. Harris frowned. "You can hardly investigate yourself, sir."

"As I certainly didn't kill my own relative, I doubt I will have any issue with remaining impartial." Lord Greenwood's usually benign expression disappeared. "And I don't take kindly to having my reputation questioned by a man such as yourself."

Dr. Harris stiffened. "I can assure you that my family does not shirk from defending their reputation either, my lord."

Caroline braced herself to intervene as the two men glared at each other like fighting cocks.

Lord Greenwood glanced out of the window where the leaden clouds obscured both the sun and the view of the horizon. "In any case, I doubt any messenger to the magistrate in the next district over would get through for days. Any investigation into this unfortunate death will have to wait until then."

"I cannot accept that, sir," Dr. Harris said.

"I believe I have stated my opinion, Dr. Harris, and as the owner of this house and the local magistrate my word is law in these parts." He glanced over at his wife, who displayed her extreme agitation by the high flashes of color on her cheekbones. "We will keep this matter between ourselves. If anyone asks after Ines—and that is most unlikely, because whoever notices she exists anyway? We will tell them that she is indisposed and currently confined to her rooms."

"Which is a lie," Dr. Harris stated.

Caroline was beginning to wonder if the good doctor had any idea of compromising with his elders and supposed betters. If he wished to have a career serving the gentry, he would soon learn that his forthright opinions would not be welcome. She almost felt sorry for him.

"It will allow our guests and our young daughter to enjoy her birthday celebrations," Eleanor said firmly. "Ines would be the last person to want Mabel to suffer over her demise. She adored all our children."

From her own experience Caroline knew that wasn't true, but people did have a tendency to want to idolize the dead. She'd frequently heard her father described as a decent, hardworking, Christian gentleman, which was about as far from the truth as possible.

Dr. Harris bowed. "As you said, the decision is yours, but when the coroner or the new magistrate do attend, I will insist on speaking to them."

"If you wish to continue to live and work in this area of the county, I wouldn't recommend that, Dr. Harris," her uncle said. "You might also wish to reconsider your combative attitude." He inclined his head. "Good day, sir."

"Lord Greenwood." Dr. Harris bowed, turned on his heel, and stalked out of the room, banging the door behind him.

"Well," Eleanor said. "What an unpleasant man."

"He merely attempted to enlighten you about a murder that took place in your front parlor, ma'am." Caroline met her aunt's glare with one of her own. "One might think you would be grateful for the information."

"Hardly," Eleanor said. "What a meddlesome busybody. If Dr. McGregor had been in attendance, none of this would've happened."

"Great-Aunt Ines would still be dead, Aunt," Caroline reminded her.

"Oh, for goodness' sake, Caroline." Eleanor rounded on her. "You are as bad as Dr. Harris. Go away and find something else to do. I am tired of listening to you both."

"With pleasure, ma'am." Caroline curtsied.

"And keep it to yourself, do you hear me?" Eleanor called out as Caroline reached the door.

"Too late," Caroline whispered to herself as she shut the door and headed for the stairs. She would caution Mrs. Frogerton from sharing the news, but if it did get out? She would certainly not deny it. Both Great-Aunt Ines and Dr. Harris deserved better.

When she reached Mrs. Frogerton's rooms she found both her employer and her daughter anxiously awaiting her.

"Ma'am?" Caroline found a paisley shawl and draped it over Mrs. Frogerton's shoulders. "That matter I spoke of earlier?"

"That a murderer is loose in the house?"

"It appears I was mistaken." Caroline met her employer's gaze head-on. "Lady Eleanor assures me that Lady Ines died of natural causes and that there is no cause for concern."

"You see, Mother?" Dorothy tossed her head. "I told you not to worry about something so fantastical." She cast a glance at Caroline. "Some people like to create problems simply to make themselves look important."

"I apologize unreservedly." Caroline curtsied to Dorothy. "You are right. I should never have mentioned the matter. The last thing I wanted to do was upset your mother."

Dorothy left the room and Caroline was just about to follow when Mrs. Frogerton held her back.

"Dotty might be convinced that everything is fine, but I am not."

Caroline grimaced. "I should not have said anything to you, ma'am. It was most indiscreet of me."

Mrs. Frogerton chuckled. "You can't fool me, missy. I know exactly why your aunt is trying to pretend nothing happened. She doesn't want a scandal to spoil her daughter's birthday. I can understand that, and I assure you that I'll keep my mouth shut, but I'll also be watching the staff and the guests very carefully."

"If I could think of any reason why anyone would want to murder Great-Aunt Ines, I might be inclined to agree with you, ma'am, but from all accounts she has lived in this house and hardly left it for the past sixty years." Caroline hesitated. "In truth, in the last few years I hardly even noticed she existed."

"What a sad legacy for the lady. To be so forgotten," Mrs. Frogerton said softly. "Now, come on, my dear, let's go downstairs and make sure Dotty doesn't start gossiping to impress her new friends."

A while later, as the guests gathered to chat and eat a light nuncheon in the dining room, Caroline took the opportunity to climb the stairs and visit the nursery. It was disconcerting to realize that her aunt had been right and that no one had noticed or commented on Great-Aunt Ines's absence. If Caroline had agreed to stay on at Greenwood Hall, would that have been her fate one day? To die alone, unnoticed, and unloved in the supposedly warm embrace of her family? It was no wonder she had chosen to avoid such an ending.

"Oh! Excuse me."

Caroline started as she almost bumped into Helen, Francis's sister, who emerged unexpectedly around the corner. Helen recoiled as if Caroline carried an infectious disease and brushed at her skirt.

"It would've been much better if you'd stayed away, Caroline. You have made Francis *most* uncomfortable," Helen scolded.

"I have made *him* uncomfortable?" Caroline raised her eyebrows. "He chose to accompany you to my aunt's home. How am I at fault?"

"We were invited! You were supposed to have . . . *gone.*"

"For the convenience of your brother and society, who do not know what to do with a woman whose own father betrayed her and spent her dowry?" Caroline raised her chin. "I am supposed to, to erase myself?"

"Yes!"

"Why exactly? Because I make you feel uncomfortable? You once claimed to be my friend, and to care about me, and suddenly I repulse you because I am no longer of value to your family?" Caroline was beyond caring who heard her now. "I have become nothing to you?"

"You hurt my brother!"

"I set him free! If you can't bear to acknowledge me as an acquaintance, Helen, how in God's name would you have treated me if I'd married your brother and this disaster had befallen me then? Sequestered me in a country house some-where? Taken my children to raise with your own?"

"That's not fair!"

Caroline stepped back; her voice was trembling despite her best efforts. "After consultation with your father, I did what I thought was required of me. If you or your brother took issue with my decision, I suggest you speak to him."

"Caroline . . ."

"Enough." Caroline half turned away. "You have made your position clear, Helen, and so have I. I wish you nothing but good in your life whereas you want me to disappear from yours. As soon as I leave Greenwood Hall, I will make my best efforts to oblige you. Good afternoon."

She stomped up the next set of stairs and almost collided with Francis, who was coming down. He opened his mouth to speak and she glared at him.

"Please do not say a word. I have had quite enough of your family for one day."

She deliberately pushed past him and continued on, tears crowding her throat as she went into the main nursery. To her surprise it was empty. She glanced at the clock and remembered that rain or shine all the children were required to take a walk at eleven. As it was currently pouring with rain, she had to assume they were amusing themselves by running up and down the long picture gallery.

As she waited for them to return, she absentmindedly set things to rights, a fallen book here, a dropped toy restored to the shelf, a half-darned stocking stuffed beneath a cushion. She almost smiled at the last item. She'd hated learning to darn and had avoided the task at all costs. She vividly remembered Great-Aunt Ines sitting by this very fireside instructing them and her acid comments and sharp slaps when they failed to live up to her exacting standards.

She found one of the small porcelain-headed dolls and picked it up, smoothing the tangled curls of the wig between her fingers as she went over to the glass cabinet that held the nursery's most treasured toys. Because they were both valuable and fragile the dolls were only supposed to be out under strict supervision on Sunday after church. She located the key in its usual spot behind the clock on the highest mantelpiece and opened the large doors.

The dolls sat in a straight row of glassy-eyed stares on the top shelf above the steam trains, clockwork toys, and musical boxes that were only played at Christmas. She replaced the doll and was just about to shut the cabinet when she noticed the front of the large doll's house that took up the rest of the cabinet was slightly ajar. She went to reattach the hook at the top of the panel and realized that something was preventing it from closing.

Opening the door more fully, she saw a strand of yarn

had fallen over the edge. Even as her gaze traveled up the striped wool to the small figure in one of the parlors her mind refused to comprehend what was right in front of her. She deliberately closed her eyes and opened them again, but nothing had changed. One of the dolls was seated in a chair by the fire, the knitting wool wrapped around her throat, and one of the tiny knitting needles had been stabbed through her neck.

Chapter 7

"Whatever is the matter, Caroline?"

Caroline gasped and spun around to find her sister, Susan, staring at her. The sound of the other children clomping up the stairs and shouting to one another echoed through the open door from the corridor as they filed in.

"Nothing!" Caroline hastily relatched the doll's house, closed the glass cabinet, and put the key in her pocket. "I found one of the dolls on the floor and was just putting her back."

Susan frowned. "They aren't supposed to be out."

"I am well aware of that." Caroline walked away from the cabinet, her heart still pounding. "I came to ask if you'd like to go for a walk with me, but it seems as though you have already been out."

"We always go at eleven, but today we had to stay in the house because it's raining. Aunt Eleanor made us walk very quietly so as not to disturb her guests." Susan helped one of the younger girls take off her shoes. "Did you know Great-Aunt Ines is dead?"

"Who told you that?" Caroline asked.

Susan shrugged. "I can't remember, but it is quite sad. She rarely came into the nursery anymore, but she still knitted a lot of stockings for everyone."

If the nursery children knew Ines had died, it was obviously common knowledge among the staff. Had Joshua blurted out the horrible truth, or had Aunt Eleanor addressed the matter herself in more measured terms? Caroline had to assume the latter. She hadn't noticed any of the guests panicking except the Frogertons, which was entirely her fault.

"Perhaps I'll come back later this afternoon and have tea with you," Caroline suggested as Susan carried on helping the children settle at the table for their lessons.

"That would be lovely." Susan smiled. "Mabel said she would pop in and bring all the others. It will be so good to see everyone again."

"Then I will most definitely attend." Caroline nodded to the two nursemaids who had shepherded the youngest children up the stairs and walked to the door. "I'll see you at three o'clock."

She escaped into the hallway and considered what to do next. Whom should she tell? Or would it be better to keep her gruesome discovery to herself? She pressed her hand over her heart, her gaze on the faded strip of carpet running along the center of the corridor. If she confided in Dr. Harris, he would immediately demand answers that were unlikely to be forthcoming, and if she told her aunt . . . she would be ordered to keep her discovery to herself.

She walked down the stairs and into her employer's suite, hoping some general tidying up would help settle her mind. To her surprise, Mrs. Frogerton was ensconced in the seat by the fire, her spectacles on the end of her nose, reading the newspaper.

"Mrs. Frogerton!" Caroline rushed over. "Did you ring for me? I was in the nursery."

"I didn't need you, lass. I just wanted a quiet hour to read the news without having to listen to all that pointless chattering downstairs."

"Then I won't disturb you." Caroline went to step back.

"What's wrong?" Mrs. Frogerton studied her intently. "Who has upset you?"

"Why would you think that?" Caroline fought to find a smile. "I merely—"

"Because you've lived with me for six months and I am beginning to understand your moods." Her employer pointed at the chair opposite her own. "Now, sit down and tell me what's going on."

Caroline sat; her hands twisted together in her lap. In truth, it was something of a relief to have the no-nonsense Mrs. Frogerton to confide in.

"It might be nothing—but, while I was in the nursery, I discovered that one of the dolls in the doll's house had wool wrapped around her throat and a needle stabbed through her neck."

"That sounds just like something one of my brothers would've done. There's no real harm in it," Mrs. Frogerton said comfortably. "Septimus told me he used to cut his sister's curls off with his pocketknife."

"That's not what upset me, ma'am." Caroline slowly inhaled and met her employer's sympathetic gaze. "That's exactly how we found Great-Aunt Ines."

"Goodness me. Then that is most peculiar indeed." Mrs. Frogerton shook her head, making the lace of her cap tremble. "There's a bad feeling in this house, Caroline. I said it before, and I still believe it. That poor butler, and now Lady Ines . . ."

"Someone must have found out how Great-Aunt Ines died and thought it amusing to mimic her death in the doll's house," Caroline said slowly. "But who would do such a cruel and unnecessary thing? The only people who know exactly how she died are my uncle and aunt, Dr. Harris, Joshua, and me."

Mrs. Frogerton shrugged. "I doubt the Greenwoods would sink to such a level. What about Dr. Harris?"

"He is far more likely to call you out for your crimes to your face," Caroline said. "He has already expressed his displeasure with my uncle and aunt for not immediately reporting that Lady Ines was murdered to the authorities."

"Which just leaves you and Joshua." Mrs. Frogerton paused. "You both have access to the nursery, and, if I might say so, lass, you do have many reasons to be angry at your treatment in this house."

"Do you think I'm a murderer then?"

Mrs. Frogerton didn't smile. "I don't, but other people might."

"But what about Joshua?" Caroline countered. "He was the one who claimed to have found Lady Ines. Perhaps he was also her murderer?"

"Far more likely." Mrs. Frogerton folded the newspaper and set it on the table. "And let's not forget what happened to Mr. Woodford."

"What does that have to do with anything?" Caroline asked.

"It's a pattern, lass, like the overlaying threads in a piece of fabric. What if Mr. Woodford was supposed to be dead as well?"

Caroline stared at her for a long moment as her stomach did an uneasy flip. "I hadn't thought of that."

"Perhaps whoever hit Mr. Woodford on the head meant to return and finish him off when he was still unconscious."

Caroline shot to her feet and began to pace the room. "But why? Why would anyone want to kill either of these people? What harm have they ever done?"

"That's an excellent question." Mrs. Frogerton sat back in her chair and contemplated Caroline. "If we can discover what the answer might be, we would surely unveil the murderer."

"With all due respect, ma'am, are you perhaps allowing your imagination to run a little wild here?" Caroline asked.

Mrs. Frogerton chuckled. "Well, I do enjoy a good gothic novel or two."

"Is it possible this is someone's idea of a joke?" Caroline ventured cautiously. "A cruel joke, obviously, but not one with murderous intent."

"How so?" Mrs. Frogerton's brow crinkled.

"Mr. Woodford wasn't murdered, he was merely made to look foolish and weak, and maybe Aunt Ines *did* die of natural causes and someone came along and found her and decided it would be . . . amusing to wrap her in wool and stick the needle in her neck."

Even as she said the words Caroline felt foolish, but she had to offer an alternative to Mrs. Frogerton's version of events. This was her family they were discussing, and she wasn't enjoying the experience at all.

"It would also explain why someone went into the nursery and did that to one of the dolls."

"I suppose you might be right, dear." Mrs. Frogerton didn't look convinced. "You know these people far better than I do. I have heard that the gentry get up to the wildest tricks during these house parties."

"I have been to several such parties in my life, ma'am, and I can assure you that murder has never been on the agenda. The most scandalous thing I've ever seen is some gentleman being caught in the wrong lady's bedchamber, and that is usually explained away in an instant."

"Not in my house," Mrs. Frogerton said firmly. "As a good Christian woman, I don't condone adultery. Anyone misbehaving themselves under my roof would be immediately cast out."

"Which is exactly as it should be, ma'am, but the aristocracy have always been a law unto themselves."

"I'd like to see this doll's house of yours," Mrs. Frogerton said.

"If you wish, we can visit the nursery later this evening when the children have gone to bed," Caroline suggested. "I still have the key for the cabinet."

"Good. Now, would you say that Mr. Woodford and Lady Ines were friends?"

"Not at all. Despite her reduced circumstances, my aunt was very high in the instep and would never have considered a member of staff a friend."

"They are from the same generation," Mrs. Frogerton mused. "One has to wonder if they ever had a romantic liaison."

"Mr. Woodford and my great-aunt? I can't think of anything more unlikely."

"You'd be surprised what goes on in these so-called great houses, lass. I read the scandal sheets."

Caroline knew this was true because they were regularly delivered to the house in Half Moon Street and Mrs. Frogerton had been known to stop on a street corner and buy one with the ink still wet. She'd regaled Dorothy and Caroline with some of the more lurid stories and eagerly awaited the next installment of each dramatic incident with great enthusiasm. Caroline hadn't the heart to tell her that most of the stories were complete fiction and had secretly quite enjoyed seeing the great and the godly unmercifully pilloried.

"I've known Mr. Woodford and Great-Aunt Ines all my life and I have never detected the slightest hint of attraction between them," Caroline repeated.

"Then what else do they have in common?" Mrs. Frogerton asked.

"They've both lived here for almost their entire lives."

"Lady Ines never married?"

"I don't believe so." Caroline frowned. "I think she is related to my uncle on his maternal side and came to live here when his mother married his father. She can't have been more than twenty at the time. I can ask my aunt, if it helps."

"And Mr. Woodford?"

"His father was the steward here. He and his sister grew up in the village down the road and both went into service at the house."

"Is his sister still alive?"

"Yes, but she's an invalid confined to her home. Mr. Woodford is a most conscientious brother and visits her regularly, in fact—" Caroline paused. "That's where everyone thought he had gone yesterday."

"Perhaps we might go and meet her while her brother is unwell?" Mrs. Frogerton suggested.

"For what purpose?"

Her employer shrugged. "You said they were close. She might know something about the current situation that we do not."

"But is it really our place to be prying into such matters?" Caroline met Mrs. Frogerton's shrewd gaze.

"You'd rather sit in that drawing room and listen to people whispering behind your back, lass?" Mrs. Frogerton snorted. "A more badly behaved bunch I have never met. Fancy blaming you for your father's sins. It is most unchristian."

"I do try to ignore them."

"As you should, but a drive out to the village in a closed carriage won't hurt, will it? Trust me, they'll be back to gossiping about us both at dinner."

Caroline stood up. "If you really wish to visit Miss Woodford, I am more than willing to accompany you. If you'll excuse me, I'll just go and order the carriage."

"That's my girl." Mrs. Frogerton gave her a nod of approval. "And mind you, don't mention it to Dotty. The last thing we need is her following us around complaining."

"I think she is too busy being charming to Lord Epping," Caroline replied.

"Who is a pleasant enough man."

"I have never heard anything bad about him, ma'am."

Mrs. Frogerton chuckled. "Don't worry, Dotty's already told me he's not grand enough to suit her tastes. She's just using him to hone her skills."

"Good for her."

Caroline set out her employer's bonnet, pelisse, and

stout boots and went down to the hall to find a footman to send a note to the stables to bring around the carriage. There was no one there so she went toward the kitchens. As she walked along the bare, echoing corridors she could already hear Mrs. Maddox's voice raised in anger.

It was not unusual for the cook to lose her temper, but this sounded far more serious. The kitchen door was open, and Caroline paused inside the door as Mrs. Maddox held forth to the entire staff, who were gathered around the table.

"What a bloody great mess! Now, who's going to own up and tell me what they did, eh?" The cook gestured at the table. "All my puddings and jellies that I left to set overnight ruined!"

She looked up and saw Caroline. "You can tell her ladyship that dinner tonight will be short of desserts because some fool thought it was amusing to upend all the molds and destroy all the puddings. Look at this mess!"

Caroline came farther into the kitchen, aware of the silent crowd of servants around her. On the table were several large metal trays containing hundreds of molds from large to small that had been knocked over, spilling ingredients into the pans.

"I left them in the cold scullery to set overnight and came into this," Mrs. Maddox said. "And we all know who her ladyship is going to blame, don't we?"

"I'm sure you've made plenty of other options, Mrs. Maddox. You are such an excellent cook." Caroline immediately attempted to soothe the angry woman. "I understand that this is upsetting, but—"

"Upsetting? Why would anyone do this?" Mrs. Maddox's gaze swept the assembled staff. "Does someone here want me to lose my job?"

"I'm sure no one wishes that," Caroline said firmly. "If someone did inadvertently ruin these puddings, they should own up."

None of the staff moved or displayed a single hint of guilt.

"Perhaps it was the cat."

Everyone turned to look at Nathaniel, the youngest member of staff, who ran errands, kept the cooking fires burning, and turned the spits when necessary.

"I suppose that is possible." Caroline turned back to Mrs. Maddox. "They do rather enjoy cream and milk."

"The cat's not supposed to be in here at night." Mrs. Maddox glared at the small boy. "Have you been letting him in again?"

"He gets cold and wet outside," Nathaniel protested. "It's been pouring with rain."

"Is it possible that the cat was trapped in the cold scullery and caused all this damage while trying to escape?" Caroline asked.

"I suppose so, miss." Mrs. Maddox didn't look as if she believed that for one moment. "But I didn't see any damned cat in there when I opened that door this morning."

"Then perhaps it would be best to put the matter behind you, Mrs. Maddox, and proceed with the day." Caroline tried to sound a positive note. She looked at the two kitchen maids. "Why don't you make a start clearing this away while Mrs. Maddox gets on?"

The cook turned her back and stalked over to the stove, still muttering while everyone else in the kitchen either started clearing the table or left as fast as they could.

Caroline saw Joshua and went toward him before he could escape.

"I need a carriage for Mrs. Frogerton. She wishes to visit the village."

"In this weather, miss?" Joshua frowned.

"I did mention that, but she insists." Caroline shrugged. "How is Mr. Woodford today?"

"Much improved, miss. Dr. Harris told him he can get out of bed and sit in the kitchen for a while if he feels up to it."

"That's excellent news." Caroline paused. "And how are you feeling after last night?"

Joshua's gaze slid away from hers. "I couldn't sleep a wink, miss. Kept seeing the lady's bulging eyes and . . . the rest of it."

"It was indeed a horrible thing to see," Caroline agreed. "I assume you've kept the details to yourself?"

"Yes, miss. I promised Dr. Harris I would." Joshua nodded. "Now if you'll excuse me, if you're still wanting that carriage, I need to get a message to the stables."

He disappeared in something of a rush, leaving Caroline staring thoughtfully after him. Her sense of unease that Mrs. Frogerton was right and that there was a bad feeling in the house was growing. Either Joshua felt guilty because he had shared the details of Great-Aunt Ines's death with someone, which was how Susan had found out, or was it something worse?

Resolving to come back and speak to both Mr. Woodford and Joshua after her trip to the village, Caroline gathered up a basket of supplies for Miss Woodford without bothering the cook further and went back to the suite to find Mrs. Frogerton ready to go out. They walked down the stairs together to await the arrival of the carriage.

Unfortunately, as they were waiting, Lord Francis walked through the hall and immediately reversed course to come and speak to Caroline.

She braced herself as he stared down at her. Mrs. Frogerton murmured something about fetching an umbrella and moved away.

"I believe I owe you an apology, Lady Caroline. My sister should not have spoken to you as she did. This is still your home and it was remiss of me to assume that you would no longer be invited here."

"If your sister has anything she wishes to say to me, I would much rather hear it from her own lips, my lord, rather than yours," Caroline said.

"She . . . was distraught."

"Why? Because I objected to her desire for me to simply fade away and stop appearing in your lives?"

He grimaced. "I agree that was an unfortunate turn of phrase for her to use."

It occurred to her that he must have overheard the entire conversation from his position on the stairs above them and had chosen neither to intervene nor reprimand his sister.

"I refuse to apologize for my father's disgraceful behavior or be humiliated by it." She held his gaze. "You see, I have already lost everything I care about and have nothing left to regret. If you will excuse me, I need to attend to my employer."

She turned away and walked back to where Joshua was opening the front door for Mrs. Frogerton.

"Lady Caroline?"

She looked back over her shoulder. "Yes?"

"What did you mean about my father interfering?"

"As I said to your sister, perhaps you should ask him."

She didn't dare look back again and continued over to where Mrs. Frogerton was trying hard not to look like she was eavesdropping and failing miserably.

"Are you ready to go, ma'am? I do hope we will be able to get over the bridge into the village. The river can flood its banks when it gets like this."

"We will do our best to get there and if we have to turn back then so be it."

Mrs. Frogerton drew Caroline under the cover of the umbrella as they ran through the sheeting rain to the covered carriage. She was puffing slightly as she sat down opposite Caroline and spread out her skirts.

"Did you settle things with your young man?"

Caroline sighed as the carriage jolted into motion. "We settled everything a year ago when I released him from our engagement. He ran away as fast as he could."

"Then he's a fool."

"He agreed to marry the dowered daughter of an earl and ended up with a millstone around his neck."

"If he truly cared for you, it should not have mattered, lass."

Caroline looked out of the window at the endless rain. "It mattered to his father and Francis has always been very proud of his family name."

Mrs. Frogerton's snort was eloquent enough to convey her feelings before she actually said a word. "You would've been a credit to him. If he wasn't clever enough to realize that, then more fool him."

"Thank you." Caroline smiled at her employer. "When I first broached the subject, I was naïve enough to think he wouldn't care—in truth—that's what he told me. It was only after he'd consulted with his family that he returned to say that he accepted my decision and wished me well."

"Did you love him, lass?" Mrs. Frogerton asked gently.

"I thought so." Caroline squeezed her gloved hands together in her lap. "But now all I feel toward him is anger."

"Because he let you down when you were counting on his support."

"Exactly."

"There's nothing wrong with being angry at someone who has hurt you."

"In my world it is not an acceptable response. I'm supposed to bow out of society, accept the blame for my father's failings, and gracefully disappear from view." She raised her chin. "But I refuse to do that. My father's disastrous choices were not my responsibility."

"Good girl." Mrs. Frogerton nodded. "When Septimus died so unexpectedly, everyone assumed I would have to remarry to get a man to take over his businesses, but I wasn't having it. I was quite capable of running everything myself—had been doing so for a decade if anyone had cared to ask. I'd acquired a taste for having my own money and making my own decisions without a man controlling everything."

Caroline didn't doubt that for a second.

"In truth, all my business interests are flourishing." Mrs. Frogerton beamed. "And I am responsible for that. I let no one forget it, least of all my son. He works for me, not the other way around."

"And does your son resent you?" Caroline asked, fascinated.

"Not if he wants to inherit anything from me, he doesn't. I own it all. He'll have to wait until I die to control the business, or if I don't think he's up to it I can bequeath it to someone else."

"I wish I'd had the power to curtail my father's excesses and consult with the family solicitor to stop him stealing funds from our dowries," Caroline said wistfully. "After our mother died, he was allowed to do whatever he wished without oversight."

"Surely there are laws against such things?" Mrs. Frogerton frowned.

"I did not have the funds to find out, ma'am, and I'm not sure how one would prosecute a man who is already dead."

Caroline looked out of the window as they approached the low bridge that linked the estate to the road into the village. "The river has almost overflowed the bank. We will have to be careful. This is the only way to cross the water in a carriage."

"How far is the village from here?" Mrs. Frogerton asked.

"It is very close." Caroline pointed at the tree line. "You can see the chimney pots of the coaching inn from here."

When they arrived at the low-sitting thatched cottage on the end of a row leading toward the village market square, Caroline alighted first and came to help Mrs. Frogerton down.

"Be careful, ma'am. It is very muddy."

"Then it's a good thing I wore my stout boots." Mrs. Frogerton took her arm. "The cottage looks in good repair."

"My uncle is a conscientious landlord."

Caroline opened the gate that led into a small front garden filled with flowers and they went up the path to the front door. She knocked on the door and waited for what seemed like forever before someone scrabbled at the latch.

"Who are you, then?" The young girl who opened the door didn't look particularly pleased to see them. "And what do you want?"

"We've come from Greenwood Hall on behalf of Mr. Woodford to ascertain that Miss Vera is still in good health," Caroline said.

"From the hall?" The girl scowled. "I suppose you'd better come in, then."

"Thank you." Caroline lowered her head and stepped through into the front room, which was obviously the best parlor and had a cold, unused feel to it. She followed the girl through to the back, where there was a warm fire in the grate and Miss Vera sat by the fire reading a book. She wore a simple lace cap over her white hair, a black gown, and a cream shawl wrapped around her bodice.

"Good morning, Miss Woodford." Knowing that the older lady was rather deaf, Caroline spoke clearly. "It is very good to see you again. May I introduce you to Mrs. Frogerton, who is staying at the hall with me?"

"It's nice to meet you, Miss Woodford." Mrs. Frogerton nodded at the elderly woman. "You have a very pleasant home."

"Thank you." Miss Woodford had sharp, intelligent eyes and a face lined with suffering. "Lord Greenwood has been very kind to our family. When my brother retires, he will move in here with me, and we'll be able to live comfortably off our pensions." She gestured at the settle on the other side of the fire. "Won't you both sit down?"

Caroline held up the basket she'd brought with her. "As

Mr. Woodford has been unavoidably detained at the hall, I thought I'd bring you some supplies and ask after your health."

Miss Woodford raised her gaze to Caroline's. "Is my brother unwell? He was supposed to visit me the other day and didn't appear."

"He had a fall in the cellar and suffered some bruising and a headache as a result," Caroline said.

"Oh, dear. I keep telling him that he is too old to manage those stone steps down into the cellars, but he will have none of it. When will he be able to come and visit me again?"

"I'm not sure, Miss Woodford. He is under the care of Dr. Harris, who will make very sure he is well enough to resume his duties before allowing him out of bed. I'm sure he will come and see you as soon as possible."

"I do hope so. I worry about him so much."

"Why is that, Miss Woodford?" Mrs. Frogerton asked.

"Because running that house is a burden for anyone and with Lord Greenwood growing more difficult to please and stingier with the staff budget, Thomas struggles to make ends meet and provide good service."

"I can imagine." Mrs. Frogerton nodded. "I did notice that the staff seemed somewhat overworked myself."

Miss Woodford's worried gaze slid to Caroline. "Not that I wish to cast aspersions on any member of your family, my lady, but I am concerned for my brother's health."

"As you should be." Caroline paused. "Has Mr. Woodford expressed any dissatisfaction with the members of his staff recently?"

"He certainly struggles to keep the younger men in order. He says they don't respect his authority and are rather too prone to answer back."

"Did he mention anyone in particular?"

"I believe it was one of the footmen." Miss Woodford's brow crinkled. "Or perhaps one of the stable hands. I can't quite remember. He does go on sometimes."

The young girl came back into the room and went up to Miss Woodford. "Do you want me to make some tea, miss?"

"That would be lovely, Ivy." Miss Woodford looked at Caroline. "If you ladies have time to join me?"

Caroline glanced out of the back window at the leaden gray skies. "We would be delighted, but if the rain continues to fall, we might have to be on our way with some haste. The banks of the river are in danger of overflowing, which would cut us off from the hall."

"Then perhaps I should not keep you." Miss Woodford sounded genuinely regretful. "You will give Thomas my best wishes, won't you? Tell him not to worry about me and that the matter we spoke of the other day can wait until he is feeling better."

"Do you wish me to take him a note, Miss Woodford?" Caroline asked. "The last thing he needs right now is to be worrying unnecessarily."

"That is very kind of you, my lady, but just tell him I have spoken to our solicitor, and that all is well."

"Then we will be off." Caroline rose from her seat and Mrs. Frogerton followed suit. "Thank you so much for seeing us."

"It was a pleasure. I was very sorry to hear about the death of your father. He was always very pleasant to me when I worked up at the hall."

"Thank you." Caroline curtsied and glanced over at Mrs. Frogerton. "Are you ready to depart, ma'am?"

"Indeed I am." Mrs. Frogerton's attention appeared to be elsewhere, but she gathered up her cloak and followed Caroline back to the front door, her gaze everywhere. She paused to look at the front parlor. "Hmm . . ."

Ivy didn't bother to show them out, which suited Caroline just fine. She helped Mrs. Frogerton up the steps of the carriage, got in, and shut the door.

"Well, that didn't accomplish much, did it?"

"I disagree. We now know that the Woodfords are engaged in some activity that necessitates the expense of a solicitor, which is a not inconsiderable sum."

"In what respect does that help with the current situation?"

"I'm not sure yet."

Caroline sat back and viewed her companion in a somewhat unfavorable light. "*I* was hoping Miss Woodford would say that she had seen her brother before his accident, tell us what he said, and that would solve everything."

"We don't know when he last saw her. It still could've been that morning. She might have been lying," Mrs. Frogerton replied. "She also confirmed my suspicion that Mr. Woodford was not at peace either with his employers or his staff, which means that your notion that he was trapped in the cellar as a horrible joke still has merit."

"As opposed to your opinion that he was supposed to be murdered like Great-Aunt Ines."

"Did you notice something odd about the cottage?" Mrs. Frogerton appeared to change the subject.

"What about it?"

"Would you say that the Greenwoods were generous with their staff? Miss Woodford appeared to imply that they were not."

"My uncle is something of a miser," Caroline agreed. "Except when it comes to his beloved game birds and stables."

"There were a lot of items in the cottage that appeared rather grand for their surroundings. Is it likely that Lord Greenwood allowed his butler to have his excess furniture and fittings?"

"I . . . didn't notice that," Caroline said slowly. "But my knowledge of my aunt and uncle would lead me to say no."

"Then I wonder how the Woodfords acquired them? I mean it is perfectly normal for servants to benefit from their employers, cast-off clothing, tea leaves, wastepaper, and other such items, but—"

Caroline interrupted her companion. "Are you suggesting Mr. Woodford takes my aunt's used tea leaves?"

"Of course he does! They can be used more than once, Caroline. Even the leftovers from a bottle of brandy or wine served at a dinner that's been decanted can be sold for a profit." Mrs. Frogerton shook her head. "I suppose you have never run your own household and can be excused from knowing such things."

"I had no idea," Caroline said. "But you think Mr. Woodford has gone beyond such petty and apparently acceptable acts to acquiring pieces of furniture and other things he has no right to?"

"I believe the word might be 'stealing' rather than 'acquiring,' Caroline. How often do your uncle and aunt visit his sister? Never, I'd wager, and how would they know exactly what had gone missing in such a large house?"

"This is all very well, ma'am, but what does it have to do with Mr. Woodford's being trapped in the cellar and Great-Aunt Ines's death?"

"I'm still not sure, but it definitely suggests that Mr. Woodford might not be the innocent victim he claims to be. Perhaps he has been taking all the perks and his refusal to share with the rest of the house has built a sizeable resentment against him." Mrs. Frogerton gasped. "Maybe Lady Ines was helping him!"

Caroline raised an eyebrow and Mrs. Frogerton chuckled.

"Perhaps I am concocting fairy tales in my head, but it does make me wonder."

Despite her initial rejection of Mrs. Frogerton's ridiculous idea Caroline found herself considering it.

"You think my great-aunt was giving Mr. Woodford things from the house for his cottage. But why would he be doing that?"

"Perhaps he offered to sell them for her?"

"But he kept them for himself. That would certainly cause friction between them."

"Goodness knows if I were trapped in a family house with no independence and money of my own, I too might try to find a way out. And I would be furious if the butler cheated *me*."

Caroline nodded. "I wonder if anyone has been through her possessions yet? Perhaps that might show if she has money tucked away somewhere."

"You could offer to do that for your aunt," Mrs. Frogerton suggested.

"I will as soon as we get back," Caroline agreed. "If we can safely navigate the bridge and not get swept away in the floodwater."

"Goodness me, Caroline, it could be fun!" her employer said brightly. "What if we ended up in the sea and were taken up by pirates?"

"Then we'd both soon be dead."

Mrs. Frogerton went off into peals of laughter and even Caroline had to smile in the end.

Chapter 8

Having secured her aunt's permission to go through Ines's possessions, Caroline let herself into the suite and leaned against the door, inhaling the smell of stale violets and musty linen. Her great-aunt's body had been taken to the family crypt to be prepared for burial. Without their owner, the rooms appeared more cluttered and cramped than Caroline remembered.

She walked over to the heavily draped window to open the lower sash but was unable to move it even an inch. She tried the second window and found it had been nailed shut. The sensation that she was trapped intensified, and she hurried through into the adjacent sitting room, where Ines kept her large workbasket and writing desk. Fortunately, the light was better in the second room and the window was already open, allowing a brisk breeze to stir the curtains.

Caroline inhaled the frigid air and stared out at the spearing gray rain. If she'd agreed to stay at Greenwood Hall, she could picture her aunt installing her in rooms just like these. Had Ines lived here from the age of twenty? She'd been in her seventies when she'd died. Perhaps it wasn't surprising that every inch was crammed full of her memories. It was the only personal space she'd been allowed to inhabit in a household that barely tolerated or acknowledged her.

The size of the task threatened to overwhelm Caroline—the mere idea that someone's entire life could be contained in two rooms was remarkably depressing. Her gaze fell on the desk and she sighed. If she was to meet with Susan and the other children in the nursery at three, she had best make a start.

The walnut and birch desk let down at the front with a key to reveal an interior of pigeonholes stuffed full of correspondence, papers, and writing implements. Caroline pulled up a chair and spent some time taking everything out until she had a considerable collection on the blotter.

She sorted out the correspondence into one pile, the copied religious tracts into another, and the various sketches and small embroidery swatches into a third. The letters would require close reading as her great-aunt's correspondents tended to cross their lines to save on paper. The sketches appeared to scan the decades and included members of the household, the nursery, and the various pets who had come and gone through the years.

It wasn't until Caroline compared her great-aunt's handwriting on the sketches to the religious passages that she noticed they had several different authors. She had some vague memory of Great-Aunt Ines teaching the children their scripture on a Sunday. Perhaps these were examples of her favorite children's work. There were also several framed excerpts on the walls.

Caroline tied up the three bundles with string, kept the letters for herself, and set the other items in a box she had brought for the purpose. The drawers of the desk proved to contain long-forgotten periodicals, damp curling parchment, and the occasional tangle of wool or embroidery threads. Considering their state, Caroline decided to throw everything away. From the condition of the items, she doubted Ines had had the strength to get the drawers open with her arthritic hands for quite a while.

The sewing basket contained two pairs of unfinished stockings, the beginnings of what looked like a shawl for a baby, and several yards of delicate white work embroidery probably destined for the baskets Eleanor graciously handed out to the new mothers on the estate. There were many handwritten patterns, knitting needles, bits of wool, a small pair of scissors, and a penknife. Caroline decided to leave everything as it was and suggest her aunt offer the basket either to another family member or to one of the staff.

Right at the bottom of the basket, Caroline found a gothic novel written by Ann Radcliffe. Great-Aunt Ines had vociferously condemned all forms of literature that weren't centered around the Bible or classical literature. If she'd ever caught Caroline reading *The Mysteries of Udolpho* in four volumes, she would have punished her severely.

After a last careful search through the basket and the desk, Caroline moved back into the darker and more claustrophobic bedroom. Every inch of the walls was covered in picture frames and embroidered texts that threatened hellfire and damnation to sinners. Caroline wondered how Ines had managed to sleep at night, but her great-aunt had been a woman of strong faith so perhaps she'd found the words inspiring.

Caroline, however, did not. The thought of taking down all the pictures defeated her, so she turned instead to the mantelpiece, where a collection of pastoral figurines jostled with statues of dogs and plaster images of saints. Most of the ornaments were chipped or damaged in some way. Had Ines collected them from the house and made them her own? If she had tended to acquire things, perhaps there might be some truth in Mrs. Frogerton's outlandish ideas after all. . . .

Caroline started putting the figurines in the box. If Mr. Woodford and her great-aunt had colluded to sell off parts of the estate and had a falling-out, she still couldn't imagine her decrepit great-aunt finding her way down to the cellar and inflicting harm on the relatively healthy butler. And, as her great-aunt had died that same night, Mr. Woodford couldn't have killed her because he'd been tucked up in bed with Dr. Harris watching over him.

Satisfied that she'd found the perfect argument against Mrs. Frogerton's rather lurid imagination, Caroline surveyed the stack of religious books her aunt had acquired on her bedside table. The Bible was well thumbed and had obviously brought her great comfort. As Caroline picked up each book, she gave it a little shake and recovered several embroidered bookmarks and folded remnants of parchment. When she reached the last book, she gently eased the last piece of paper free and discovered it was a banknote for two hundred pounds.

Such a large sum of money confounded her. The average servant's salary was about twenty pounds a year, and even she, a very accomplished companion, only received eighty pounds per annum. How had her aunt acquired the money? Caroline glanced uncertainly at the box of her aunt's possessions. Should she place the note in there or hand it over to Eleanor to pay for a decent funeral and headstone in the graveyard? She had a horrible suspicion that her aunt would simply take the note and do no such thing.

Caroline put the money in her pocket, where it nestled uneasily against the key to the glass cabinet in the nursery. Another melancholy thought struck her as she opened the bedside drawer. Although two hundred pounds was a sizeable amount of money, enough to buy a small property in the countryside, it probably represented everything Ines had accumulated in her long life. Caroline doubted the value of her own possessions amounted to that much.

Had Ines planned an escape from Greenwood Hall? The very idea seemed as farfetched as one of Mrs. Frogerton's flights of fancy, but what other use would Ines have for the money, and how had she acquired it? Caroline realized she was staring into an empty drawer as if it might have the answers to her questions and quickly shut it. Just to make certain that she hadn't missed anything, she checked beneath the pillows and under the mattress.

Her fingers touched something fuzzy jammed up against the headboard and, hoping it wasn't a dead mouse, she reached farther, grasped the object in her hand, and drew it out. It was a small velvet drawstring bag with some weight to it. As Caroline released the drawstring a glint of gold caught the light.

"Goodness me," Caroline breathed as she stared at the gold sovereigns. "Great-Aunt Ines, whatever have you been up to?"

Caroline took the letters to her room, made sure that Mrs. Frogerton and Dorothy were comfortably established in the drawing room enjoying their afternoon tea, and went to the nursery. There was a burst of laughter as she approached the half-open door, which made her smile because she knew Mabel was there. She'd always cheered up the nursery children and was definitely much adored.

Caroline quietly eased the door fully open to see Mabel, Harry, and Tina Brownworth already seated at the nursery table surrounded by children. Dan and Joshua stood just in front of Caroline and had obviously not noticed her arrival as their attention was fixed on the activity in front of them.

"I'm glad the old bitch died," Dan murmured. "She got what was coming to her and so will the rest of them."

Even as Caroline went to remonstrate with him, Harry glanced over and frowned at his brother. "Don't speak ill of the dead, Dan. Especially not in front of the children."

"Why not? Everyone who lives in this house knows what she was like."

"How so?" Caroline inquired.

Dan started and turned to look at her. Joshua stammered something about having to fetch more cake and rushed past Caroline into the corridor.

"If you don't know, my lady, I can't help you." Dan inclined his head. "My brother, here, says I shouldn't say another word." He sauntered toward the table, his hands in his pockets, whistling. "Now, where's this tea I've been hearing about?"

Tina grabbed his hand and pulled him down to sit beside her. "If you stop blathering for a minute, I'll pour you some."

Mabel smiled at Caroline. "Susan said you were going to join us. Come and sit here!"

"Thank you." Caroline took her seat and nodded to everyone at the table. "How nice it is to see you all back here."

Harry laughed and looked around the room. "It hasn't changed a bit. I wonder if it ever will."

"I don't know," Dan said. "The staff have changed." He looked over at Susan. "Are they kind to you?"

"Very." Susan nodded. "They also let me help as much as I want."

"Well, that hasn't changed," Dan said. "The Greenwoods always encouraged unpaid labor."

"Dan . . ." Harry again intervened. "Not now, please. We are here to celebrate Mabel's birthday, not dig up old grievances."

"Hard to ignore when it appears history is repeating itself," Dan muttered.

Tina kissed his cheek. "Oh, Dan. You are such a miserable sod, but I still love you."

Dan smiled and kissed her back. "That's the truth." His gaze swept the table. "I'll keep my mouth shut now."

"Thank you." Mabel beamed at him. "I want my birthday celebration to create new and happy memories for all of us."

"Amen!" one of the smaller children said, and everyone laughed, breaking the tension Dan had created.

Caroline helped Mabel and Susan distribute the tea, cakes, and sandwiches around the table.

"Mrs. Maddox said she didn't have much to offer us today, but I think this spread is quite splendid," Mabel said.

Tina giggled. "Poor Mrs. Maddox—having to cater for us lot. She must hate it. She probably decided she didn't want us to have her best offerings and sent up the scraps."

"There was an accident in the kitchen last night," Caroline said. "Apparently, a cat got in and upset a lot of her jellies and puddings that were left to set overnight."

"A cat, eh?" Tina smirked. "How unfortunate. That's probably why she was in such a bad mood when I popped in earlier to remember myself to her."

"I don't think she was very pleased," Caroline agreed. "It can't be pleasant to do all that work and then have it spoiled."

"I know the feeling, miss." Tina sipped her tea. "When I worked in the kitchen, she could be very difficult to please. But I suppose she did train me well enough to get my current position."

"Which you manage very well," Dan said. "The vicar and his wife have nothing but good to say about you."

"That's only because they're frightened I'll leave them soon to marry you," Tina teased. "They even offered to increase my wages!"

"As soon as I get that promotion and the cottage on the estate that goes with it, I'll be setting a date for the banns to be read," Dan said. "I promise."

"Good for you!" Mabel raised her cup. "I can't wait to attend your wedding."

Caroline smiled along with everyone else, but she couldn't help but feel that Dan's grudges against the Greenwoods and the staff were rather more serious than anyone else appeared to believe. He'd actively been celebrating Great-Aunt Ines's death—gloating even. Had Joshua told him the truth? Or had Dan known about the death even earlier?

Caroline could just imagine the two men working together to kill her aunt, but did Dan's apparent grievances against the old woman justify murder? Perhaps if she talked to him away from the nursery, he would reveal more to her. His apparent anger and disgust for everything connected to the Greenwoods could not be ignored.

"Caroline?"

"Yes, Susan?" She set down the teapot and smiled at her younger sister. "Are you enjoying the tea party?"

"Very much so. Mabel has always been very kind to me. When you left, she'd let me come into her bed and sleep with her when I was sad."

"I'm sorry I had to leave you," Caroline said.

"It's all right. Mabel explained why you had to go."

Caroline glanced over at their cousin, who was now walking around the nursery with one of the youngest children on her hip, pointing out items of interest.

"I promise that as soon as I can support us both, I will come and take you away with me." Caroline held her sister's gaze. "Us being together is all that I dream of."

Susan smiled. "I know, and I wish for that, too. Mabel says I should never give up hope." She stood up. "Now I really must help clear the table or we will never be ready for our afternoon reading."

Caroline wanted to tell her sister that it was not her job to do anything of the kind, but she was unwilling to stir up more controversy. She might not agree with Dan on much, but she couldn't ignore the fact that the Greenwoods did like to get value for money from their "charitable works."

The clock chimed the hour and Caroline rose from the table.

"Please excuse me. I have to help Mrs. Frogerton prepare for the dinner this evening."

Harry looked up. "Is it true you're employed now, my lady?"

"Yes indeed," Caroline answered with a smile.

"That must be hard." Harry paused. "If you don't mind me asking, did Lady Eleanor offer you a home here with your sister?"

"She did, but I decided I'd rather find my own way in the world."

Harry nodded slightly. "Good for you, my lady. Better not to be beholden to anyone and to be away from this place."

"I quite agree." Caroline smiled down at Susan. "And once I have my sister with me again, I will be even happier."

"Amen to that, miss," Dan said. "She doesn't deserve to be stuck here either."

"I'll keep her safe for you, Caroline." Mabel put her arm around Susan. "Don't you worry about that."

Susan smiled adoringly up at her cousin. "Mabel's going to tell us some ghost stories tonight."

Caroline pretended to shudder as Mabel laughed.

"You used to tell them to me, Caroline. Do you remember the one about the headless nun who walks the long gallery at night bewailing her fate? It gave me nightmares for weeks."

"I can't say that I do," Caroline said. "But I apologize for the nightmares."

"We loved those stories, didn't we, Dan?" Harry grinned at the children seated around the table. "The scarier the better. Drowned bodies in the lake, ghosts under the floorboards, Black Shuck roaming the fens and howling outside the nursery door."

"Who's Black Shuck?" Susan asked.

"Well, legend says he's a giant black dog who came with the invaders from the north. . . ."

Caroline left the nursery just as Joshua returned with an empty tray to start clearing the table. He avoided looking at her and rushed over to the table. She contemplated speaking to him and realized she wasn't sure exactly what she wanted to say, or whether it was any of her business.

Even if Joshua and Dan had decided to murder Great-Aunt Ines, Caroline had no proof, and confronting them with her lack of evidence might place her own life in danger. Aware that she was beginning to sound remarkably like her imaginative employer, Caroline strove for some common sense as she went down the stairs.

The banknote in her pocket rustled as she walked and she stopped suddenly on the steps. If she kept the money, she'd have a head start on the savings necessary to begin a new life somewhere with Susan. Ines wouldn't know . . . she might even approve. No one else appeared to have knowledge of her great-aunt's secret fund, so why shouldn't she benefit from it?

A year ago, the thought of such deception would have horrified her, but she was in a different world now—one where her survival depended on her ability to succeed against the odds. If anyone inquired as to the missing money, Caroline would gladly hand it over, but if no one knew of its existence, then perhaps she would keep it for herself.

Mrs. Frogerton and Dorothy were already in their suite of rooms when Caroline arrived and were involved in a vigorous discussion.

"I want to wear it for dinner tonight." Dorothy glared at her mother.

"It's meant for the grand dinner and the ball, Dot!"

"Don't call me that!" Dorothy snapped. "I've noticed that my clothing is vastly inferior to the other ladies', and I want to impress them now."

Caroline hastened to intervene. "Your clothes are perfectly acceptable for a house party in the countryside, Miss Frogerton. In fact, I have heard many approving comments from the older ladies about how well you deport yourself."

"Who cares what they think?"

"Everyone who wants to have a successful first Season." Caroline met Dorothy's defiant gaze. "Trust me, if the mothers and grandmothers don't approve of you, they will never allow their sons, brothers, and grandsons to dance with you, let alone court you."

For the first time, Dorothy looked thoughtful and Caroline held her breath.

Mrs. Frogerton poked her daughter in the ribs. "See? Listen to Lady Caroline. She knows what she's talking about. Save your grandest gown for the ball and leave them with the best impression of you."

"All right then." Dorothy nodded and turned back toward her room. "I'll wear the lemon silk tonight and leave the rose pink for the ball."

"An excellent decision," Caroline agreed. "You are very wise."

Mrs. Frogerton managed to keep a straight face until Dorothy shut the door behind her.

"Did the crusty old dowagers really say that about my Dotty?"

"They said she was much less showy than they had anticipated and would not disgrace any family she chose to marry into."

"High praise, indeed." Mrs. Frogerton, who had no illusions as to the value the aristocracy placed on her and her daughter, chuckled. "I suppose the lure of her dowry must be very strong."

"There is that," Caroline conceded. "In my opinion, introducing a straightforward woman like Miss Frogerton into any aristocratic household would enliven it considerably."

Mrs. Frogerton drew her over to sit by the fire. "Did you find anything interesting in Lady Ines's rooms?"

"I have her letters to read. It might take some time but could be helpful."

"Indeed."

"I also found a large bag of gold sovereigns tucked under the mattress," Caroline said. "I suppose I should hand them over to my aunt. I assume Great-Aunt Ines must have had a will somewhere."

"I wonder where she acquired those?" Mrs. Frogerton asked.

"I doubt they came from her nefarious dealings with Mr. Woodford, ma'am," Caroline replied firmly. "And, as to that, I also doubt my aunt had the strength to go down into the cellar and knock the butler unconscious."

"That would've been difficult for her," Mrs. Frogerton admitted, and then noticeably brightened. "Perhaps she had an accomplice in her schemes?"

"I did think about that," Caroline admitted. "Joshua is behaving oddly and he's avoiding me."

"Joshua also works for Mr. Woodford. Perhaps he is the connection between them?"

"In that he both assaulted Mr. Woodford and murdered my great-aunt?"

"He could have done both of those things," Mrs. Frogerton agreed. "Perhaps he was being paid by both of them and decided he wanted more."

"We have no proof that any of this is true, ma'am," Caroline reminded her employer.

"Which is why we probably need to pay a visit to Mr. Woodford before dinner." Mrs. Frogerton rose from her chair. "I'm sure he'd like to hear about our conversation with his sister."

"Are you quite certain?" Caroline called after her employer, who was already heading for the door. "Mrs. Frogerton?"

With a sigh, she picked up her skirts and hurried after her.

There was no sign of Dr. Harris when they reached the butler's private quarters. Caroline wondered if he had returned home. She doubted the Greenwoods had offered him any hospitality after he'd accused them of covering up a murder.

Mr. Woodford was sitting up in his chair, a rug tucked over his legs as he read the newspaper. He looked up as Caroline entered.

"Excuse me if I don't get up, miss. I'm still a bit wobbly on my feet."

"Please don't exert yourself on our account." Mrs. Frogerton smiled warmly. "We visited your sister in the village this morning. She was most insistent we reassure you that she is well."

"You visited Vera?" Mr. Woodford didn't look as pleased as Caroline had anticipated. "Whatever for?"

Mrs. Frogerton took the seat opposite the butler. "We understood that you had received a message from your sister on the morning you were injured. Miss Morton was worried that if Miss Woodford didn't hear back from you as expected she would become alarmed." She reached over and patted his knee. "We were on a mission to see if the road was still passable and it was no trouble to pop in and ascertain that your dear sister was safe and well."

"Did she want to tell me anything in particular?" Mr. Woodford looked distinctly worried.

"Only that she wished you a swift recovery and that she would be praying for you." Mrs. Frogerton paused. "Oh, and she did mention that matter about the solicitor."

The silence grew as Mr. Woodford stared into space. Eventually he cleared his throat. "She . . . told you about that?"

"Yes, after she reassured herself that Miss Morton would never reveal any private conversations between us to her uncle and aunt." Mrs. Frogerton glanced over at Caroline. "You did promise to keep everything to yourself, didn't you, my dear?"

"Yes, of course. I no longer live here, Mr. Woodford, and I'm not beholden to the Greenwoods," Caroline said even as she admired Mrs. Frogerton's artful presentation of the facts.

"I just wanted to protect my sister," Mr. Woodford whispered.

"Perfectly understandable," Mrs. Frogerton said warmly. "I would do exactly the same in such a situation."

"I can't have the Greenwoods threatening her like that."

"Of course not. You were very wise to seek a legal opinion to consider your options." Mrs. Frogerton nodded.

"From what I observed of Miss Woodford's demeanor, the solicitor offered her some encouraging news." She paused delicately. "Such matters between employers and their staff are often . . . misinterpreted, but unfortunately the power still remains with the gentry."

"That's the truth, ma'am." Mr. Woodford nodded. "But we acted in good faith."

"I am quite sure you did. Why would you jeopardize your position by acting otherwise?"

There was a knock on the door and Dr. Harris came in looking rather wet and windswept. He frowned at Caroline.

"I thought I told you to leave Mr. Woodford alone to convalesce?"

Mrs. Frogerton stepped in front of Caroline. "I asked her to bring me to see Mr. Woodford, Doctor. I had a message to convey to him from his sister."

"In the village?"

"Yes, we visited her earlier today."

"Well, you won't get back there now," Dr. Harris said. "The bridge isn't safe and the river's overflowed its banks. I can't get home and will have to beg the Greenwoods to put up with me for another night or two."

"I'm sure they'll be delighted," Caroline murmured, and received a glare in return. "My aunt is a great admirer of the medical profession."

She turned to Mrs. Frogerton. "Perhaps we should go, ma'am? It must be time to dress for dinner."

Her employer could barely contain herself until Caroline shut the door of her suite behind her.

"I knew I was right. Mr. Woodford and his sister have been helping themselves to items from the house and your aunt has consulted her solicitor and is having none of it!"

"You now think it is my aunt who shut her butler in the cellar and murdered a relative just because they made a few coins from selling old furniture?" Caroline asked. "If she has any suspicion of fraud or theft within her house-hold, she could simply turn them all out on their ears."

"I'm not sure about the details, yet, Caroline, but we are definitely onto *something*." Mrs. Frogerton smiled, her confidence obviously unbowed. "Now, please ring for Peggy, and then go and get yourself ready for this grand dinner."

Caroline went to ring the bell. "Do you still wish to visit the nursery later, ma'am?"

"Of course I do!" Mrs. Frogerton pointed at the door. "Now hurry along with you."

Chapter 9

Caroline tapped gently on the door of the nursery, opened it a crack, and went in followed by Mrs. Frogerton. Hetty, one of the nursemaids, sat by the fire darning a stocking by the light of a candle and the fire. At almost ten o'clock, the nursery was uncommonly quiet and still. Hetty looked up and smiled.

"Lady Caroline."

"Good evening, Hetty." Caroline gestured at her employer. "This is Mrs. Frogerton. I was telling her about the doll's house, and she expressed a great desire to see it."

To Caroline's relief, Hetty didn't seem to find that odd and simply nodded.

"If you need to fetch anything from the kitchen, I can watch the children for you while you're gone," Caroline offered.

"I could do with a scuttle full of coal to keep the fire going." Hetty pointed at the low flickering flames. "I'd hate to have to wake the children up to a cold room tomorrow morning."

Knowing her aunt's renowned meanness about supplying the nursery with sufficient fuel to heat the large, open rooms, Caroline nodded. "Then go and get your coal and we'll await your return."

"Thank you, miss." Hetty set her darning down on the table, bobbed a curtsy, and exited the nursery, leaving Caroline and Mrs. Frogerton alone in the silence.

The children's bedrooms were on both sides of the main room where they now stood. The charity children shared their beds with however many others needed them, whereas the Greenwood children and Susan had their own rooms. Mabel had recently moved out of the nursery into her own bedroom on a lower floor. According to Susan, Mabel often returned to the nursery and slept in Susan's bed. She claimed it was too quiet in her own room, and that she missed being on hand to help out with the younger children, especially if they needed comforting in the night.

"Quickly now," Mrs. Frogerton murmured. "Do you still have the key?"

"Yes." Before going down to dinner Caroline had transferred the key to the pocket of her second-best evening gown and secreted the two-hundred-pound bill in her stocking drawer.

She unlocked the cabinet, took a deep breath, and unlatched the front of the doll's house.

"There."

"Oh, my," Mrs. Frogerton said. "That is quite macabre." She peered closely at the little figure with the wool wrapped around its neck, but didn't reach in to touch it, which Caroline quite understood.

"And what is this?" Mrs. Frogerton pointed at the kitchen. "Someone has upset all the food in the pantry."

"What?" Caroline tore her gaze away from the parlor and looked down a level. Just as Mrs. Frogerton had said, the kitchen was in some disarray while the cook stood by the table, her wooden arms up in the air. "Good Lord."

"Caroline . . ." Mrs. Frogerton whispered. "Look at the cellar."

Even as she turned to stare at the basement of the house, Caroline already feared what she might see.

The butler was locked in a little wooden cage.

She carefully shut and locked the doll's house door and closed the glass cabinet, her hands shaking.

"What on earth—?" Mrs. Frogerton whispered with some agitation.

Caroline held a finger to her lips as the door opened and Hetty returned with a scuttle full of coal.

"Thank you, miss." Hetty scattered some of the coal on the fire and put the rest in the bucket. "Did you like the doll's house, ma'am?"

"It is very fine," Mrs. Frogerton said. "In truth I don't think I have ever seen anything quite like it."

Caroline linked her arm through her employer's and drew her firmly toward the door. "We should be going, ma'am. You need your sleep. Thank you, Hetty."

She marched Mrs. Frogerton all the way down the stairs and into her suite before releasing her. There was no sign that Dorothy had returned. She'd been practicing a duet to sing with Lord Epping and was eager to show off her quite unremarkable singing voice.

"What on earth is going on?" Mrs. Frogerton started to pace the carpet, her hand pressed to her ample bosom over her heart. "I told you there was an unpleasant atmosphere in this house, Caroline. It's as if someone finds this whole business *amusing*."

"I agree," Caroline said slowly.

"And should we be worried about the safety of the cook, next?"

"I believe that scenario has already happened, ma'am. Yesterday when I went into the kitchen, Mrs. Maddox had gathered the staff together to find out who had gotten into the cold pantry and destroyed all her jellies and puddings. I thought—we all thought—that the scullery boy had accidentally let the cat in there."

"Do you believe that now?" Mrs. Frogerton shook her head as she continued to walk the room. "Don't you think it has the same spiteful feeling as what happened to Mr. Woodford?"

"Yes," Caroline said simply. "It's as if someone is enjoying inflicting pain on members of this household."

"Does Joshua get on with the cook?" Mrs. Frogerton asked.

"He probably resents her authority as much as any other member of staff. Mrs. Maddox does have something of a temper. But why air all his grievances now?"

"Perhaps he wishes to cause the maximum of embarrassment for his employers during the birthday celebrations before he leaves—possibly with his share of Mr. Woodford's and his sister's money."

"With all due respect, ma'am, we still have no evidence that Joshua is involved in a scheme that might not even exist."

"Well, something is going on," Mrs. Frogerton declared. "And someone needs to be held accountable!" She sat down in her chair. "Should I speak to Lord Greenwood or Lady Eleanor?"

"My aunt would probably be more receptive to such a confidence, ma'am," Caroline said carefully. "But I doubt she will believe you without any evidence to support your claims."

"Then we will have to find something to convince her that we are right. What do you know about Mrs. Maddox?"

"She's been here since I was a child. She worked her way up to become cook."

"So, she and Mr. Woodford have known each other for years?"

"Yes, indeed." Caroline nodded.

Mrs. Frogerton frowned. "Does it feel to you that this matter is very much centered on this house and its occupants?"

"The Greenwoods currently have guests," Caroline reminded her employer. "Including you and Miss Frogerton."

"But so far everyone who has been targeted has lived here for years." Mrs. Frogerton waved Caroline's objection away. "Most of the staff are local people. Did Joshua grow up here as well?"

"Yes. He was one of the orphan children my aunt housed, fed, and educated. I remember him quite well as a child." She paused. "He was friends with Dan Price."

"That rather angry young man your cousin invited to her birthday celebrations?"

"Yes."

"I met him at the first dinner, and he didn't have a nice word to say about anyone except Mabel."

"He says he wasn't happy here and seems eager to let everyone know that," Caroline said slowly. "The thing is—I overheard Joshua and Dan laughing together about Lady Ines's death. They were being most unkind."

"Then perhaps we have our answer." Mrs. Frogerton folded her hands in her lap. "Either Joshua or Dan Price might be a grudge-bearing murderer with a malicious streak."

Caroline raised her eyebrows. "Have you given up on your theory that Mr. Woodford and his sister were in ca-hoots with my great-aunt to defraud the Greenwoods?"

"Oh no, dear. I am just advancing an *alternative* theory. There might be more than one thing wrong in a household this size." Mrs. Frogerton smiled for the first time since they'd seen the doll's house. "In my experience, it never hurts to suspect as many people as possible."

"Which still leaves us with the question of what to do about it," Caroline said. "We have no evidence to support *any* of your theories."

"I have an idea," Mrs. Frogerton said thoughtfully. "But it will require your cooperation."

"I am willing to do whatever you think fit, ma'am, al-though I doubt we will have much success."

"We shall see about that." Mrs. Frogerton rose to her feet. "Now, shall we join the others in the drawing room? I did promise Dotty I would be present when she sings."

Caroline followed her employer down the stairs into the drawing room where the guests were currently grouped around the piano or playing cards at small tables. She noticed Lord Francis and his sister almost immediately. They were seated to the right of the door, their fair heads close together as they talked. Neither of them appeared to be listening to the vicar's daughter's singing or aware that Mrs. Frogerton and Caroline had entered the room.

She waited for the familiar pain of his loss to overcome her and felt nothing. He'd made his decision and so had she. If his family were truly more important to him than she was, she was glad to be free of him.

"Miss Morton."

She jumped as Dr. Harris appeared beside her. He was dressed in his usual old coat and trousers, but at least, thanks to her, his shirt was clean.

"Good evening, Dr. Harris. How is Mr. Woodford?"

"His injuries are healing nicely, but he's still quite fearful."

"Of what?" Caroline looked up at him.

"I thought you might tell *me* that."

"I wish I knew, Dr. Harris." She paused. "Has he confided anything at all to you?"

"If he had, I wouldn't betray a confidence, Miss Morton."

"Yet you would expect me to betray mine."

His quick smile transformed his face. "Very good, ma'am. I stand corrected."

"I wish I knew what or who he was afraid of," Caroline said quietly. "I suspect he knows very well who trapped him in the cellar, and is either pretending to have forgotten, or is too scared to admit the truth."

"I would have to agree with you." Dr. Harris paused. "If he does confide anything to me, Miss Morton, may I ask for your opinion again?"

She curtsied. "I would be delighted to help you, sir."

"Thank you." He nodded, his gaze sweeping disapprovingly over the assembled guests. "I suspect Lady Eleanor would prefer me to stay and be sociable, but I don't have the stomach for it."

"Knowing your views, Doctor, I suspect she would much prefer it if you didn't," Caroline murmured, her gaze on the regal sweep of her aunt's piled-up hair as she listened to the music.

Dr. Harris gave a short bark of laughter that turned several heads and then exited the drawing room, leaving Caroline exposed to the stares. She smiled back serenely and walked over to where Mrs. Frogerton had seated herself in the second row next to Mabel as Miss Frogerton came forward to sing her duet.

Just before she reached her destination, her cousin Eliza caught hold of her elbow, halting her progress.

"It's nice to see you socializing with your equals rather than your betters, Caroline."

Caroline eased free of her cousin's grip, but Eliza kept talking.

"Dr. Harris has no money or standing but he would probably be delighted to obtain the favor even of an impoverished, disgraced woman such as yourself."

"There is no disgrace in being the daughter of a reprobate, Cousin. It was hardly my doing."

"But you must admit it does reflect badly on you." Eliza looked around the room. "I mean, we all feel sorry for you, but the general consensus is that hanging around begging for scraps of attention makes everyone uncomfortable."

"Surely that is their problem and not mine?" Caroline asked. "I am merely doing my job and attending to my employer's needs. Why would anyone care?"

"Because—" Eliza spluttered as if Caroline's continued refusal to accept her place was completely unacceptable to her. "Because you don't belong here anymore!"

"Thank goodness for that." Caroline smiled at her enraged cousin. "I must confess I have never been happier. I no longer have to deal with the shame of a drunken debt-ridden father, I earn my own money, and I enjoy my occupation." She raised an eyebrow.

"Perhaps you should attend to your own situation, Cousin, rather than worry about mine?" She gestured toward the rear of the room where Eliza's spouse was playing cards with a bottle of brandy at his elbow. His face was already flushed, and he was arguing loudly with his partner across the table, his words already slurring. "Your husband might soon require your assistance to help him to bed."

"You . . ." Eliza hissed. "How dare you!"

Caroline curtsied and went to sit down between Mabel and Mrs. Frogerton. Her employer patted her hand.

"Well done, lass. You certainly put her in her place."

"I have no idea why she dislikes me so intensely," Caroline murmured.

"Because you're prettier, nicer, and more intelligent than she is?" Mabel joined the conversation. "And Mama always held you up as an example to Eliza?"

"Oh, dear Lord, that's all I need." Caroline sighed.

She was relieved when the music started up again and Miss Frogerton and Lord Epping sang two ballads together in remarkably good harmony. Even Lady Eleanor clapped and nodded graciously as Dorothy rushed over to her mother, her cheeks flushed with victory.

"Well?"

"Nicely done, Dotty. Nicely done indeed." Mrs. Frogerton smiled up at her daughter.

"You sounded very well together," Caroline added.

Dorothy sat down and fanned herself vigorously. "Thank you. I enjoyed learning the songs with him. He was most patient and kind."

When Dorothy went off to find Lord Epping with Mabel, Mrs. Frogerton lowered her voice.

"After some reflection, I think it would be best that next time I talk to Mr. Woodford I am alone, Caroline. I fear he is less likely to be honest when he sees you because of your connection with the Greenwoods."

"As you wish, ma'am." Caroline nodded. "Dr. Harris said he will let me know if Mr. Woodford says anything of interest to him."

"Excellent." Mrs. Frogerton rose to her feet. "I will speak to him before I go to bed."

"Ma'am?" Caroline looked up at her. "Be careful."

Her employer patted her cheek, her brown eyes kind. "Don't you worry about me, lass. I'm well able to take care of myself."

Caroline only waited a moment longer before she too left the drawing room. The idea that all the ladies wished her gone didn't bother her as much as Eliza probably hoped. She'd already said goodbye to that world and if truth be told had already felt like a fraud and an outsider because of her father's behavior.

As she walked out into the silent hallway, she noticed her uncle disappearing down toward his study. On impulse, she followed him and knocked on the door.

"Come in."

She went inside to find him pouring himself a large drink from the cut glass decanter on the sideboard under the window.

"Caroline, what a pleasant surprise. Are you here on behalf of my wife or daughter?"

"Neither, Uncle Nicholas." Caroline smiled at him. "I just wanted to share something that has been concerning me and ask for your advice."

He waved her toward a seat as he lit a cigar and sat behind his desk.

"What is it, my dear? Are you regretting your decision to leave and wish to know how to get back into your aunt's good graces?" He chuckled. "If it's that, then please don't ask me."

"No, Uncle, it's more to do with what's been going on in this house."

"How so?" His amused expression disappeared.

"There have been several unpleasant . . . incidents this week," Caroline said carefully. "Not only was Great-Aunt Ines killed in a particularly horrible way, but Mr. Woodford was attacked in the cellar, and all Mrs. Maddox's jellies were deliberately overturned."

"Sometimes a house party can get out of control, Niece." He glanced toward the curtains. "Especially when the weather is this atrocious and the guests can't get outside to kick up a little."

"So, you don't think there is anything to worry about?" Caroline asked.

"Well, I do think what happened to poor Ines was somewhat beyond the pale, but sometimes people do cruel things. I remember when I was at Eton some chaps played the ghastliest pranks on others." He shifted something on his desk. "Your aunt Eleanor is in charge of the indoor household. You should really bring such matters to her attention, not mine."

"I will certainly do that, but I did want to make sure that you were aware of what was going on." Caroline paused. "My aunt seems somewhat out of sorts. Is she concerned about the threat of legal action from the Woodfords?"

"I have no idea. You'll have to ask her about that yourself."

"You were unaware that she had sought advice from a solicitor about suing them?"

He flicked ash from his cigar onto the carpet. "She probably mentioned it at some point, but I can't be expected to remember such minor domestic matters."

"Of course not." Caroline nodded. "You have far weightier matters to consider—such as your work in the House of Lords."

"Indeed." He picked up his pen. "Speaking of which, I do need to write this letter."

"Then I shall leave you in peace." Caroline immediately got to her feet. "Thank you for listening to my concerns."

"Rest assured, as soon as the guests leave any silliness will end and the house will return to normal."

"*If* the guests can leave," Caroline said. "I understand that the bridge across the river is unsafe."

"I'm sure it will be fixed by the end of the week." Her uncle dipped his pen in the inkwell and started to write. "Don't forget to close the door on your way out."

Caroline did as he requested and stood for a moment outside his door before walking back into the main hall. At least she'd done her duty and informed him about what was going on in his own house even if he had no interest in it. She supposed she should speak to her aunt. There was still the matter of the bag of coins to discuss.

There was no sign that Mrs. Frogerton had returned to the drawing room. Caroline decided to go back upstairs and make a start on reading the letters she'd found in Ines's rooms. She was halfway up the second staircase when she heard Eliza's voice. She had no desire to speak to her cousin and quickly retreated down to the first landing and cravenly concealed herself among the window drapes.

As Eliza swept past, Caroline instinctively turned her face into the shadows so she wouldn't be seen. A sharp screech followed by a series of bumps made her turn around and run toward the top of the staircase. Her cousin lay in a crumpled heap at the bottom of the stairs. Caroline picked up her skirts and ran down to Eliza, who was already stirring.

"Get some help!" Caroline shouted out to a startled footman who had just entered the hall. "Find Dr. Harris!"

She gently put her arm around Eliza's shoulders and encouraged her to sit up. A stream of guests emerged from the drawing room headed by Eleanor. There was no sign of Eliza's husband.

"Are you hurt?" Caroline asked. "Did you catch your skirt on your heel?"

Eliza struggled to free herself from Caroline's embrace. "Don't touch me!"

Caroline eased herself free, went to stand up, and was assisted by Lord Francis.

"Thank you."

Dr. Harris arrived wearing his usual impatient expression. "What's going on?"

"My cousin fell down the stairs," Caroline explained.

"Fell?" Eliza screeched. "You deliberately pushed me!"

Francis dropped Caroline's elbow and stepped back as everyone else stared at her. She kept her gaze on Dr. Harris.

"I was on the landing waiting to go up the stairs when I heard my cousin cry out. By the time I turned around she had already fallen."

"You are lying! I distinctly felt a hand on my back pushing me!"

"Most unlikely, ma'am," Dr. Harris said briskly. "If someone had shoved you, I suspect you would still be unconscious. It's far more likely that you caught your shoe on the hem of your gown and tripped yourself up."

"How dare you suggest that I am lying!" Eliza's voice rose with each word. "She deliberately pushed me! She's full of spite and resentment!"

Caroline noticed several of the women nodding and staring at her.

Eleanor stepped forward. "Hush, now Eliza. You are overwrought." She gestured at Joshua. "Please carry Lady Theydon up to her bedchamber where Dr. Harris can attend to her privately."

Chapter 10

As the whispering crowd started to disperse, Caroline
went over to her aunt, who had remained at the bottom of
the stairs.

"I swear I didn't push her."

"Of course you didn't." Eleanor raised her voice to address the departing guests. "Eliza has become quite fanci-
ful during her pregnancy." She gripped Caroline's elbow.
"Come upstairs and we will make sure your cousin is
being properly attended to."

"I doubt Eliza will wish to see me," Caroline said as she
mounted the stairs beside her aunt.

"She owes you an apology."

"I don't think she'll see it like that."

"Which is beside the point." Eleanor knocked briskly
on Eliza's bedroom door and went in without waiting for
an invitation.

Eliza lay on her bed, her skirt tucked up to her knee
while Dr. Harris felt her right ankle.

"I repeat. I don't think it's broken, or even sprained.
You might have some stiffness or soreness overnight, but
other than a possibly bruised posterior, you will be fine."

"Dr. Harris!" Eleanor spoke sharply. "Your language!"

He looked inquiringly up at his hostess. "How else would you prefer me to refer to it, ma'am?"

"I would prefer it if you didn't mention a lady's anatomy at all."

"But that is my diagnosis." He stepped back. "Lady Theydon will recover completely. Because of her pregnancy I would advise a day of rest in bed, but that is entirely up to her. I don't believe in coddling gestating women."

Eleanor opened her mouth and Dr. Harris held up his hand.

"I apologize in advance, my lady, and I will take my leave." He turned back to Eliza, who was glaring at him from her bed. "If you have any concerns tonight, do not hesitate to call for me."

"Thank you."

"Miss Morton, Lady Theydon, Lady Eleanor." He bowed and left the room.

"Well." Eleanor let out her breath. "If this is an example of the new breed of supposedly scientific physicians, then I cannot say I am impressed. He is far too . . . explicit."

"He was very kind when he examined me," Eliza said.

"One would hope he treated your person with the reverence it deserves." Eleanor sniffed. "Now, I wish you to apologize to your cousin and then we will leave you in peace."

Eliza stiffened. "Apologize to *her*? She tried to kill me!"

"Nonsense," Eleanor said briskly. "You sound quite unhinged, dear, and the last thing we need in this house right now is another scandal."

"The only scandal is you allowing Caroline back into this house," Eliza snapped, her cheeks flushing as she struggled to sit up.

"It is as much her home as it is yours, Eliza." Eleanor said severely.

"It is not!"

"She is my niece and I value her greatly." Eleanor looked down her nose at her daughter. "You have everything she will never have, and it behooves you to be the gracious one, Eliza."

Caroline tried not to wince as Eliza studied her, a small smile on her face as she pretended to sigh.

"You are correct, Mama. I should feel sorry for her, but I fear she has turned against us."

"How so?" Eleanor frowned.

"Have you not noticed what's been going on? The staff are all gossiping about it," Eliza asked. "Mr. Woodford was badly injured, Cook's kitchen has been turned upside down, and Great-Aunt Ines is dead!"

Eleanor drew herself up. "I am well aware of all those things, Eliza. I am the mistress of the house. What I fail to understand is what it has to do with you and your silly grudge against Caroline."

"Because *she* comes here, and all these terrible things happen. Don't you see it yet? She hates us and is taking her own petty revenge on us all."

"You are accusing *me* of killing Great-Aunt Ines?" Caroline asked. "Why on earth would I do that?"

"I don't know, but I'm sure you have your reasons," Eliza shot back. "We should watch her carefully, Mama. I can guarantee that when she leaves all this nonsense will stop!"

"Don't be ridiculous, Eliza." Eleanor took Caroline's arm and turned to the door. "Pregnancy has obviously addled your brain. Come along, Caroline. Your cousin needs some restorative sleep."

She shut the door behind them and sighed. "Poor Eliza."

"I appreciate your trust in me, Aunt," Caroline said. "I have no idea why Eliza would accuse me of any of that."

"She has never been satisfied her entire life." Eleanor walked back toward the stairs, her back ramrod straight. "I will do my best to squash any gossip. I expect you to do the same."

"Naturally." Caroline hesitated and then went after her aunt. "May I speak to you for a moment?"

"What is it now?" Eleanor pressed a hand to her brow and gestured for Caroline to follow her down to her suite. "Mabel is already worried the ball will not take place because of the appalling weather, Eliza is behaving badly, and half my staff are missing or incompetent."

"I did as you asked and went through Great-Aunt Ines's possessions," Caroline said as she hurried along with her aunt. "I found a bag of gold sovereigns under her pillow."

"Gold?" Eleanor stopped walking. "Where on earth did she get that from? And why did she conceal it? One might think she would've offered it to us to cover the cost of her room and board for the past half century, but no."

"I wondered if perhaps it was a gift from her mother or her dowry from her father?" Caroline asked.

"I suppose that is possible. That generation did prefer to keep their money in gold, which I quite understand." Eleanor held out her hand. "Do you have it with you?"

"No, ma'am, it's in my room. I didn't want to leave it with Great-Aunt Ines's boxed-up possessions and it is too heavy to carry around in my pocket."

"Then bring it to me in the morning." Eleanor sighed. "I do hope this awful rain lets up or else Mabel's ball will be very poorly attended indeed."

"I suspect she would be more than happy if it went ahead with just the people present at the house party, ma'am," Caroline suggested.

"You are probably right." Eleanor paused. "It might even be better if no one from society *does* attend. I would hate for Mabel to be labeled as 'odd' because she chooses to associate with her inferiors, but this is what she and her father wanted."

Caroline could only nod.

"Is there anything else?" Eleanor asked as she stopped outside her bedroom door.

"Not at this moment, ma'am," Caroline said.

"Then I'll bid you good night. I have something of a headache. George said he would supervise the remaining guests until they retire."

Caroline couldn't think of a worse idea but resisted the urge to offer to supervise in his stead. The house was no longer her concern. It was also unlikely that any of the guests would heed her suggestions because they considered her beneath them.

"Good night, ma'am."

Caroline curtsied and went back toward the landing that overlooked the ground floor. A glow of light from the open doorway into the drawing room illuminated the hallway below. From the sound of it the only guests still up were Mabel and her friends. Caroline decided to leave them to their own devices and walked onward to Mrs. Frogerton's suite of rooms.

Dorothy was not yet present, but Mrs. Frogerton was seated by the fire, writing busily in a notebook.

"Ah! There you are, lass. I spent an illuminating quarter of an hour with Mr. Woodford before Dr. Harris appeared to shoo me away."

Caroline sat opposite her employer, suddenly aware of how tired she felt after a long day of dealing with people who were reluctant to acknowledge her very existence.

"He is remarkably rude," Caroline said.

"I don't mind a straightforward man," Mrs. Frogerton said. "In truth I prefer it."

Caroline leaned her aching head back against the chair. "I spoke to my uncle about our concerns. He dismissed them all as due to childish pranks at a house party."

Mrs. Frogerton snorted. "Of course he did. No man likes to admit that he doesn't know what's going on in his own house." She consulted her notes. "Mr. Woodford was not as helpful as I had hoped either, although he did admit that there was a conflict between his sister and the Greenwoods."

"Which we had already speculated about." Caroline

half closed her eyes and appreciated the warmth of the fire.

Mrs. Frogerton smiled. "But he said it was a *financial* matter and suggested they had been misled by another member of the household."

"Who exactly?"

"Lady Ines." Her employer was looking positively triumphant now. "He only told me because as she is now deceased, he doesn't believe the Greenwoods have a case against him and his sister."

"Then surely we have solved this mystery. Mr. Woodford murdered Great-Aunt Ines to prevent her from testifying against him and his sister in court."

"Ah, but as you pointed out earlier, Mr. Woodford was under the care of Dr. Harris and could not have gone upstairs and killed Lady Ines."

"Dr. Harris was sleeping when I went in to see Mr. Woodford," Caroline said. "He didn't hear me, so it is possible that Mr. Woodford managed to creep past him."

"After being dosed up to the eyeballs with laudanum?" Mrs. Frogerton sniffed. "Someone in the house must have been in league with him and we both know who that was, don't we?"

"Joshua?"

"Exactly." Her employer nodded. "Now, all we need to do is get him to admit the truth!"

"Good luck with that." Caroline was almost too tired to be polite. "He scuttles away like a scared rabbit every time he sees me."

"Then I will speak to him myself."

"With all due respect, ma'am. You have no authority here. Joshua might just laugh at you, or even worse, kill you," Caroline pointed out.

"Then I will make sure I am not alone when I confront him."

"I doubt that even if I am concealed in the vicinity, Josh is strong enough to overpower both of us. Perhaps we should go to my uncle with our suspicions and ask for his assistance. He *is* the local magistrate."

"And he has already told you he believes nothing is wrong."

"Then what do you propose?" Caroline asked.

"The only person here who is rightfully angry about Lady Ines's death is Dr. Harris. I'm sure that if we ask him to accompany us, he'll gladly agree."

"Dr. Harris?" Caroline considered that. "I suppose that is possible."

"Good, then you will seek him out in the morning and ask for his help."

"*I* will seek his help?"

"Yes, indeed. He will listen to you." Mrs. Frogerton set her notebook to one side and stood up. "Now, good night, my dear. There is no need for you to linger. I will wait up for Dotty."

"Are you quite sure?"

"Yes, indeed. You look quite done in." Mrs. Frogerton patted her shoulder and turned her toward the door. "Sleep well, lass."

Caroline lit a candle from the fire, left the suite, and walked back to her bedroom, her thoughts in an uncomfortable jumble. The house was quiet around her, the only sounds the faint ticking of a clock somewhere and the soft rustle of her petticoats beneath her serviceable blue evening gown. Her employer's optimism about Joshua readily confessing to his crimes seemed somewhat debatable, but as Caroline didn't have an alternative plan, she could hardly complain.

The notion that she should involve Dr. Harris in her employer's madcap scheme to bring Joshua to justice didn't sit well with her, but at present she couldn't conceive of any other solution. Perhaps if she slept on the matter, she might think of something new.

She opened the door to her room and even in the soft glow of the inadequate candle noticed something was different. Someone had been in and banked up the coal fire, which had warmed the room quite considerably. Had that someone also searched her room for the missing money from Great-Aunt Ines's rooms? She locked the door, set the candle on the mantelpiece with unsteady hands, and rushed over to the chest of drawers. The two-hundred-pound note was still securely rolled up in her stocking. The velvet bag of coins sat on the dressing table, which was not where she had left them.

She checked the contents of the bag, but all the coins were present. Perhaps one of the maids had moved them while attending to the fire and dusting without realizing what she held in her hand? It was not usual for the maids to be in the bedrooms in the evening unless someone rang the bell, but the shortage of staff might have meant that Caroline's room had been left until last.

Convinced that she was overreacting, and glad of the roaring fire, Caroline turned to the bed and went still. There was a small bound book sitting on the pillow that definitely did not belong to her.

She approached it warily, supremely conscious of the silence and the knowledge that whoever had been in her room had deliberately chosen to leave something behind. She had a sudden urge to fling open the door to the walled cupboard just in case someone was hiding there watching her reaction. The sense that something was deeply wrong increased with every step she took toward the bed.

She sat on the patchwork quilt and forced herself to pick up the book and examine it. The cover was a mottled brown with no identifiable title. When she opened the book, it appeared to be a collection of sermons until she realized that someone had written on the back of each piece of paper in small, almost indecipherable handwriting. She found her spectacles and attempted to puzzle out the first page.

The witch was horrible to everyone. Given no dinner and made to hem sheets until my fingers bled and I could barely see. Went to bed hungry. D gave me some bread which helped.

Caroline paused in her reading to quickly scan the page. It appeared to be some kind of diary, but it wasn't dated.

Cook felt sorry for me today and let me help in the kitchen instead of the endless sewing. At least it was warm, and I had three good meals. T glowered at me the whole time and will make me pay, but it was worth it.

Caroline raised her head and briefly shut her eyes as a headache threatened. It was almost impossible to decipher the faint scrawl in the flickering light of the candle and the red glow of the coal fire. She closed the book and stared down at it. Who had placed it with such care on her pillow and why had they done so?

She flicked back to the inside cover of the book and discovered a small drawing of a single rose done in faded colors. The inscription was in different handwriting from the rest of the book. Caroline read the words aloud.

" 'A rose for a rose. With my love. N.' " She peered at the faded script. "Or is that an M?"

A sharp knock on her door made her startle like a wild hare. She shoved the book under her pillow and leapt to her feet.

"Who is it?"

"Dr. Harris wants you, miss." Hetty opened the door. She was already dressed for bed and had her hair bundled up in a cap. "Says it's urgent."

"Where is he?" This time Caroline made sure to lock her door and keep the key as she left the room.

"In the kitchen last time I saw him. I was down there getting warm milk for some of the little ones Harry and Miss Mabel scared out of their wits with their ghostly tales." Hetty gave Caroline a strange look as she pocketed her key but didn't comment further. "Do you want me to come down with you?"

"No, you go off to bed." Caroline mustered a smile. "I can find my own way."

"Then take my candle and be careful on the stairs," Hetty warned, as if Caroline was one of her nursery charges.

"Thank you. I will."

Caroline took the fresh candle and turned toward the main stairwell, her heart still beating far too fast for her own comfort. Despite her annoyance at Dr. Harris's high-handed manner, she was secretly relieved to not have to go to bed just yet.

Shielding the candle flame against the drafts in the stairwell, she made her way down to the shadowy basement. There was still activity in the main kitchen where the footmen and kitchen maids were putting away the dinner service and polishing the silverware, but there was no sign of Dr. Harris.

Unwilling to disturb the hardworking staff, Caroline proceeded down the echoing central corridor until she reached the butler's quarters. The candle flickered and almost went out, and she caught her breath as the blackness closed around her. Dr. Harris poked his head out from the door, offering a welcome beam of light, and frowned at her.

"Wherever have you been?"

"I was about to go to bed," Caroline replied as he held the door open for her to enter the butler's sitting room. "What is so urgent that it cannot wait until morning?"

"This." Dr. Harris went to the internal door that led to Mr. Woodford's bedroom and flung it open. Caroline followed with some reluctance. "He's dead."

Chapter 11

Caroline stared down at Mr. Woodford's peaceful face. He lay on his back, his hands crossed neatly on his chest like one of the medieval knights in the family graveyard.

"Did he die in his sleep?" Caroline asked.

"I assume that's what I'm supposed to believe."

Caroline turned to look at Dr. Harris, who looked furious. "I don't understand."

"It's mightily convenient that a man who was recently trapped in a cellar and barely escaped with his life suddenly passes away."

"He doesn't look as if he suffered."

"That's because I laid him out properly. When I came to check on him, his eyes were wide open, the bedclothes were disarranged, and he was gripping the sheets so hard I had to prize each finger free of the threads." Dr. Harris paused. "He looked terrified."

"He's been afraid ever since the accident." Caroline paused. "Are you suggesting he died of fright?"

"Don't be ridiculous." Dr. Harris pointed at two pillows on the floor beside the bed. "If I was going to end an old man's life, I'd suffocate him, which is what I assume happened here. Unfortunately, unless you catch someone in the act, it's very hard to discern why someone stopped breathing just from an external examination."

"Then what do you intend to do if you can't prove anything?" Caroline asked.

Dr. Harris shrugged. "I'll tell the Greenwoods what I suspect happened, but they won't listen to me."

"Maybe he did just pass away," Caroline said hopefully. "Perhaps his heart couldn't take the shock of his incarceration."

Dr. Harris just looked at her before raising the bedsheet to cover Mr. Woodford's face.

"I examined him on several occasions, Miss Morton. He was a relatively healthy man with a strong heartbeat for his age. I wonder if the Greenwoods will care enough to start an investigation into this matter when they refused to believe their own blood relative was murdered?"

"My aunt simply wishes to avoid a scandal during her daughter's birthday celebrations," Caroline said.

"Yes, because not upsetting Miss Mabel and her guests is *far* more important than bringing a murderer to justice," Dr. Harris snapped as he picked up his bag and walked through into the sitting room.

Caroline followed him. "There is no need to be so scathing, Doctor. I did not say I *agreed* with her, just that this is how she will see the matter and my uncle will not argue against her."

Dr. Harris sat down abruptly in one of the chairs and shoved his hand through his thick dark hair. "Here I go again, shouting at you rather than addressing the real problem because for all intents and purposes these people are my benefactors and the success or failure of my medical practice is in their hands."

"If I may be frank, Dr. Harris, have you perhaps considered finding employment in a hospital rather than in the countryside? I understand that there are some excellent teaching establishments in London."

"I might have no choice in the matter now." He sighed.

"I wish I could just ride away from this damned house and leave Dr. McGregor to deal with everything."

"I suppose you could do that." Caroline tentatively sat down opposite him. "Dr. McGregor would certainly pander to my uncle and aunt's demand for silence."

He raised his head to look at her. "But would it be right? What kind of doctor would I be if I ignored the basic promises I made to heal the sick and do no harm?"

"I believe you have fulfilled your side of the bargain admirably, sir. It is hardly your fault if someone keeps murdering your patients."

He held her gaze for a long moment. "You are an interesting woman, Miss Morton."

"Hardly." She shrugged. "But I have learned to be a practical one. I cannot allow you to blame yourself for trying to do your best in very difficult circumstances."

"Thank you." He inclined his head.

"You're welcome." She rose to her feet. "Both my aunt and uncle have retired for the night, so perhaps this news could wait until the morning?"

"Why not? It makes no difference to Mr. Woodford now. I will stay here and make sure no one discovers him in the morning and makes a scene."

"But what if the murderer comes back to make sure Mr. Woodford is dead?" Caroline asked.

"Then we'll be having a very interesting conversation." He suddenly looked rather formidable. "In truth, I'd quite welcome such an encounter."

"I should go to bed," Caroline said as she hastily smothered a yawn. "There was something I wished to discuss with you, but it will wait until morning."

"You might as well tell me now." He stood as well and towered over her.

She suppressed a sigh at his return to bossiness. "As you wish. The short version is that my employer, Mrs. Frogerton, is convinced for a variety of reasons that Joshua is the person who murdered Lady Ines. She wants to confront

138 *Catherine Lloyd*

him with this information and requires someone who believes that a murder was committed to be by her side in case Joshua decides to run or retaliate."

"And apart from you I'm the only person who agrees Lady Ines was murdered." Dr. Harris nodded. "Might I ask how Mrs. Frogerton became involved in what I thought was a family matter?"

Caroline bit her lip. "I might have inadvertently alerted her to the murder before I realized my aunt and uncle would fail to take the matter seriously."

"Ah."

"She would like to speak to you about the matter at your convenience," Caroline continued.

"I can see why she might suspect Joshua, who was the one who found Lady Ines in the first place," Dr. Harris said. "I've met many a murderer who has loudly proclaimed their own crime."

"My cousin Eliza believes I am the murderer," Caroline said.

"I know." He smiled. "She told me."

"Did you believe her?"

Dr. Harris looked down at her. "I could see you murdering someone if you had to, Miss Morton, but a defenseless old woman? No."

"Thank you for that, at least." Caroline turned to the door.

"But I can also see how you might have returned to this house with grudges and old scores to pay off. Lady Ines wasn't known for her sweetness of temper. It's possible you might have strangled her in a fit of rage." He looked her up and down. "You have the physical ability, and you could definitely have overpowered Mr. Woodford."

"Really, Doctor?" Caroline asked and he raised his eyebrows.

"I am merely exploring all the possibilities."

"Good night, Dr. Harris."

He had the audacity to smile at her again. "Good night, Miss Morton."

After a restless night's sleep, Caroline woke to a cold gray dawn and dressed quickly before going down to the kitchen to collect Mrs. Frogerton's breakfast tray. There was no sign that anyone in the kitchen knew of Mr. Woodford's death yet. Caroline assumed Dr. Harris was still guarding the butler's door. She'd decided she should be the first person her employer spoke to that morning because she had a lot to impart.

She wasn't surprised Dr. Harris had agreed to aid Mrs. Frogerton. He'd already struck her as a man who hated injustice and one who was more than willing to right a wrong. On their last encounter he'd shown a harder side she hadn't seen before.

"I'll take that up to Mrs. Frogerton, Peggy," Caroline called out to the maid who was just placing a jug of milk on the tray.

"You sure, miss?" Peggy looked doubtfully at her and then at the tray. "It's heavier than it looks."

"I'm certain I'll manage," Caroline said brightly. "Perhaps you might bring Miss Frogerton her breakfast?"

"She won't ring until ten at the earliest, miss. She didn't get to bed until after midnight." Peggy smothered a yawn. "I had to wait up for her."

Caroline took the tray and set off up the first flight of stairs. She wasn't going to admit it to Peggy, but the cumbersome tray did appear to become heavier with every step, and she had quite a long way to go.

"May I help you?"

She glanced up to find Francis looking down at her—his expression concerned.

"No, I am quite capable, thank you." She gave him a dismissive smile.

"I suppose I should have expected that a woman such as

Mrs. Frogerton would have you performing all kinds of menial tasks to satisfy her every whim."

She frowned at him as she balanced the tray. "I have no idea what you are talking about, or why it is any concern of yours whatsoever."

"She demeans you."

"She pays my wages."

"Which is intolerable. If I'd known—"

Caroline cut him off. "What else did you think would happen to me when my father died, and his financial indiscretions became known?"

"I thought you would have the good sense to come and live here with your aunt and uncle."

"Thus, absolving you of any responsibility for my downfall?"

He frowned. "That's hardly fair."

"And what exactly did you expect me to do here? Pine away while I worked just as hard but without the dignity of a wage?" She readjusted the tray and started back up the stairs. "I'd rather be at Mrs. Frogerton's beck and call than my aunt's."

She kept walking until she reached Mrs. Frogerton's room and managed to open the door. She'd never imagined Francis would become an irritant. She was fairly certain that his expressed outrage over her current circumstances had more to do with his own guilt than any real concern for her.

"Good morning, ma'am. I have your breakfast here."

To her surprise her employer was already awake and sitting up against her pillows. Her hair was covered by a lace cap and she wore her spectacles on her nose as she perused yesterday's paper.

"Why are you carrying that heavy tray?" Mrs. Frogerton demanded. "You'll put your back out, and then where will we be?"

"I wanted to make sure I was the first person to awaken you."

"Why?" Mrs. Frogerton immediately brightened. "Do you have news?"

"You could say that." Caroline set the tray over her employer's knees and offered her a cloth napkin. "Dr. Harris says he would be happy to accompany you when you interview Joshua."

"Excellent." Mrs. Frogerton poured herself some tea and offered Caroline a cup, which she declined. "I knew he would prove to be useful."

"Something else happened last night," Caroline continued. "Mr. Woodford is dead."

"Of natural causes?"

"Dr. Harris doesn't think so, but he says he doesn't have the evidence to prove foul play."

"Why ever not?" Mrs. Frogerton's brow creased.

"Because he believes Mr. Woodford was suffocated."

"Oh, dearie me. Exactly the same thing happened to an acquaintance of mine when her husband wanted to get rid of her and marry his mistress. The only reason he was convicted was because her maid came in unexpectedly and witnessed the whole thing." Mrs. Frogerton grimaced. "I would hate to think that my interactions with Mr. Woodford caused the murderer to return and finish him off."

"I doubt that, ma'am." Caroline hastened to reassure her. "One has to assume Mr. Woodford knew his assailant. And if that was the case, then his life was already at risk regardless of whether he spoke to you or not."

"I suppose you are right," Mrs. Frogerton said. "I wonder if anyone has thought to tell Miss Vera?"

"I don't think his death is widely known about yet," Caroline said. "Dr. Harris was going to wait until my aunt and uncle came down to breakfast to tell them."

"Well, may his soul rest in peace." Mrs. Frogerton set her cup back on the tray. "I'm sure he will be missed and mourned by many."

Caroline glanced out of the window where it had at least stopped raining. "I doubt the river is crossable. We might have to wait until tomorrow to share the sad news with his sister and the rest of the village."

Mrs. Frogerton nodded. "Which also means I need to speak to Joshua today. If he believes he has gotten away with two murders, I doubt he will be hanging around waiting to be caught, do you?"

"Do you believe he killed Mr. Woodford as well?" Caroline asked.

"Of course he did." Mrs. Frogerton looked surprised at the question. "There can't be two murderers running around this house at the same time."

"It would be something of a coincidence," Caroline agreed. "The fact that this is happening at all is quite fantastical."

"You would prefer it to be one of those ghosts your cousin is so fond of?" Mrs. Frogerton shivered rather dramatically.

"We might as well be dealing with ghosts as no one in my family seems to believe us anyway," Caroline retorted.

"I need to speak to Dr. Harris as soon as possible," Mrs. Frogerton said.

"Yes, ma'am." Caroline went to remove the tray and her employer held up her hand.

"But not until I have finished these excellent coddled eggs and ham."

After assuring Mrs. Frogerton that she would ask Dr. Harris to meet with her at his earliest convenience, Caroline checked the time and went up to the nursery. The children were absent on their morning walk and the place was deserted. She still had the key for the doll's house in her pocket and approached the glass cabinet with some trepidation. The door opened easily, and she unlatched the front panel of the house.

The butler doll had disappeared from the basement and was tucked neatly into one of the beds with a pillow over his face. Caroline shuddered as she hurriedly closed the door and locked it.

"Are you looking for the other key, miss?" Hetty called out from the door as she came in. "It's been missing for a while now."

"Really?" Caroline tried to look concerned. She wondered if she should be concerned with her descent into being comfortable with deceit. "I'm sure I put it back on the mantelpiece behind the clock after I showed Mrs. Frogerton the house the other day, but I will check my pockets just to make certain I didn't inadvertently steal it."

"There used to be three or four copies of that key, so I wouldn't worry yourself too much, miss. I'm sure one will turn up soon." Hetty picked up a wooden block from under the table. "Were you looking for your sister?"

"Yes," Caroline smiled. "I presume she is off on her walk?"

"They are all marching up and down the long gallery like soldiers under the watchful eye of her ladyship." Hetty chuckled. "The poor dears have been cooped up in here for days now. If it wasn't for Miss Susan, Miss Mabel, and Danny Price inventing all these new games for them to play, I don't know how I'd manage."

"I should imagine it is quite frustrating," Caroline agreed. "It has been raining less today so perhaps the weather is about to take a turn for the better."

"His lordship doesn't think so, miss. The bridge into the village is still impassable and might need repairing before anyone even attempts to get across it again."

"I didn't realize that. I wonder if any of the guests will be able to get to the ball?"

"I don't see how they will manage it, miss." Hetty looked glum. "And we were all looking forward to seeing everyone in their fancy gowns and jewels."

"I think the ball will still take place if that is what Mabel wants." Caroline made sure the key was firmly in her pocket. "She said that everyone she cares about is already here and that is good enough for her."

"Sounds just like her, miss. She was always good with the children."

Caroline made her way back to the door. "Do you ever remember a child named Rose living here, Hetty?"

"Rose?" Hetty wrinkled her nose as she considered the name. "Not in my day, miss, but her ladyship has been taking in her waifs and strays for thirty years or so. You should ask Mr. Woodford or Mrs. Maddox. They've been here the longest."

"Thank you, Hetty. I'll go and see if I can intercept Susan on her way back up here. Mrs. Frogerton was asking after her," Caroline said. "Perhaps you can tell Mrs. Whittle that she is with me if she inquires."

"I will, miss."

Caroline went all the way down to the main hall and was just about to go and search for her sister again when Dr. Harris appeared at her side.

"I just spoke with Lord Greenwood."

"And?"

"He suggested that I not only leave his house at the earliest opportunity, but that he will do everything in his power to make sure I never practice medicine in his vicinity again."

"I'm sorry."

He shrugged. "It wasn't exactly unexpected. I'm beginning to believe that coming back here was a terrible mistake."

"Coming back?" Caroline asked.

"I was born about ten miles away. My parents moved away when I was a child." He frowned. "I can't say I had good memories of the place and things certainly haven't improved."

"I think you will be far happier in a teaching hospital in London," Caroline said firmly. "Where you will be valued for your insights and intelligence."

"Thank you." He sighed. "I offered to leave straight-away, but was reminded that the bridge is unstable, and that Miss Mabel wishes me to be present at her ball. I have no idea why."

"She thinks very highly of you."

Dr. Harris raised an eyebrow. "I doubt it."

Caroline went to turn away and he cleared his throat. "Would you mind coming with me to speak to the staff about Mr. Woodford's death? Lady Eleanor is indisposed, and his lordship seemed to think it's beneath him to deal with his own employees."

"My aunt is ill?" Caroline asked.

"Not to a degree that requires my services, apparently. She is simply overtired and is spending the morning in bed."

"I must go up and speak to her."

Dr. Harris took a firm hold of her elbow. "Not until you help me first."

"I am certainly willing to do that if you accompany me afterward to speak to Mrs. Frogerton."

"As you wish."

Caroline allowed herself to be led toward the kitchen where Mrs. Maddox had assembled the staff.

"Well, what is it then, Doctor?" the cook asked. "I do have a dinner to get on the table tonight if you don't mind."

Dr. Harris looked at Caroline, who stepped forward.

"I regret to inform you that Mr. Woodford died during the night."

There were a couple of gasps and one of the kitchen maids burst into tears.

"Dr. Harris was with him," Caroline continued.

"The poor old man." Mrs. Maddox wiped a tear from her cheek. "I've known him most of my life and while he could be exasperating, he served this family well for years, and should be remembered with respect."

Caroline glanced over to where the footmen stood gath-ered in a group and noticed Joshua's white face. Even as she looked at him, he turned on his heel and left the kitchen. She made no attempt to follow. Dr. Harris and Mrs. Frogerton would deal with Joshua without her help, but if a man ever looked consumed with guilt, Joshua was that person.

She turned to Dr. Harris. "Have you finished with the staff, Doctor?"

"Indeed, I have. Shall we go and find Mrs. Frogerton?"

He followed her out of the kitchen and up the stairs to Mrs. Frogerton's rooms. Caroline knocked and went in to find her employer sitting by the fire.

"Dr. Harris, ma'am."

"Oh good!" Mrs. Frogerton gestured for him to take a seat opposite her. "I need your help."

"So I hear." With a flick of his coattails Dr. Harris sat down. "Although I must say that the notion of confronting Joshua with his supposed crimes is remarkably dangerous."

"How else are we going to persuade him to admit to being a murderer?" Mrs. Frogerton asked.

"By finding some evidence, perhaps?"

"Like what exactly?"

Dr. Harris shrugged. "Written accounts of his misdeeds? Large amounts of money on his person? Bloodstains on his linen?"

Mrs. Frogerton turned to Caroline, who had lingered by the door. "Perhaps while the good doctor and I are interrogating Joshua you could search his room?"

"Wouldn't that be unlawful?" Caroline asked.

Dr. Harris snorted. "Of course not. He's in your uncle's employ and thus subject to his authority. And Lord Greenwood is the local magistrate. No one around here would dare to question him about how he deals with his own staff."

"Then I will take myself up to the servants' quarters and investigate while you talk to Joshua," Caroline said. "The faster we can solve this matter the sooner everything can go back to normal and Mabel can enjoy what remains of her birthday."

"With two lives already lost, I doubt things will ever be the same," Mrs. Frogerton added. "But bringing a criminal to justice might help."

"I agree." Dr. Harris nodded and rose to his feet. "Shall we find Joshua, ma'am, and hold him to account?"

"Good luck with that," Caroline said. "He bolted like a rabbit after your announcement earlier."

"We'll find him," Dr. Harris announced as he offered Mrs. Frogerton his hand to help her rise. "He can hardly have gone far in this atrocious weather." He glanced toward the window where it had been raining steadily since dawn. "I attempted to get back over the river again this morning, but the current was too fierce for my horse to navigate."

Caroline opened the door. "I will speak to my aunt and then, if all is clear, I'll proceed as planned to the servants' quarters."

It was still early in the morning, and the majority of the houseguests were in bed as Caroline traversed the quiet corridors. It was unusual for her aunt not to come down for an early breakfast and a consultation with her staff, but perhaps the trying nature of the last few days had taken their toll on Eleanor's nerves. She had certainly not been herself since Caroline's arrival at the house.

She knocked gently on her aunt's door and went in. Eleanor was still in bed with the curtains half-drawn. Unfortunately, Eliza was sitting beside her gesticulating wildly. Even from the doorway, Caroline could see her aunt's pained expression and that her cousin hadn't yet noticed her arrival.

"She needs to go, Mama. She hates us!"

"Eliza . . ."

Caroline walked toward the bed. "Good morning, Cousin, Aunt."

"What are you doing here?" Eliza asked. "Have you come to gloat over Mr. Woodford's death?"

"I came to inquire as to my aunt's health," Caroline said. "Have you recovered from your fall, Cousin?"

"Keep away from me!" Eliza screeched, and held up her hand as if to prevent Caroline's approach.

"Oh, for goodness' sake." Eleanor sounded exhausted and Caroline wondered how long her cousin had been haranguing her mother. "If you won't stop this nonsense, Daughter, I will ask your husband to take you home for the good of your health."

"It isn't nonsense! She is laughing at us as she wreaks havoc on your household."

"Why would I do that to the woman who offered me and my sister a home when my father was too incompetent or too broke to care for us?" Caroline asked. "My aunt will always have my gratitude for that."

"Because you've always resented the fact you weren't part of the family," Eliza countered.

"I admit I found that difficult when I was a child, but, in truth, you were the main reason for that. You never failed to point out my inferiority. I believe you even instructed the staff not to treat me like a member of the family."

"See?" Eliza turned back to her mother. "She holds on to every little grudge and has allowed her mind to become distorted by hatred."

"Why would you think that?" Caroline didn't allow herself to become angry. She was genuinely curious as to why her cousin had such a ridiculous opinion of her. "I have never done you or anyone else in this house harm."

"Don't pretend you don't know," Eliza said. "I have evidence."

"Of what?" Caroline asked.

"Your perfidy," Eliza snapped. "Did you think I would burn those horrible little notes you used to send me? Or the new ones that have arrived in my room since your return?"

"Notes?" Caroline frowned. "I have no idea what you are talking about."

Eleanor waved a weary hand toward her dressing table. "I have them in the second drawer on the right. Eliza insisted I read them last night."

Caroline went to retrieve the letters.

"Don't throw them on the fire, now!" Eliza warned as Caroline approached the bed with the bundle of papers.

"May I read them, Aunt?" Caroline inquired.

"Of course, my dear."

Caroline sat in the chair Eliza had vacated and sorted through the pile as she read. Eventually, she looked up.

"I can see why they would have upset you, Cousin, but I can assure you that I didn't write them. They don't even attempt to mimic my handwriting."

"I told her the same thing, Caroline. Your script is far neater than that."

"She is hardly going to admit it, is she?" Eliza scowled. "Who else would've written such horrible things?"

Caroline set the letters back on her aunt's bed. "That is the question, isn't it? One has to ask whether there were any other children you bullied as well as me?"

"I simply made sure that everyone knew their place, Caroline." Eliza raised her chin. "My mother did not intend for her charity brats to take precedence over her own children. Order needed to be maintained."

"It was not your place to assume such authority, Eliza," Eleanor said.

"Someone had to."

"That was the job of the nursery staff."

"And I can assure you that everyone knew where they came in the social order." Caroline met her cousin's gaze. "It was enforced with relentless regularity."

"Hardly. Boys like Dan and Harry Price were always disrespectful."

"That might be true, but they always knew their future was different to yours and never expected anything better."

Eliza looked away. "It is pointless arguing with you, Caroline. You are never going to admit to your part in this."

"That is because I had no part to play," Caroline repeated. "I am truly sorry that someone sent you those unpleasant notes, but as you just pointed out, you never wanted to be friends with anyone in the nursery who wasn't directly related to you anyway."

"I just find it odd, that you return to the house and the notes begin again."

"I agree that is odd," Caroline conceded. "But I'm not the only additional guest in the house at present."

Eliza frowned. "I did notice that Dan Price has not had a kind word to say to any of us as he enjoys our hospitality. Perhaps I should talk to him."

"Or you could just let things be?" Caroline suggested. "You are soon to celebrate the birth of your first child, Mabel wishes to enjoy her birthday with her friends, and surely my aunt deserves some peace."

"I suppose I am the lucky one," Eliza said reluctantly. "Perhaps everyone is simply jealous of my good fortune and should be ignored."

"I am sure that is correct." Caroline nodded. "In a few days all the guests will depart, and you will have nothing to vex you."

Eliza didn't look much happier but at least she had stopped suggesting Caroline was a murderer. Eliza walked toward the door and then paused to look over her shoulder.

"I do not need advice from you, Cousin. If anything else goes wrong in this house while you are in it, I will be speaking to my father."

Caroline waited until Eliza shut the door before walking over to the bed.

"May I get you anything, Aunt? Have you had your breakfast yet?"

"I've not done anything except be shaken awake by Eliza so that I could listen to her call you a murderer." Eleanor drew her shawl tightly around her shoulders and sat bolt upright against her pillows. "Good Lord, that girl is tiresome. I don't know how her husband puts up with her."

"She is simply concerned for her family, ma'am. That is quite understandable." Caroline hesitated. "Did you know she had received those notes at the time?"

"She never mentioned it. She said I wouldn't have listened to her, which is quite untrue. If I'd known someone in the nursery was being so spiteful, I would've investigated the matter until I'd found the culprit and dealt with them."

"I didn't write those letters."

"Of course you didn't." Eleanor offered her an impatient glance. "I brought you up far better than that."

Caroline forbore to mention she'd received the same upbringing and schooling as Eliza.

"It is strange that the notes should start up again while I am here."

"I suspect Eliza wrote those herself," Eleanor said. "She seemed hell-bent on getting rid of you."

"I suppose if she felt I'd written the earlier ones she felt justified in doing so," Caroline said. "Would you mind if I took the notes to read through again? I knew all the children in the nursery well and even helped some of them with their letters. I might find some clue to the author from the handwriting."

"As far as I am concerned you can take them away and burn them." Eleanor pressed her fingers to her brow. "I have a terrible headache."

"Then may I suggest you stay in bed and I'll ask your maid to bring you up some soothing tea?" Caroline offered. "None of your guests are up yet and your absence will not be noted."

"Yes." Eleanor leaned back and closed her eyes. "That would be most helpful. Despite insisting we hold the ball here, your uncle is offering me no assistance at all. Perhaps you might act as hostess in my stead."

Caroline lightly pressed her aunt's shoulder and went toward the door. Finding her aunt's maid gave her an excellent excuse to visit the kitchen and inquire about Joshua's whereabouts.

Ten minutes later, after relaying her aunt's wishes to her maid, and ascertaining that Joshua was currently closeted with Mrs. Frogerton and Dr. Harris in the housekeeper's study, she went up the back stairs to the servants' quarters on the very top floor of the house. Even though her uncle kept the house in relatively good condition, it was bitingly cold up in the rafters and the stained wallpaper was evidence of leaks in the ceilings and roof.

Joshua was the most senior of the current footmen, which meant his room would probably be the biggest one at the end of the row. It was unlikely that any member of staff would be present in the attics at this time of day unless they were ill, but she proceeded as quietly as she could.

None of the doors were locked so she unlatched the door to Joshua's room and went inside. There was a small, recessed window set into the thick wall that looked out over the parapet into the gardens behind the house. The window was open, and the thin curtain flapped in the stiff breeze bringing in the scent of the fens. An iron bedstead with two quilts and two pillows sat in the center of the room. Against the wall was a small chest of drawers and there was a trunk under the bed.

Leaving the door slightly ajar in case anyone ascended the stairs, and still feeling slightly guilty, Caroline started to look through the drawers. To her surprise, Joshua kept his belongings very neatly and in good condition. He had a Bible and a copy of the Pugilistic Club's rules for boxing on his bedside table and not much else.

She went down on her knees and pulled out the battered trunk with some effort. It was an old piece of luggage with several faded address labels on the outside that she assumed had either belonged to one of Joshua's parents or been appropriated for his own use at some point. To her relief it wasn't locked as she was able to ease the lid free. The stale smell of hair pomade, sandalwood, and pipe smoke clung to the silk lined interior.

A new pair of boots, two crisp white shirts, and a fashionable black coat had been carefully placed inside. Caroline took each item out, noting its position so that she could return it to its exact place. There were several pockets within the silk interior. She checked each one, revealing a tortoiseshell cigarillo case, a tin box containing some kind of male invigorating pills to combat baldness, and a silver-backed hand mirror. She frowned as she contemplated the strange mixture of items.

Had Joshua helped himself to these things from the house to sell on later? Or were they more personal? From what Mrs. Frogerton had told her it was not uncommon for servants to benefit financially from items thrown away or forgotten by their employers. There was nothing else in the pockets to discover and she replaced each item in the correct place before turning to the boots.

The right boot was heavier than the left. She delved inside it until her fingers brushed against something soft. She almost wasn't surprised when she drew out a red velvet bag full of gold coins and ten carefully folded five-pound notes. The similarity to what she had found in her great-aunt's room was too hard to ignore.

After replacing all the other items and pushing the trunk back under the bed, she left the room, the money concealed in her pocket, and went back down to the kitchen area. Even though the door to the housekeeper's rooms was closed, she could hear Dr. Harris speaking. She knocked and waited until the doctor came to the door. When he raised his eyebrows at her she beckoned for him to join her in the corridor.

"You were supposed to leave this part to Mrs. Frogerton and me, Miss Morton."

"I am well aware of that. Has he confessed yet?"

"Not at all. He's currently whining that we are being

unfair and that he's never had a bad thought about anyone in his life."

Caroline took out the velvet bag. "You said we needed evidence. I found these gold coins and fifty pounds in his bedroom."

"Gold coins?" Dr. Harris held out his hand and Caroline dropped the bag into his palm. "Good Lord. Did you count them?"

"Not yet. I thought it more important to come and ask Joshua why he had them." Caroline hesitated. "I found a similar velvet bag amongst my great-aunt's possessions."

She didn't mention the two-hundred-pound note, or the fact that she had still failed to hand over the other coins to her aunt.

"What an interesting coincidence." Dr. Harris indicated the door. "Do you care to come in and continue this conversation in front of Joshua? I must confess that I am eager to hear what he has to say about this discovery, too."

"I would be delighted." Caroline inclined her head as Dr. Harris stepped back to allow her through the door. "Thank you."

Joshua was leaning up against the table, his arms crossed over his chest and his expression sullen as he stared at Mrs. Frogerton.

"I keep telling you. I don't know nothing about Mr. Woodford's death. I was asleep and dreaming of better things when he kicked the bucket."

His wary gaze flicked to Caroline and then back to the door.

"Morning, miss."

"Good morning, Joshua," Caroline said, and took the seat beside Mrs. Frogerton, who looked at her inquiringly.

"I know you might not believe me, Joshua, but no one here wishes you harm," Dr. Harris said. "We simply wish to know what happened to Mr. Woodford."

"You think I don't want to know that, too?" Joshua asked. "I didn't like him, but I didn't want him dead."

"Then who did?" Caroline leaned forward. "And why?" She held his gaze. "Does it have something to do with the scheme hatched between the Woodfords and Lady Ines?"

Joshua's expression froze. "I don't know what you're talking about, miss. I already told the doctor and the lady that."

"The Woodfords and Lady Ines might have profited from the sales, but they needed someone younger and fitter such as yourself to participate for it to be successful."

"I'd never do that." Joshua looked revolted.

"I know that it is not uncommon for staff members to . . . help themselves to their employer's castoffs and sell them on," Caroline suggested.

"That's what you think I've been doing?" Joshua looked around the room. "Pilfering stuff and selling it?"

"Well, that's what it appears the Woodfords and Lady Ines were doing," Dr. Harris spoke up. "One assumes you were getting paid for physically moving the items along from the house to Miss Woodford's cottage in the village."

Joshua remained silent for a long time before he finally raised his head.

"So what if I did? Who cares if someone profits from the rubbish of the rich?"

Dr. Harris shrugged. "We certainly don't, but it's possible that the Greenwood family might take another view. Were you aware the Greenwoods had consulted their solicitor about the matter?"

Joshua blinked. "I beg your pardon?"

"I assume Lady Eleanor believes the Woodfords went well beyond the accepted practices and should be classified as thieves—which, if you are involved with them as seems likely—means that you, too, could be prosecuted."

"For the removal of a few broken cups and chipped figurines?" Joshua snorted. "That's ridiculous."

"No doubt it is, but you must know that the law isn't fair, and that such a sentence might end in your transportation," Caroline spoke up. "And I don't believe it was simply broken china you were handing over to them. I doubt that would make you much money."

Dr. Harris held up the velvet money bag. "Is this yours?"

Joshua lurched forward and tried to grab the bag. "Give that to me!"

"Unfortunately, I can't do that. It might be considered as evidence by the courts." Dr. Harris tucked the money into his waistcoat pocket.

"You have no right to go through my things!" Joshua said.

"I had my aunt's authority to do so," Caroline replied, which was stretching the truth somewhat, but Joshua didn't need to know that. "Who gave you the gold coins?"

"That's none of your business!" Joshua was shouting now, his fists clenched at his sides. "You interfering bunch of busybodies!"

"May I remind you that two of the people you were helping to steal are now dead?" Caroline stood and blocked Joshua's exit.

"You trying to pin that on me now?" Joshua turned to Dr. Harris. "If I'd killed the old bitch, why would I come and tell you about it, sir?"

"It would be an excellent alibi to prove your innocence."

"I didn't kill no one!"

"Somebody did." Caroline held his angry stare. "If they were paying you to help them—perhaps you decided it would be better to take all of the profits?"

"That's a lie, miss. I had no need to kill them when they needed my help and paid me well." He shrugged. "I mean I will admit to scaring Mr. Woodford in the cellar the other night but it was just harmless fun."

"He was hurt and terrified," Caroline said evenly.

"Nothing more than he's done to people like me his whole life, miss, and gotten away with." Joshua's gaze was cool. "Maybe it was time he got a taste of his own medicine." He turned to Dr. Harris. "But I didn't kill either of them. I swear."

"I wish I could believe you," Dr. Harris said. "But the evidence points to a different conclusion."

"I'm no murderer!" Joshua shoved Caroline to one side, making her stagger against Dr. Harris and grab hold of his coat. "Now, leave me be!"

Dr. Harris was too busy untangling himself from Caroline to be able to stop Joshua's hasty exit.

"Well, I never!" exclaimed Mrs. Frogerton. "Where does the silly boy think he's going now?"

"In this weather?" Dr. Harris set Caroline back on her own two feet and scowled at the doorway. "Not far. And, as I have his money, I suspect he'll be back."

"You believe he did kill both Great-Aunt Ines and Mr. Woodford?" Caroline asked.

"Who else could it have been?"

Mrs. Frogerton cleared her throat. "But there is the matter of the money."

"What about it?" Dr. Harris turned to look at her.

"I doubt Joshua earned all that money just by stealing from the Greenwoods."

"If he was taking fine porcelain, works of art, and jewelry, he might have," Caroline said. "But I'm fairly certain that my aunt would notice if such items were disappearing from her house. She is a very careful and conscientious housekeeper."

"If Joshua's money isn't from Mr. Woodford and your great-aunt, then where else would he get it?" Mrs. Frogerton asked.

"Maybe it isn't so much a question of who gave it to him as what was it for," Caroline said thoughtfully. "Is it possible someone else was involved?"

"You think half the village is in on it now?" Dr. Harris asked. "I sincerely doubt it. I think our duty here is clear, don't you? We inform Lord Greenwood that we have discovered a murderer."

Chapter 12

As predicted, Joshua hadn't gotten far. He'd tried to help himself to the petty cash in the butler's pantry, which was where he'd been discovered by one of the maids, who screeched loud enough to wake the dead. Even though Lord Greenwood had him confined to the cellars, Caroline was well aware that her uncle didn't really believe anyone had been murdered. In truth, he'd been quite angry with her when she'd approached him for assistance.

"You do realize this whole thing is ridiculous?" Eleanor paused her walking long enough to glare at Caroline. After hearing the news from her husband, who had departed in something of a huff for the stables, she had asked Dr. Harris and Caroline to present themselves in his study. "Mr. Woodford died in his sleep after the unfortunate incident in the cellar and Ines was simply old."

Dr. Harris went to speak and then raised his eyebrows at Caroline, who reluctantly entered the conversation.

"Is it true you believed Mr. Woodford and his sister were selling items from the hall to enrich themselves, Aunt?"

"What?" Eleanor stopped pacing and swung around.

"Miss Woodford mentioned that she and her brother had received a letter from your solicitor threatening them with legal action."

"Even if that was the case, what would it have to do with Joshua?"

"One has to suspect that if Mr. Woodford was taking items from the hall then he would need an accomplice— someone young and healthy like Joshua—to aid him."

"And then Joshua murdered the man who was making him rich?" Eleanor asked, unconsciously echoing Joshua's own argument. "Why on earth would he do that?"

"Perhaps he decided he could do better by himself," Caroline said. "We also wondered if Great-Aunt Ines was helping them."

Eleanor pressed two fingers against her temple and let out her breath. "We as in you and Dr. Harris, Niece?"

"Yes, Aunt."

"Might I ask what any of this has to do with either of you?"

Caroline shared a quick glance with the doctor. "Even though I no longer live here, I wouldn't wish for you or anyone in this family to come to any harm."

"From the butler, an old lady, and a footman?"

"If they truly were conspiring together to defraud you, then yes, ma'am." Caroline held her aunt's skeptical gaze. "And if the footman decided to murder his coconspirators I'd prefer to know. Wouldn't you?"

Eleanor took another brisk walk around the room and paused to look out of the window at the sodden garden beyond. Even with all the windows closed, the drumming of the rain and the howl of the rising wind were clearly audible.

"You will both come with me and speak to Joshua."

"As you wish." Caroline hesitated. "Do you want me to send someone to fetch another magistrate?"

"Not yet." Eleanor was already in motion, her back straight, her chin in the air like a soldier advancing into battle. "Come along."

Dr. Harris let Caroline walk in front of him as they descended the stairs into the kitchen wing and down again into the cold, echoing confines of the cellar below. Joshua was sitting within one of the cages, his head bent, and his hands clasped loosely together between his knees. He stood up as Eleanor approached.

"Morning, Lady Eleanor."

"Good morning, Joshua." Eleanor unlocked the cage door and opened it wide. "Please step out."

"What for?" Joshua looked wary. "You carting me off to the assizes in this weather?"

"I merely wish to ask you a question."

Joshua emerged from the cage and Dr. Harris straightened up beside Caroline, his hands flexing at his sides.

"Now, then. Tell me what happened in your own words."

"Dr. Harris accused me of murdering Mr. Woodford and Lady Ines, ma'am. I told him that was a lie and he threatened to turn me in anyway."

"That's not—" Caroline went to interrupt and was ignored by her aunt.

"Then tell me what did happen."

"I might have teased Mr. Woodford by locking him in this cage. He used to do it to us when we misbehaved in the nursery." Joshua pointed behind him. "But I didn't kill him."

"Why would you lock him up?"

"Because he wasn't being straight with me, ma'am." Joshua kept his gaze on his employer. "He was asking me to steal things for him, and I didn't like it."

"Steal from this house?"

"Yes, ma'am. It was all right when he just needed a hand taking a broken footstool or a piece of cracked china to his sister in the village to sell on, but when he was after new and bigger things, I didn't want nothing to do with it."

"So, you trapped him to teach him a lesson?"

"Yes, ma'am." Joshua swallowed hard, his expression so virtuous Caroline almost wanted to scream. "I didn't expect him to take it so hard and worry himself to death over it, but that's hardly my fault, is it?"

"It certainly isn't your fault." Eleanor nodded and stepped aside. "You may go about your business."

"You aren't going to dismiss me?"

"Not at this moment. You are the senior footman and with Mr. Woodford gone you will have to act as his deputy." Eleanor fixed Joshua with a hard stare. "If I find out you have continued this practice of stealing from your betters, then I will dismiss you without a reference and blacken your reputation with the entire county. Do you understand me?"

"Yes, my lady. Thank you. I swear I will not let you down."

Joshua bowed low and took the opportunity to scurry past Caroline and Dr. Harris, pausing only to offer them a very cheeky wink.

Caroline waited until the sound of his footsteps faded before facing her aunt.

"I believe you are making a terrible mistake."

"And I believe you are making a mountain out of a molehill and I wish you would stop. No one has been murdered and there is nothing to investigate." Eleanor turned toward the stairs.

"But what about all the money Joshua has accumulated?" Caroline asked. "You cannot believe he acquired it from Mr. Woodford?"

"It depends how much the Woodfords were making at my expense, doesn't it?" Eleanor brushed off a cobweb that had attached itself to her skirt. "With Mr. Woodford gone, and his sister living in fear that I might choose to evict her, I doubt their scheme will continue."

She started up the stairs, the oil lamp in her hand, as Caroline and Dr. Harris exchanged frustrated glances.

"I doubt we will hear any more from Joshua, Niece. Now perhaps you might turn your attention to your cousin's birthday ball instead of fabricating murders out of nonsense?"

Caroline didn't reply, and Eleanor continued on her way, leaving Dr. Harris and Caroline in the cold darkness of the cellar.

"Well, that's the end of that," Caroline said. "My aunt has spoken."

"She's wrong, you know."

"Of course she is, but we're guests in her house and we have no power here."

"Strange how Joshua changed his story when confronted by your aunt."

"Yes, he almost made his lies sound plausible." Caroline sighed.

"Do you happen to know the name of the next county's magistrate?" Dr. Harris asked.

"I can probably find out who it is. Why?"

"Because I intend to write them a letter."

Caroline shivered as the dampness seeped into her bones. "Much good that will do."

"If the Greenwoods refuse to believe the evidence right in front of them, maybe someone else will."

"They'll believe my uncle, you know that." Caroline went up the stairs.

"Sometimes I wish"—Dr. Harris let out an exasperated sigh—"I was a powerful man and not a lowly physician."

"Don't we all." She arrived on the top step and welcomed the warmth emanating from the kitchen beyond. "It is quite extraordinary how far my aunt will go to pretend that everything is fine. I thought better of her."

"I didn't." Dr. Harris moved past her. "I have to attend to Mr. Woodford's body. He's being taken to the chapel crypt until the rains let up for his burial."

"Has anyone notified his sister?" Caroline asked.

"I believe so." Dr. Harris was already moving past her, his attention elsewhere. "I would suggest you look for more evidence, but I doubt it makes any difference now."

Left to herself, Caroline made her way up to Mrs. Frogerton's suite, where she knew her employer would be waiting to hear the latest news about Joshua. She opened the door and went in to find Mrs. Frogerton in conversation with Peggy about the gown she intended to wear to the ball.

"The purple with the red sash, I think," Mrs. Frogerton said. "And my hair up under the matching turban."

"You will look very fine, ma'am." Peggy nodded. "I'll make sure your gown is freshly pressed and ready to wear."

"Thank you. My daughter intends to wear the pink tulle with the deep lace borders and embroidered roses."

"So she told me," Peggy said. "It is very grand indeed."

Peggy noticed Caroline had entered the room and bobbed a curtsy. "Good morning, miss. Have you decided which gown you intend to wear to the ball?"

"As I only have one, the choice is easily made." Caroline smiled at Peggy.

"I'm sure Miss Eliza would have something you could borrow, miss, if you'd like me to ask her dresser."

"I doubt my cousin would lend me a shift."

"She wouldn't have to know, miss. Martha could find something Miss Eliza wore before she got married, and left behind, and make it nice for you."

"Go on, lass. Take up this offer," Mrs. Frogerton urged. "I've been nagging you to have another gown made for months."

Caroline addressed Peggy. "If you can do it without incurring my cousin's wrath, then please go ahead. But I don't want Martha getting into any trouble."

"Yes, miss." Peggy positively beamed at her. "I'll make sure of it."

"I'm trying to save my money, ma'am." Caroline waited until Peggy put the dress away and left before continuing the conversation. "Another ball gown seemed like an extravagance."

"You make me feel like a miserly employer." Mrs. Frogerton took her usual seat by the fire.

"You certainly are not. You pay me very handsomely."

Caroline sat opposite her. "It is just that I want to ensure Susan's future away from this house."

"And very wise that is, too. This place has a bad feeling to it." Mrs. Frogerton gathered her silk shawl closer around her bosom. "Did you find Joshua?"

"He was trying to pilfer the butler's household account and was locked in the cellar." Caroline sighed. "Unfortunately, my aunt decided that the worst he could have done was frighten an old man. She reprimanded him and let him go."

"Lady Eleanor let him go?" Mrs. Frogerton gasped. "I can't believe it!"

"Neither can I. He told her some fairy tale about heroically refusing to steal any more from his employers and Mr. Woodford not accepting that. He confessed to locking him in the cellar to frighten him, but nothing else. And my aunt let him get away with it," Caroline concluded glumly. "She dismissed our concerns and suggested it was none of our business—which is true, by the way."

"Did you tell her about the money?"

"Yes, but she didn't seem to think it was significant."

"If one of my footmen had fifty pounds in his possession and a bag of gold coins, I'd be very suspicious *indeed*."

"I think my aunt just doesn't want to deal with anything unpleasant while she has guests in the house and is holding a ball."

"Not even murder?" Mrs. Frogerton asked. "And theft?"

"Apparently not. In truth, I do not know what else we can do about the matter if she refuses to acknowledge it even happened."

"What if now that Joshua is free, he decides to murder someone else? Will she pay attention then?"

"As it would probably be me, you, or Dr. Harris, who ended up dead, I sincerely doubt it."

"It makes no sense." Mrs. Frogerton shook her head.

"Perhaps we should stop worrying about it." Caroline rose to her feet. "Do you need me for anything, ma'am?"

"What if your aunt is the murderer?" Mrs. Frogerton was obviously not quite ready to give up. "If that is the case, then Joshua is the one who is not long for this world."

"I cannot see my aunt murdering anyone." Caroline sighed. "And if it isn't Joshua, then who else could it be?"

"Dan Price?" Mrs. Frogerton suggested. "He looks like a bad 'un to me."

"He is friends with Joshua." Caroline considered the matter. "But even if he is somehow responsible, how am I supposed to find that out?"

"Have you spoken to him?"

"About what exactly? I can hardly walk up to him and casually ask if he happened to kill my great-aunt and the butler."

"I suppose that's true." Mrs. Frogerton looked positively crestfallen. "I'll think on the matter."

"As you wish." Caroline smiled at her. "Is there anything else I can do for you right now? Would you like me to fetch you the morning paper?"

Mrs. Frogerton rose from her chair. "Not at the moment, but I would like to see you at lunch, lass. With Dotty off enjoying herself with all the youngsters and no Lady Ines to talk to I am left somewhat on my own."

"Of course." Caroline immediately felt guilty. "I will join you there at twelve after I have seen Susan."

"Good." Mrs. Frogerton waved her on her way. "I look forward to it. In truth, you're the only person worth speaking to anyway."

Aware that not only was her aunt annoyed with her, but that she was neglecting her duty toward her employer, Caroline's spirits were remarkably low. The sight of Susan in the middle of the nursery surrounded by a crowd of excited faces did much to cheer her. Despite the insecurities of her childhood, Susan had a gift for making others happy. She was particularly sensitive to the needs of the waifs and strays who regularly arrived and departed the hall.

She still hadn't handed over either the gold coins or the two-hundred-pound note to her aunt. Caroline recalculated how soon she could remove her sister from Eleanor's home and live a modest but secure life. The money meant nothing to her aunt and everything to her. If it was forgotten in her aunt's continued annoyance with her, Caroline would not bring it to her attention.

"Caroline!" Susan caught sight of her and came over, a small boy still hanging on to her skirts. "Aunt Eleanor says that if we behave ourselves, we may all watch the ball from the balcony above the ballroom!"

"How lovely!"

"Mabel was worried it wouldn't go ahead at all, but she managed to convince Aunt Eleanor to allow it to proceed."

Caroline glanced out of the window at the leaden skies. "It will certainly be hard for most of the guests to get here."

"Mabel doesn't care. She'd much rather it was a small and intimate party."

Susan sounded like she was directly quoting her cousin. Not for the first time, Caroline wondered whether Mabel was replacing her in her sister's affections.

"Have you seen your cousin this morning?" Caroline asked.

"Yes, she came in for breakfast with Dan, Harry, and Tina. She was in excellent spirits."

"Did Joshua come in at any point?"

"Yes, he came rushing in looking most mysterious and asked to speak to Dan and they went off together."

Caroline nodded as if this all made perfect sense. She did wonder whether Dan Price had offered Joshua advice as to how to deal with the accusations against him. Why else would Joshua have come directly to the nursery after leaving her and Dr. Harris? He'd certainly come up with a glib story to fool Eleanor.

"I suppose they are having their breakfast downstairs now?" Caroline asked.

"I think they were going to risk an outing to the stables. Mabel said she was tired of being stuck in the house and everyone agreed with her." Susan sighed. "I wish I could've gone with them, but Mrs. Whittle said I needed to stay behind and help with the little ones." She patted the tousled red hair of the small boy who was still firmly attached to her side. "Liam only just arrived last night, and he is very fearful."

"Poor Liam," Caroline said as she glanced at the nursery clock. "I have to go and attend Mrs. Frogerton now. I will make sure to visit you later."

Susan kissed her cheek. "I am so glad to see you here, Sister. I wish you could come home for good."

Caroline cupped Susan's chin and met her sister's hopeful gaze. "This isn't my home and at some point, it won't be yours, either. Please don't forget that."

"Mayhap I want to stay here forever." Susan eased away. "Mabel says that if I want to I can."

"Mabel isn't in charge here, either," Caroline reminded her gently. "And, when she marries, she'll be leaving this house. What will you do then?"

"She says I can come with her." Susan positively glared at Caroline. "And unlike some people, she never *ever* breaks her promises." She spun on her heel, grabbed Liam's hand, and headed back toward the table, leaving Caroline staring helplessly after her.

Had she broken any promises to her sister? Quite possibly. But she'd had no choice. Susan wouldn't understand that yet. Caroline could only hope that any damage she'd done would be repairable in time.

"What's with the glum face?" Hetty, who had just arrived in the nursery with a pile of fresh linen, glanced over at Caroline.

"Nothing in particular." Caroline rearranged her expression into her usual calm lines.

"Did you hear about Joshua?" Hetty set the pile down and began to sort it out.

"What about him?"

"The doctor tried to tell Lady Eleanor that Joshua murdered Mr. Woodford." Hetty chuckled. "Her ladyship sent him about his business, I can tell you that."

"Is it so far-fetched?" Caroline asked.

"Well, they certainly didn't like each other, but that's only because Joshua was impatient for Mr. Woodford to retire so that he could take his position. It's hardly a reason for killing someone though, is it?"

"I suppose not."

Hetty leaned in close. "Her ladyship told me on the quiet, like, that she thinks Dr. Harris is stirring up trouble."

"Why on earth would he do that?"

"On account of what happened to him and his parents."

Caroline frowned. "What happened?"

"Apparently, years ago Dr. Harris's parents were evicted from their cottage and Lady Eleanor took him and his sister in."

"*Here?*"

Hetty nodded. "Yes, miss. But they weren't at the hall for long because their parents came back for them. There was an almighty row when Lady Eleanor refused to release them, saying the parents weren't capable of bringing them up. They had to get a local magistrate involved to prove their financial stability and take possession of their own children."

"Who told you all this?" Caroline asked as Hetty continued her sorting and folding.

"Mrs. Maddox. She was a nursery maid at the time Dr. Harris and his sister lived here and remembered him right off."

"How extraordinary." Caroline struggled to reassemble what she knew about Dr. Harris with these startling revelations. "He did mention he grew up in this area."

"As soon as Mrs. Maddox heard that Joshua was being accused of murder, she went and told Lady Eleanor about her memories of Dr. Harris."

"I'm surprised my aunt didn't remember him herself."

"He was only here for a month or two and there have been so many children. When Mrs. Maddox reminded her ladyship of the circumstances, she certainly realized why he was so intent on causing mayhem in this house." Hetty lowered her voice. "She even wondered whether if there *had* been a murder, the good doctor was the one who did it."

"Goodness me," Caroline said. "Poor Joshua being accused of something he didn't do."

"He's fine, miss. I just saw him heading down the stairs with a big smile on his face whistling like a nightingale."

"How nice for him to be exonerated." Caroline headed for the door. "I have to go to Mrs. Frogerton."

She was halfway down the stairs before she paused to consider what she thought she was going to do. She continued and paused on the landing that overlooked the main entrance hall to gather herself. Bert was coming up the stairs with a loaded tray in his hands.

"Morning, miss."

"Good morning. Do you happen to know where Dr. Harris might be?"

"He's in the kitchen having his breakfast."

"Thank you."

Caroline already had her palm against the kitchen door when she hesitated again. What exactly did she intend to do? Barge in and accuse Dr. Harris of what, exactly? Simply lying to her, when she'd begun to imagine they trusted each other, or much worse? Before she could even decide, the door was jerked inward and the gentleman in question was suddenly staring down at her.

"Miss Morton."

"Dr. Harris."

"Why are you scowling at me? It's hardly my fault that Joshua got away with murder."

"Are you quite certain about that?" Caroline asked. "Because it appears to me that it might *indeed* be your fault."

He took hold of her elbow, marched her down to the deserted butler's room, and closed the door behind them.

"Explain yourself."

"I beg your pardon?" Caroline jerked free of his grip and raised her chin. "If anyone should be explaining themselves, it should be you. Why didn't you mention that you lived in this house as a child?"

He frowned. "Because it isn't something I care to dwell on? And it has nothing to do with how I conduct myself as a physician."

"My aunt would not agree with you."

"Your aunt tried to steal me and my sister from our parents. My father's employers defrauded him. It took a while to make things right with the law and for him to be reinstated and financially solvent. She tried to stop him reclaiming his own *children*." His slight smile disappeared, revealing the harsher lines on his face. "You can hardly expect me to like your aunt for that, but it certainly doesn't affect how I treat your family as my patients."

"She thinks you are the one disturbing the tranquility of the house."

"Does she now?" His smile was both unexpected and full of charm. "Next you'll be telling me she thinks I'm a murderer."

Caroline just looked at him and his smile grew.

"She truly believes that I murdered her butler. Whatever for? I admit he was not very kind to me or my sister when we resided here, but he was unpleasant to all the children in the nursery as were most of the staff. If I were to hold a grudge, I wouldn't bother with the butler, I'd murder your aunt for her thoughtless and invasive charitable works."

"That is hardly a good recommendation for your current mental state, Dr. Harris."

"I can't believe you even brought this up," Dr. Harris continued as if oblivious to Caroline's right to be indignant. "I thought we were colleagues in arms."

"So did I, but perhaps I was mistaken. The mere fact that you 'forgot' to inform me that you lived in this house as a child indicates your lack of trust," Caroline snapped.

"I didn't think it was relevant." He'd returned to frowning now. "It was a minor aberration in my life that I don't care to dwell on."

"Do you remember Lady Ines being in the nursery, too?"

"Yes, she taught my sister how to sew, and supervised our Sunday scripture lessons. She had a short temper and a very heavy hand for a supposedly Christian woman. What of it?"

"Was she also unpleasant?"

"Of course she was. You must have dealt with her yourself." Dr. Harris paused. "Although I seem to remember that family members in the nursery were treated far more gently than the waifs and strays."

Caroline was well aware that was true and still felt guilty about it.

"I assume you're about to tell me that your aunt thinks I murdered Lady Ines, too."

"Not that I have heard, but it seems likely," Caroline admitted.

"What did I do to make Lady Eleanor suddenly remember me?" Dr. Harris demanded.

"She didn't. Mrs. Maddox mentioned it to her after she found out about Joshua."

"That makes sense. Ruth Maddox is a hard woman."

Dr. Harris grimaced. "Well, I am devastated to inform you that I didn't kill either of them. If you wish to pass that information on to your aunt, be my guest." He bowed and flung open the door. "Trust me, Miss Morton. If I could get out of this damn house, I'd be gone in an instant!"

Caroline didn't attempt to stop him leaving. What else was there to say? He'd admitted he'd lived at the hall and in his typical fashion couldn't imagine why that made a difference to how his actions might be perceived. She stomped back up the stairs to Mrs. Frogerton's room and went inside.

"Dr. Harris neglected to mention that he and his sister lived here as children under somewhat contentious circumstances."

Her employer, who was busy composing her daily letter to her son, looked up. "He *lived* here?"

"Apparently, my aunt now believes that if any murders were committed, they were done by the good doctor because he bears a grudge against this family."

"That does seem rather far-fetched," Mrs. Frogerton commented as she removed her spectacles and set the quill pen back in the inkwell.

"No more than your suggestion that my aunt was the murderer." Caroline was beyond being considerate of her employer's feelings. "Dr. Harris lived in the nursery with his sister for a few months when his parents were evicted from their cottage. When they successfully restored the family fortunes and asked for their children to be returned to them, my aunt refused, citing her concern that they were too degenerate to be trusted. The Harrises had to turn to the law to regain possession of their own children."

"One can see why Dr. Harris might have resented that," Mrs. Frogerton said thoughtfully. "And, one has to say, my dear, that if anyone was in a good position to murder Mr. Woodford it would be the doctor who was watching over him." She turned in her seat so that she could see

Caroline more completely. "He wouldn't be the first doctor to murder his own patient. It happens quite often."

"I just wish he'd mentioned that he'd lived here." Caroline continued her pacing of the carpet. "I feel . . . deceived."

"Quite understandably." Mrs. Frogerton nodded so energetically the lace on her cap trembled. "And here I was thinking he rather liked you, and that you liked him back."

"I—" Caroline stopped moving and glared at her employer. "That isn't it at all, ma'am. He is quite insufferably rude."

"If you say so, love," her employer said sympathetically. "It still has to sting."

Caroline decided that her best course was to ignore Mrs. Frogerton's romantical notions and move on.

"If Dr. Harris is the murderer, then Joshua really is in the clear."

"I suppose that's true." Mrs. Frogerton frowned. "Somehow that doesn't sit right to me—what with the money you found, and Joshua's general behavior. I still believe he's more likely to have done it than the good doctor."

Caroline couldn't help but agree with her. "Perhaps my aunt is right, and I should just let the matter go. It's hardly my business, is it?"

"I like to think that getting to the truth of a matter is everyone's business, but that might just be me," Mrs. Frogerton said. "If you want to continue to investigate, I'm not going to stop you."

"You don't feel as if I am neglecting my duties?" Caroline ventured to ask.

"Not at all, lass. I haven't been so entertained for years!" Her employer waved her hand around to encompass the room. "Here I am staying in a fancy country house full of peers of the realm while my daughter hobnobs with an earl's son—what's not to enjoy?"

"You are no longer worried about being murdered in your bed?"

"Not at all." Mrs. Frogerton smiled broadly. "Now, if you wish to hurry off and investigate something then go ahead. I'll meet you in the salon for luncheon at noon."

"I thought it was time to talk to Dan Price," Caroline said. "After Joshua left us this morning, the first thing he did was seek out his friend to get his story straight."

"Then off you go, lass. I can't wait to hear what he has to say for himself."

Chapter 13

Caroline put on her pelisse, stout boots, and most rain-proof bonnet and made for one of the lesser exits from the hall that led directly to the stables. There were several umbrellas in a stand beside the door, most of them already dripping wet from regular use. Caroline selected one and was just about to brave the rain when someone behind her cleared their throat.

"Lady Caroline?"

She spun around, the umbrella clutched to her chest, to find Francis looking down at her. He held up his hands.

"I apologize if I frightened you."

"Not at all." Caroline brought the tip of the umbrella down to the floor and grasped the handle firmly. "I was just about to go out."

"So I see. I just wanted to clarify something with you."

Inwardly she sighed. "Please, go ahead."

"You suggested that my father had some influence on your decision-making regarding our impending marriage."

Caroline frowned. "You must know that he did. You are always mindful of obeying his instructions to the letter, and he was very clear to me that the marriage should not take place."

"You believed he was speaking on my behalf?"

"He is the head of your family."

"And he indicated what to you? That I no longer wished to marry you?"

"Francis . . . you had already 'indicated' the same thing by letting me hang out to dry for a week after I told you what had transpired with my father's affairs," Caroline said carefully.

"And what if my silence was an attempt to discover how to resolve our difficulties and marry you anyway?"

Caroline stared at him for a long moment. "You said nothing about that at the time. The only communication I had throughout that long, horrible week was with your father."

"And you chose to believe him rather than wait to hear from me."

"I heard from you." Caroline spoke more strongly. "You wrote to me, remember? You said you would be consulting with your father and asked me to be patient."

"While I attempted to find a way out of our 'difficulties.' "

"Maybe it would have helped if you'd been more specific." Caroline wasn't going to allow him to make her feel guilty. "Your father chose to communicate with me in a very direct manner that left no doubt of his contempt for me and my family. How could you think I would marry you knowing that?"

"Because you cared about me?"

"Francis . . ." Caroline held his gaze. "You were my world. I couldn't in all conscience allow the marriage to proceed knowing it would alienate you from your father and everyone you loved."

"You're suggesting you gave me up because you loved me?"

"*Yes.*"

"One might think that if that were true you would've trusted me to make things right."

"How, Francis? How could you possibly reconcile those two things? If I'd thought of a way—"

He cut across her. "But you didn't, did you? And you gave me no time to find one, either."

Caroline took a deep breath. "I refuse to allow you to blame me for wanting you to continue to enjoy the love of your family—something I never had. I thought I was doing the best for you, and your father encouraged me to believe that it was what you wanted, too."

"I wanted to marry you," Francis said.

"But you didn't, Francis, did you? If you'd found an acceptable solution to our issues, you would have shared it with me and your father, and we would now be married. There *was* no middle way. The society we live in wouldn't allow it. We both know that."

A muscle twitched in his jaw. "Perhaps if I'd felt you believed in me, I would've fought harder."

"Maybe our attraction to each other wasn't strong enough to weather such storms."

"Then you do accept some of the blame?"

"If it matters to you, then yes."

He inclined his head a stiff inch. "Thank you for that."

"I wish you nothing but the best, Francis." Caroline reached out to touch his arm. "If I hurt you, I am truly sorry."

He nodded and turned on his heel, leaving her standing there still gripping the handle of the umbrella. It took her a few moments to realize that yet again she'd been the only one apologizing. Such pointless conversations had to stop. She'd said everything that needed to be said and he deserved nothing more from her.

She opened the door, stepped out into the drizzling rain, and opened the umbrella. After that bruising encounter, a quick walk to the stables and a conversation with Dan Price suddenly seemed far more inviting. She eyed the distance between the two buildings, picked up her skirts, and made an undignified but very necessary run for shelter.

She arrived somewhat out of breath, and went into the main stable yard, her boots slipping and sliding on the wet cobblestones. She heard voices and headed toward the row of stalls where both the carriage and riding horses were kept. Her uncle's obsession with fox hunting and grouse shooting ensured that the stables were always kept in excellent order and were well staffed. Several of the orphan boys had started work here and either stayed or gone on to other more lucrative positions.

"I remember when this mare was born."

Caroline recognized Harry Price's voice and went toward the door of the stall.

"She's lovely," Mabel replied. "I ride her almost every day when the weather is fine."

"I like to think of that," Harry replied. "You, with your hair streaming down your back riding like the hellion you are. When I used to accompany you on your rides, you'd give me conniptions."

Mabel laughed. "I was rather reckless, wasn't I?"

"Yeah, and I was the one who would've lost my job if you'd had an accident."

"I'm ashamed to say I never thought about that," Mabel sighed. "I just wanted to feel free."

"Never you mind," Harry said. "It was a pleasure to be with you."

"Now, what is it they say about eavesdroppers, Miss Morton?"

Caroline started as Dan's voice came from behind her.

"Isn't it that they never hear good about themselves?" He continued to talk as she turned around to face him. "I'd thought better of you, miss."

"Why?" Caroline shrugged. "I had no idea that your brother and my cousin had formed such a close relationship."

"Are you going to tell her ladyship, then?"

"Why would I do that? It has nothing to do with me."

Dan raised his eyebrows. "That doesn't seem to have

stopped you interfering with my friend Joshua's life. You and that doctor, claiming he was a murderer."

Caroline held Dan's derisive gaze. "And you didn't interfere yourself? Weren't you the first person Joshua came running to when he needed advice?"

"As I said. We're friends." He shrugged. "What about it?"

Caroline decided she had nothing to lose.

"Did you know how much money Joshua accumulated from his scheme with Mr. Woodford and Lady Ines?"

"None of my business," Dan retorted. "If they needed his help, what they paid him is up to them."

"You believe they paid him hundreds of pounds to help them steal old china and broken furniture?"

A flicker of surprise flashed across Dan's smiling features but was quickly gone. "How do you know how much money Joshua has? You been through his things?"

"That's irrelevant," Caroline said.

"It damn well is not, miss, if you'll excuse my language. What right did you have to nose around in his bloody room?"

"My aunt and uncle gave me permission."

"I thought you just said you didn't work for them anymore." Dan snorted. "Sounds like you are still eager to do their bidding."

"I simply want to know why Mr. Woodford and Lady Ines were murdered," Caroline said. "Is that honest enough talk for you? And I'd also like to know how you were involved."

"Me?" Dan burst out laughing. "That's a good one, miss."

"You bear a grudge against everyone in this house because of the way you claim you were treated here as a child."

"Claim?" The amusement drained from Dan's face. "You were there. You damn well know how we were treated."

"I wasn't there during most of the years you spent at the hall."

"Lucky old you."

"If I had been there and I'd seen any mistreatment, I would've immediately brought it to the attention of my aunt."

"Who would've done nothing." Dan wasn't backing down an inch. For the first time Caroline felt a shiver of fear as he towered over her. "She never gave a damn about any of us."

"That's not fair. She *tried*—to save you from the work-house or an orphanage."

"Maybe some of us would've been better off in there. Goddamn Christian ladies and their good works."

Aware that the conversation was veering off course and desperate to avoid the hint of violence infusing each combative interaction, Caroline spoke again.

"I am not responsible for my aunt's actions. All I want to know is why two members of this household who interacted with Joshua suddenly died within a few days of each other."

"Coincidence?" Dan was back to smiling at her now, which was irritating but definitely less threatening. "You need to calm down, miss. Imagining things that don't exist and have nothing to do with you. Wouldn't want you ending up dead as well, now would we?"

"Dan!" Harry spoke from the door of the stall and strode over toward them, Mabel at his side. "What the devil are you saying to Miss Morton?"

"Just suggesting she keeps her thoughts to herself, Brother." Dan winked at Caroline. "And maybe tell that doctor friend of hers to keep his trap shut as well."

"Why? Because you know he is right, and someone did murder Mr. Woodford and Lady Ines?" Caroline asked. "Something is very wrong in this house."

"Murdered?" Mabel came over to stand by Caroline. "Are you feeling quite well, Cousin?"

"Yes, indeed." Caroline kept her attention on Dan and his brother, who now stood shoulder to shoulder. "Don't you think it's strange that Dan returns to the house and his best friend, Joshua, is suddenly implicated in two murders?"

"Josh didn't murder anyone," Dan scoffed. "He might have diddled those two old fools out of their money and then threatened to turn them in to the Greenwoods, but they deserved it."

"So, you believe they both died from natural causes." Caroline didn't even try to keep the skepticism out of her voice. "How convenient."

"They were old, miss, and riddled with hatred for others." Dan shared a glance with his brother, who frowned down at his boots. "I'm not going to pretend I'm sad about their deaths. If seeing us all here again hastened their ends, then I'm pleased as punch to hear it."

"Dan, shut your mouth." Harry raised his gaze to meet Caroline's. "He means nothing by this, miss. He's just blowing off steam."

Caroline didn't say anything, and Mabel slipped her hand into hers.

"They are both being very silly, Cousin." She addressed the brothers. "I am surprised at you, Dan. Caroline and her sister, Susan, are my favorite relatives. I will not allow you to speak so disparagingly to her."

Dan grimaced. "I admit I got a bit carried away when she started in on our Joshua." He bowed his head to Caroline. "I should apologize, miss. I was only funning."

Mabel beamed at him. "Thank you, Dan. It's only two days to my ball and I want everyone to enjoy it."

"Oh, we will." Dan's smile for Mabel was full of warmth. "I wouldn't miss it for the world."

Mabel kept hold of Caroline's hand and drew her away from the brothers and toward the coachman's cottage. "Will you come and have tea with me at Mrs. Butterfield's in the coachman's house before you return to the hall? She'll be delighted to see you."

Caroline checked the time on the large stable clock. She

had almost an hour before luncheon would be served. "If you wish."

It occurred to her that it might be interesting to speak to Mabel alone and see if she had any insights to offer about Joshua or the Price brothers.

"You mustn't mind Dan," Mabel said as they went through into the kitchen. "He is very passionate about everything and meant no harm."

"I cannot agree with you, Cousin." Caroline shut the door behind her and bent to pet the Butterfields' large dog, who was attempting to put his muddy paws on her skirts. "Does it not concern you that two members of your parents' household have died in mysterious circumstances?"

"I only know Mr. Woodford had a bad heart, because he complained about it quite often, and that Great-Aunt Ines was very old. Isn't it possible that all the sudden activity in the house was simply too much for them?" Mabel looked hopefully at Caroline. "I can't bear to think that my desire to have my birthday celebrated at home caused their deaths."

"I'm sure there is some reasonable explanation," Caroline said. "Unfortunately, I still have no idea what it is." She hesitated. "Joshua said he shut Mr. Woodford down in the cellars to teach him a lesson."

"I know. Harry told me recently that Mr. Woodford used to leave the children in the cages overnight if they misbehaved. It must have been terrifying." Mabel shivered. "But I told him that was a dreadful thing to do even if he did have good reason to dislike the man."

Mrs. Butterfield came into the kitchen.

"Miss Mabel and Miss Caroline! How lovely! Now let me make some tea and then we can sit down, and you can tell me all about your adventures."

While Mrs. Butterfield was occupied with the kettle, Caroline lowered her voice and leaned in toward Mabel. "Did you hear that someone wrapped knitting wool around Great-Aunt Ines's neck and stabbed her with her knitting needle?"

Mabel gasped and pressed her fingers to her mouth. "That's . . . *horrible*."

"Indeed," Caroline agreed. "Would you condemn Joshua or Dan if they had done such a thing?"

"Of course I would!" Mabel said earnestly as she took Caroline's hand between both of hers. "But I cannot believe they would be so underhand."

The conviction in Mabel's voice rang true to Caroline. But Mabel always thought the best of everyone—particularly those she considered friends. She was such a gentle soul that the idea that anyone could behave so despicably was probably beyond her imagining. Caroline, however, was quite convinced that Dan and Joshua were murderers, and nothing would persuade her otherwise.

"I know you are close to Dan and his brother, Cousin, but you would tell me if they were planning any other such pranks, wouldn't you?" Caroline asked.

"I would never permit them to do such a thing again," Mabel said firmly. "And if Dan does tease you again then you must tell me so immediately!"

Caroline feared that after Dan was done with her, she might not be in a fit state to tell Mabel anything, but she nodded, and Mabel's face relaxed.

"They are good men, Caroline. I can assure you of that. It's just that their time here at the hall was not always happy and coming back has stirred up a lot of their old memories and resentments."

"I can certainly understand that," Caroline said.

"Yes, because Eliza and my mother weren't always very kind to you, were they?" Mabel searched her face. "Just imagine how much worse it was for poor Dan and Harry."

"Did you know that Dr. Harris and his sister spent a few months at the hall when they were children?" Caroline asked.

"How interesting!" Mabel frowned. "Do you remember him?"

"I don't remember either of them," Caroline said. "But in my earlier years I was often with my father when he had money and a home to put us in. The Harrises were only here for a couple of months and I believe Dr. Harris is older than I am."

"I was probably not even born when he was here."

"Probably not," Caroline agreed.

"And there were so many children who came and went through the nursery. It is sometimes hard to remember them all."

"You appear to have stayed connected with as many as possible," Caroline noted.

"I have tried," Mabel said. "Some of them became good friends of mine."

"Like Harry and Dan."

"Yes." Mabel's expression softened. "Harry's taught me so much."

"Do my aunt and uncle know that?"

Mabel chuckled. "I hope not and please do not enlighten them. They would consider him far below them in rank and status."

"I have no intention of telling them anything."

"Thank you." Mabel met her gaze. "Dr. Harris seems very taken with you. Did he tell you himself that he'd lived at the hall?"

"He mentioned that he grew up around here, but it was Mrs. Maddox who recognized him and told your mother."

"Was she hoping to get him into trouble?" Mabel made a face. "That would be just like her. Tina says she was a difficult woman to work for."

"Apparently, Mrs. Maddox was attempting to shift blame from Joshua to the doctor. She suggested he not only had a reason to hate our family, but the opportunity to kill."

Mabel looked thoughtful. "I suppose she is right. I hadn't considered that."

"If you don't believe Joshua capable of murder, then how can you doubt Dr. Harris?" Caroline asked. "He prides himself on caring for others and saving lives, not ending them."

"True." Mabel went back to drinking her tea and carried the brunt of the conversation while Caroline's mind worked furiously.

She had no way of proving Joshua had murdered anyone, especially as her aunt and uncle refused to admit any such thing had taken place. Mabel would not support her either, as she believed Harry and Dan to be honest and straightforward men. Dan's cocksure attitude and attempts to intimidate her only underlined her certainty that he would never be asked to pay for his crimes. It was remarkably infuriating.

"Would you like milk in your tea, miss?" Mrs. Butterfield asked, drawing Caroline out of her thoughts.

"Yes, please." Caroline summoned a smile. "Now, how is your Daisy? Last time I saw her she had just learned to walk."

Chapter 14

As she was still not speaking to Dr. Harris, Caroline joined her only ally, Mrs. Frogerton, for luncheon at twelve as planned. Although the other guests were polite to her employer, they made no effort to involve either her or Caroline in their discussions or invite them to join their party. Caroline was becoming so used to being ignored that it no longer bothered her, but she was offended on Mrs. Frogerton's behalf.

"Please come and sit here by the window, ma'am. There is a very pleasant view of the slope down to the lake." Caroline maneuvered her way past Helen and claimed the prized table.

"Thank you, my dear." Mrs. Frogerton peered doubtfully out at the grounds. "There is a lake?"

"Indeed." Caroline set her employer's plate on the table and then her own. "If the sun ever shines again, you will be able to see it very clearly."

A footman came past and offered them something to drink. Caroline was still full of tea and cake and declined the offer, which Mrs. Frogerton accepted.

"How did your morning progress, lass? Did you make any headway?"

Caroline grimaced. "Dan Price threatened me and when

Mabel told him off, he tried to turn everything into a joke."

"Then you must be doing something right. I've noticed that men often become abusive when they are avoiding confronting an obvious truth," Mrs. Frogerton said.

"I am quite convinced that Dan and Joshua conspired to murder Mr. Woodford and my aunt," Caroline stated.

"I can't disagree with you, dear. The problem is, where's the proof?"

"There isn't any." Caroline stabbed her fork into a piece of ham. "And even if there were, my aunt and uncle will blame Dr. Harris."

"It all seems remarkably unfair."

"As my father often told me, ma'am, life isn't fair."

Caroline chewed slowly, her gaze passing over the other occupants of her aunt's dining room. Dorothy was sitting with Lord Epping and his sister at one of the other tables. Helen and Nora sat together beside the fire and Eliza occupied the sofa opposite them. Dr. Harris came in, took one appalled look at the assembled company, and promptly turned on his heel and left. Caroline couldn't blame him.

"Dan Price did say one interesting thing."

"What was that?" Mrs. Frogerton asked.

"He suggested that Joshua might have extorted money from the Woodfords and Great-Aunt Ines by threatening to turn them in to my aunt and uncle."

"That sounds very likely. It might also account for the excessive amount of money Joshua had in his possession," Mrs. Frogerton agreed.

"He had the same velvet purse as my aunt," Caroline said. "I wonder if she gave him the coins?"

Mrs. Frogerton chuckled. "Well, I doubt he gave them to her."

"It does make more sense if Joshua was blackmailing his coconspirators, doesn't it?" Caroline said slowly, her gaze drifting to the door where Mabel and her friends had just appeared. Dan was smiling and joking with Tina while Harry sauntered over and chatted away to Lord Epping as if they were equals.

"Not really, dear."

Caroline switched her attention back to her employer, who raised her eyebrows.

"Why would Joshua kill the fatted calf, so to speak?"

"There are many reasons," Caroline replied. "He could have decided he'd made enough money to plan his escape, or he might have been egged on by Dan Price to finish the deed once and for all."

"It takes two men to kill a frail old woman and an elderly man with a heart condition?"

Caroline shrugged. "Perhaps Joshua lacked the nerve to do it himself and asked Dan to help him."

"Joshua doesn't strike me as a terribly strong man so you might be right." Mrs. Frogerton sighed. "Perhaps when the ball is over and everyone returns to their own homes, Joshua will simply move on and everyone will forget what happened."

"I suspect that's what my aunt would prefer," Caroline said. "I must confess. I am at a loss, ma'am."

"Then perhaps you should turn your mind to what you are going to wear to the ball." Mrs. Frogerton patted Caroline's hand. "Sometimes I find that when I stop thinking about something directly the answer pops into my head when I'm least expecting it. Peggy said she has found the perfect dress for you and that Martha wishes to fit the gown on you this afternoon in my chamber."

"I am looking forward to it, ma'am." Caroline gestured at her employer's empty plate. "May I get you something else to eat?"

"No, thank you, dear." Mrs. Frogerton set her knife back on the plate. "One good thing I have to say about your aunt is that she doesn't skimp on her hospitality."

"She has always prided herself on being an exemplary hostess." Caroline stood up and then hesitated. "I know you suggested I should stop thinking about this matter, but I still feel there is more to all of this than we suspect."

Mrs. Frogerton regarded her keenly. "Then I suggest you keep looking for answers, lass. There's nothing worse than something niggling at your brain like a worm on a hook." She linked her arm through Caroline's. "I can't tell you the number of nights I've woken up with some mathematical calculation solving itself correctly in my head."

"I cannot say that has ever happened to me, ma'am." Caroline found herself smiling at her employer as they progressed through the room to the open door. She didn't even need to look at Eliza to know that she was glaring at her. Her cousin had always resented her ability to be happy despite her often adverse circumstances.

"I think I might take a restorative nap after Martha and Peggy fit you for the dress," Mrs. Frogerton confided as they climbed the stairs together. "I have some correspondence to deal with from my son, but it can wait until this evening."

"You don't wish to sit in the salon and play cards or chat with the other guests?" Caroline asked. "I am more than willing to accompany you."

Mrs. Frogerton gave her a droll look. "I want to do that about as much as you do, my love. I'd much rather count my blessings and my pennies than mingle with women who don't like me."

"Do you regret coming here, ma'am?"

"Not at all! Dotty is having a wonderful time and I am involved in an intrigue right out of the pages of one of my favorite gothic novels."

Caroline suppressed another smile as they turned to ascend the second set of stairs. She briefly caught a glimpse of Mabel in the hall below talking earnestly to Dr. Harris. She already knew him well enough to notice he was half-turned to flee, not being comfortable with emotional females. Mabel was probably commiserating with him about his stay at Greenwood Hall and that was a subject he was not interested in reopening.

Could he have murdered Mr. Woodford and Ines? He certainly was strong enough and had the opportunity. But Caroline simply couldn't believe him capable of such a thing. Joshua and Dan Price were a different matter. Their obvious malice and glee at the misfortunes of others didn't sit well with her and echoed the unpleasantness in the house itself.

Another thought occurred to her. Mrs. Maddox had recognized Dr. Harris and her kitchen had been deliberately ransacked. Was the doctor responsible for that, or was it Dan Price? Now that Caroline thought about it, both men shared a common grievance against the Greenwood family. . . .

"Come along, dear."

Caroline realized she'd slowed down and that her employer was looking at her inquiringly and was already standing by the open door to her chamber.

"Sorry, ma'am." She increased her pace. "Shall I ring the bell for Peggy, or have you already arranged for her to meet us in your room?"

"I'll ring the bell. I can't wait to see you in a new outfit, lass."

After trying on the dress, which Martha assured her would be unrecognizable after she removed half of the fussy trim, Caroline went up to her bedchamber. She locked the door and immediately checked to see if the velvet bag and banknote were still secreted in their hiding places. She still hadn't handed over Ines's gold to her aunt and after their recent conversations she had no intention of doing so unless directly asked.

She had no idea how much the gold coins were worth, but she was certain that on her return to London a discreet inquiry to a jeweler would reveal that information. Sometimes the anonymity of the capital city alarmed her, but on this occasion, it might stand her in good stead if she wished to conduct her business privately.

Her gaze went to her narrow bed. She sat on the quilt and slid her hand under the pillow where she'd put the small book someone had left her. As she drew it out, she almost wished it wasn't still there. The anguish concealed within the faded covers was unsettling and the thought that someone who had lived in the house had written it was worse. But someone wanted Caroline to know what it contained, which meant she was obliged to read it.

He says he wants to give me special lessons, but we all know what he really wants. Sit on my knee, he says, let me touch your hair, give your uncle a kiss. It's always the same. He never goes any further, so we put up with it and accept the boiled sweets with a smile and a curtsy before we run away as fast as possible. Who would listen to us anyway?

He's not like the other one, who truly listens and encourages me to make the best of myself.

Caroline raised her head from the text and took a deep, slow breath. Who was the girl referring to? A long-gone member of staff or someone who was still here at the hall? She remembered enduring such unwanted attentions herself—the drunken friends her father brought home, the elderly relatives who had abandoned her and Susan when they were desperate for sanctuary.

Smile, curtsy, and run away as fast as you can.

Caroline shuddered and shut the book. What was she supposed to do with this information? Did it somehow tie in with Mr. Woodford's and Great-Aunt Ines's deaths? She had to think there was a connection; otherwise why would someone deliver the book to her room?

Did Joshua and Dan want her to know why they had decided to act? Had it been Mr. Woodford who had abused the trust of the children in his care? He had once worked in the nursery as had Great-Aunt Ines. Caroline flipped back a few pages to check on the initials the author had used and stopped at the T. Mr. Woodford's first name had been Thomas. . . . Could it possibly be him the girl was alluding to?

Another image flitted through her mind. She slipped the book into her pocket and left her room. She walked along the corridor, away from the nursery, and entered her great-aunt Ines's suite where she had left the box of her aunt's possessions. There was no fire to welcome her and it took a moment to find a flint and candle to illuminate the afternoon gloom.

Her gasp echoed around the enclosed space. Even with the inadequate light of the single candle it appeared that the place had been ransacked. The drawers of the tallboy were hanging open like jagged teeth and the covers on the bed had been thrown to the floor. Caroline pressed a hand to her fast-beating heart and backed away to lean against the wall.

Who had done this? She had a fair idea what the person or persons involved might have been looking for, seeing as the money was securely in her possession. But to leave the room in such a state? It smacked of someone thinking they were untouchable. Had the Price brothers come up here while she was at lunch with Mrs. Frogerton to make sure there was nothing left to tie them to the woman who had died?

She gathered her courage and walked through into the adjoining room, which had received the same treatment. Should she tell her aunt? The Greenwood household was no longer her concern, but such deliberate destruction might finally convince Eleanor that something was very wrong. Caroline spied the box of Ines's possessions she had left on the desk and picked it up.

If she were to speak to her aunt, it might be for the best that both Ines's letters and drawings were safe in Caroline's hands. She hurried back through the door, went down the stairs, and knocked gently on Mrs. Frogerton's door. The only response was a slight snoring sound from the bed where her employer had retired for her nap. Caroline placed the box in the back of the armoire so that it was well hidden behind the clothes and tiptoed out.

She paused to consider the current time. Would her aunt have retired to her room to rest before dinner, or would she still be in the drawing room offering tea and conversation? A knock on her aunt's bedchamber door received no response so Caroline went down the main staircase to the more public rooms. There was no sign of Eleanor in the main drawing room but one of the maids said she was in the back parlor.

Caroline made her way to the back of the house, which usually caught the last rays of the sun, and found her aunt at her desk perusing the household accounts. Unfortunately, Eliza was with her.

"Good afternoon, my dear." Eleanor looked up. "Have you recovered from your fit of the sullens yet?"

Eliza stifled a snort, and Caroline ignored her.

"I went to finish clearing out Great-Aunt Ines's room and found that someone had been in there and ransacked the place."

"What?" Eleanor set her pen on the desk. "Who on earth would do that?"

"We all know the answer to that, Mother." Eliza spoke up. "Caroline destroyed the room and now she's trying to place the blame elsewhere—probably on this supposed 'murderer.'"

"That is not true." Caroline held her aunt's gaze. "Will you please come and see what has been done?"

"For goodness' sake, Niece." Eleanor slammed her palm flat on the desk, making everything rattle. "Why must you constantly bother me? If there is a mess, then tell one of the staff to clear it up!"

"It looks as if someone was searching for something," Caroline persisted. "One has to wonder if it is connected to the manner of my great-aunt's death."

Eleanor stood up so suddenly that Caroline had to take

a quick step backward. She followed her aunt up the stairs to Ines's apartment.

"Get me some more light," Eleanor demanded.

Caroline obliged and waited as her aunt surveyed the damage, her expression difficult to read.

"Why would anyone do this?" Eleanor eventually asked.

"Because they were looking for something?" Caroline replied. "Maybe evidence that would connect them to Ines's murder?"

"She was not murdered!" Eleanor snapped, and swung around to confront Caroline. "Perhaps Eliza is right for once. *You* did this."

"That's ridiculous!" Caroline gasped.

"You are deliberately attempting to cause chaos and misunderstanding in my house and draw attention to your outlandish claims."

"I am trying to hold someone accountable for *murder*!" Caroline refused to back down. "Something you continue to deny simply because you don't want to disrupt a social occasion and upset your guests."

"Don't be ridiculous." Eleanor's gaze swept the room again and then returned to Caroline. "I've just remembered something. You said that you found gold coins here. Where are they?"

"In my room—what does that have to do with—"

Eleanor pushed past her. "Were you hoping to enrich yourself further, Niece? Did you become impatient when you couldn't find anything else to steal from your own family or did you find more?"

"Aunt Eleanor . . ." Caroline ran after her aunt, who was already on her way down the corridor to Caroline's bedroom. "What are you doing?"

"I'm going to search *your* room, Caroline. It only seems fair. Ring the bell and ask Peggy to come and help me."

"This is not acceptable," Caroline said desperately. "I am here as the employee of another person. You no longer have the right to treat me like a member of your own household."

"Then ask your employer to be present!" Eleanor yanked on the bell with some force. "If you're a thief, then surely she should know?"

Caroline took one look at her aunt's furious expression and ran along the corridor and down the stairs to Mrs. Frogerton's suite.

"Ma'am." She approached the bed, her breathing uneven. "Please wake up. My aunt has gone mad and I need your assistance most desperately."

By the time Mrs. Frogerton had woken up, been apprised of the situation, and agreed to accompany Caroline to her room, Eleanor had already started going through Caroline's possessions. Mrs. Frogerton was puffing from climbing the stairs and sat down heavily in a chair beside the fire, her lace cap slightly askew.

"What exactly is going on, your ladyship?"

Eleanor, who was standing in the middle of the room supervising Peggy, looked down her nose at Caroline's employer.

"My niece is suspected of stealing. She insisted that you be present while I searched her belongings."

"The very idea that Caroline is a thief is nonsensical, my lady. She's your own flesh and blood and you must know that," Mrs. Frogerton said robustly.

Peggy cleared her throat. "I just found this in Miss Caroline's drawer." She held up the velvet drawstring bag.

"I believe that is mine." Eleanor took it from the maid.

"I told you I had found this money," Caroline said. "I've simply not had the opportunity to give it to you in private."

"A likely story." Eleanor sniffed. "Carry on, Peggy."

Peggy offered Caroline a sympathetic grimace before she delved back into the drawers.

"Caroline also told me about this money, Lady Greenwood. She had every intention of returning it to you. In truth I'm glad she had the sense to keep it in a secure place what with all the goings-on in this house," Mrs. Frogerton said as she watched Peggy move onto the top drawer of the chest. "I confess I have kept her too busy to deal with the matter."

"Hmph." Eleanor kept her attention on the maid.

Caroline tensed as Peggy carefully unrolled her best silk stockings and revealed the banknote.

"Lady Eleanor?"

Her aunt took the note, glanced at the value, and immediately turned to Caroline.

"Where did you get this?"

"I don't believe that is any of your business, ma'am." Caroline met Eleanor's furious gaze.

"It is a two-hundred-pound note!"

"I am well aware of that," Caroline replied.

"You can hardly pretend you earned it."

"I—"

Mrs. Frogerton spoke over Caroline. "I gave it to her."

"I beg your pardon?" Eleanor said.

"It was her Christmas gift. Would you like me to verify the number for you with my bank, my lady?" Mrs. Frogerton held out her hand and Eleanor passed over the note. "Yes, this is the same one. I always mark the corner with an x."

Mrs. Frogerton handed the note to Caroline. "I am glad to see you are saving the money, lass, rather than wasting it on trinkets like my Dotty." She turned back to Eleanor. "Are you done here now, my lady? Perhaps you might take your little bag of coins and allow my valued companion the privacy she deserves."

For a moment, Caroline held her breath as the two older women locked gazes. To her amazement, Eleanor was the first to back down. She offered them both a stiff nod and turned toward the door.

"No more of this nonsense, Caroline. And you will

clean up the mess you made in your aunt's suite by tomorrow morning."

Peggy followed her mistress out, leaving Caroline alone with Mrs. Frogerton, who was surveying her bedchamber with great interest.

"I expected your aunt to put you up somewhere nicer than this."

"It's been my room since I left the nursery." Caroline sat down abruptly on the bed, her knees shaking. "At the time I was simply delighted not to have to share with anyone else."

"It's remarkably bare." Mrs. Frogerton's voice was surprisingly comforting. "But I'll wager your aunt doesn't spend money on anything she doesn't have to."

"You would be correct about that. She is all about appearances." Caroline took a deep breath. "About the banknote—"

"Hush, lass." Mrs. Frogerton brought her finger to her lips. "I don't need to hear anything about it. You keep it and do with it what you will."

Caroline stared at her for a long moment. "Thank you."

"You're welcome. I'm just sorry I couldn't get the gold coins for you as well."

"I did intend to give those to my aunt at some point," Caroline said carefully.

"But if she'd forgotten, you wouldn't have minded either, would you, miss?" Mrs. Frogerton winked as she got to her feet. "I don't blame you. In this world I truly believe that every woman has a right to look out for herself."

Somewhere down below the clock struck six times.

"I need to change for dinner," Mrs. Frogerton announced. "Come to my suite when you're ready and we'll go down together."

"I still have to clean up my great-aunt's rooms," Caroline said.

"No, you don't," Mrs. Frogerton said. "I employ your

services, not your aunt. If she wants it done, she can tell one of her own staff to do it."

"Thank you, ma'am." Caroline rushed to open the door for her employer. "Thank you for everything."

"Think nothing of it." Mrs. Frogerton paused to look searchingly up at Caroline. "You're no more of a thief than Dr. Harris is a murderer, and don't you forget it."

Caroline nodded, shut the door behind her employer, and leaned back against it fighting the urge to cry. Her aunt's behavior had been both humiliating and inexcusable. In two days, she would leave Greenwood Hall, and, if she had her way, when she returned it would be to collect Susan and take her away forever.

Chapter 15

"Are you going to ignore me all evening, Miss Morton?"

Dr. Harris handed Caroline a cup of tea and didn't move away. It had already taken all Caroline's resolve to sit through dinner with her aunt and uncle at the head and foot of the table pretending nothing was wrong. Eliza had been whispering to the other female guests and Caroline had a fair idea of what she might be implying. Joshua was also serving the meal and made sure to smile at Caroline every time he offered her something to eat or drink.

"I would still be ignoring you if you hadn't deliberately accosted me," Caroline replied.

"With a cup of tea? It's hardly an offensive weapon."

"Maybe not to you—a man who's never witnessed two women fight over who gets to pour the tea."

He frowned. "Why would anyone care about that?"

"Because she who commands the teapot rules the house, Dr. Harris."

"I've never thought of it like that." He looked back over his shoulder to where Eleanor was dispensing the tea from her seat by the fire. "I doubt anyone is likely to challenge a formidable woman like your aunt."

"Wait until my cousin Nick or his brother George get married and introduce a new woman into the household,"

Caroline said grimly. "Then you might witness a battle *royale*."

She surprised a chuckle out of Dr. Harris, which was somewhat gratifying, even though she was still at odds with him.

"I've been thinking about what you said to me, Miss Morton." Dr. Harris had somehow maneuvered her into a corner. "I might have been at fault."

"Good Lord, Dr. Harris. Are you admitting you were wrong?"

"Not about everything, but I perhaps should have clarified earlier that I'd lived in this house. It was twenty years ago, and I've tried to forget it." He paused. "Even though it pains me to admit it because the experience was not pleasant, I should have trusted you with the information."

"I appreciate that," Caroline said slowly.

"I can also see why it might have made you suspicious of my motives for returning to this place. But, in truth, due to my lack of connections it was extremely hard to secure a medical position. It was only because my father was still friends with Dr. McGregor that I ended up here. It was also an opportunity for me to face my past and overcome it." He held her gaze. "I reasoned that if I could be successful here caring for people I despised, then I could be successful anywhere."

"I can quite understand that." Caroline nodded. "I came back to this house for similar reasons."

His eyebrows rose. "You despise your own family?"

"Not exactly. My aunt has always been very gracious, but her kindness is tied to an obligation—the idea that both Susan and I should repay her by staying here and serving her family as required."

"And you don't want that."

"No." She looked up at him. "I don't want to be obliged to anyone."

"Now, that I can appreciate."

For a long moment they simply looked at each other before Caroline remembered she must still be wary.

"Thank you for the tea."

"You're welcome." He paused. "Are you telling me to
go away again?"

"Yes."

"Am I forgiven?"

"Possibly."

He bowed, turned on his heel, and walked away, leaving
Caroline staring after him. He was an infuriating man, but
his directness was quite refreshing after dealing with her
previous acquaintances. She drank her tea and set the cup
on a table before returning to Mrs. Frogerton's side.

"I see you and Dr. Harris have made up," her employer
commented.

"He admitted he was at fault." Caroline surveyed the
room, noting that Mabel was again talking earnestly to
Dr. Harris.

"What an unusual man. Did he say why he omitted to
mention the time he spent at Greenwood Hall?"

"I believe he saw returning here as something of a test
of his character."

"Ah." Mrs. Frogerton slowly fanned herself, her gaze
on the doctor and Mabel.

"And it didn't occur to him that his motives needed explaining to anyone, including me." Caroline continued
even as she wondered why she was defending Dr. Harris.

"He must have known someone might recognize him.
One might think he would've had a story prepared."

"But he doesn't think like that," Caroline said.

"Or he is a lot cleverer than we give him credit for."
Mrs. Frogerton frowned. "He is a highly intelligent gentleman, Caroline. We should not forget that."

"Which only means that if he did murder Mr. Woodford
and Lady Ines we are just as unlikely to prove it as we are
for Joshua and Dan," Caroline said. "In fact, our chances

of holding anyone accountable for these murders is minis-cule."

"But it is enjoyable trying." Mrs. Frogerton elbowed her gently in the side.

"Until I end up murdered in my bed," Caroline mur-mured. She smiled sweetly at her employer. "Would you like another cup of tea, ma'am?"

"No, thank you." Mrs. Frogerton's attention was on the entrance to the room. "I see my friend the vicar has ar-rived. I will go and speak to him."

Caroline watched Mrs. Frogerton head directly for the vicar, who did look pleased to see her, which was some-thing of a relief.

"Where is my mother?" Dorothy appeared beside Caro-line.

"She is over there, Miss Frogerton." Caroline pointed toward the group by the door. "Is something amiss?"

"I . . . just wanted to tell her that I'm retiring early."

Caroline looked properly at her companion's face for the first time. "Are you not feeling well?"

"I just need some time to myself." Tears glinted in Dorothy's blue eyes.

"Did something happen with Lord Epping?" Caroline had to ask.

"Why would you think that? Do you think I'm the kind of girl he'd treat badly?"

"No, not at all. I just . . ." Caroline held Dorothy's of-fended gaze. "I know how gentlemen can behave some-times. If you need someone to listen to you or advise you, then I would be more than willing to help."

Dorothy stared at her and then nodded abruptly.

"Come upstairs with me."

"If you wish."

Caroline followed Dorothy up to her bedchamber and closed the door behind them. Dorothy immediately went to her chest of drawers, retrieved a clean handkerchief, and loudly blew her nose.

"Did Lord Epping offend you in some way?" Caroline ventured to ask.

"He has been nothing but gracious and kind." Dorothy half turned away and looked out of the window. She looked very fine in a blue satin gown with large puffed sleeves and a heavily embroidered hem.

"Then who upset you?"

"Do I look upset?" Dorothy asked. "I'm actually quite angry."

"With whom?"

"His sister."

"I thought Miss Baskins was your friend."

"So did I." Dorothy swung around, her arms folded over her chest. "She *said* she wanted to give me a gentle hint that I should not take anything her brother says seriously because their father has already decided whom he will marry, and it certainly won't be me. I told *her* that as I had no intention of marrying her brother because he wasn't of sufficient rank to interest me, that was perfectly fine. Her mouth hung open like a fish and she blurted out how most people thought I'd be lucky to get any gentleman to marry me even with my fortune."

Caroline winced. "She is quite immature."

"If she's old enough to be looking for a husband," Dorothy retorted, reminding Caroline forcibly of her mother, "she's definitely old enough to keep a civil tongue in her head."

"I can't argue with that," Caroline said. "Did you tell her so?"

"As she looked as if she was going to cry because of what I said about her precious brother's prospects of marrying me, I didn't bother."

"That was good of you."

"I thought so," Dorothy agreed.

"She is hardly worth your attention. When we return to London you will encounter many gentlemen who would be delighted to add you to their families."

"Do you really think so?" For the first time ever, Dorothy looked uncertain. "I thought it would be easy. I am well spoken with barely a hint of a northern accent, I've had excellent schooling, I'm quite beautiful, and I'm worth a fortune. Who would not want to marry me?"

"Society can be . . . quite complicated sometimes," Caroline said slowly. "There is a reluctance to admit and embrace newcomers and a tendency to close ranks when presented with a choice."

"They did nothing to save you," Dorothy said. "You can't imagine the snideness of the gossip I've heard about you and your family this week."

"Oh, I can imagine it all too well," Caroline said. "The problem is that my father committed the ultimate sin of going bankrupt and killing himself in full public view. There was no way to cover up his misdeeds or transgressions, so they dealt with it by pretending that he, and by extension his children, no longer existed in their world."

"That's cruel."

"That's why society continues to thrive and survive by driving out the undesirables and presenting a united front." Caroline smiled at Dorothy. "People like you and your mother are considered as much a threat as I am—especially when they refuse to bow down and accept society's dictates."

"You could help me navigate these stormy waters, couldn't you?" Dorothy said.

"In truth, Miss Frogerton, it would be my pleasure to watch you storm the barricades and take possession of a dukedom."

"Then perhaps I will take more heed of your advice from now on."

"As you wish."

"You do not intend to stay on here at the hall as your aunt desires?"

"This is the last place on earth I wish to be," Caroline

said. "I am looking forward to returning to London most ardently."

"Good." Dorothy nodded. "Now, do you think I should tell Lord Epping what his sister was saying before she does?"

"Personally, I would say nothing at all. The worst thing you could do is come between a beloved brother and sister. I doubt she will want to repeat a conversation where she was made to look foolish and her brother's status was considered inadequate."

"That's true," Dorothy said. "I'll just pretend that nothing happened and treat them both with the greatest consideration."

She smiled at Caroline, who smiled back.

"I am glad we had this conversation." Dorothy blew her nose again, checked her reflection in the mirror, and turned back toward the door. "I feel ready to go down again, now."

"I'm glad I was able to help," Caroline said. "Although, I must note that from what I have seen, Lord Epping *is* very taken with you. His sister's attempt to deflect that attention might be because she is aware of his attraction for you, too."

"Really?" Dorothy perked up. "Now, that would be a coup, wouldn't it? Him declaring he loves me and me getting to turn him down flat."

"Indeed." Caroline found herself smiling again. "It would certainly declare to everyone that you have set your standards very high."

"As I have." Dorothy opened the door and Caroline followed her out. "I'm sure there is a duke or a marquess out there just waiting to meet me."

"Hopefully a very elderly one who will die quickly and leave you with an infant son, an immense fortune, and control of his estate," Caroline murmured as they descended the stairs together and headed toward Mrs. Frogerton and the vicar.

"One can but hope." Dorothy laughed so heartily that several people turned to look at her. "Good evening, Vicar, Mother. Are you enjoying yourselves?"

After making sure that both Dorothy and Mrs. Froger-ton were happily engaged with their friends, Caroline slipped out of the drawing room. Dr. Harris was in the hall and came over to her.

"You look tired."

"It's been a difficult day. My aunt accused me of being a thief."

His faint smile died. "Your aunt is a fool."

"She went through my possessions as if I were . . . nothing." Caroline shivered. "It reminded me of the time the bailiffs came into our London house and removed half our possessions to pay my father's outstanding debts. They even took my favorite doll."

"What was Lady Eleanor hoping to achieve by alienating you?"

"To put me on my notice and stifle my claims of there being a murderer amongst us?" She sighed as she turned toward the stairs, the doctor at her side.

Dr. Harris snorted. "I have to suspect that her machinations will have the opposite effect on you, Miss Morton. You have never struck me as the kind of woman who will allow herself to be intimidated."

"I'll take that as a compliment, Doctor," Caroline said. "And you are correct. I am more intent on exposing this murderer than ever."

"My only advice is to be careful." Dr. Harris paused on the landing. "I would hate to be the one writing your death certificate for the local coroner."

Caroline winced. "Thank you."

"I also offer my help." He looked down at her. "If you have decided I am trustworthy, of course."

"What was Mabel talking to you about?" Caroline asked.

His eyebrows flew up. "What does that have to do with my trustworthiness or lack of it?"

Caroline continued to stare at him until he sighed.

"She was commiserating with me about the time I spent at Greenwood Hall and apologizing on behalf of her parents."

"That sounds just like Mabel."

"I thanked her for her concern and assured her that my life had turned out remarkably well since then."

"And your sister's?" Caroline asked.

He frowned. "What about her?"

"Did her life turn out just as well as yours?"

For a second he said nothing, and Caroline instinctively braced herself.

"She never fully recovered from being forced to live here, Miss Morton." He inclined his head. "And now I will wish you good night."

He stalked away up the stairs, leaving Caroline feeling more bewildered than ever. Had she somehow hurt him? And what on earth had happened to his sister?

She counted to a hundred before she followed him up the stairs and went into Mrs. Frogerton's suite to collect Ines's possessions. Now that Eleanor had searched her room it would perhaps be safe to keep them there. Caroline tried to remember what had initially drawn her to reexamine the boxes before she'd been confronted with the destruction in her aunt's rooms.

She locked her own door, took the book out of the pocket of her gown, and retrieved the bundle of letters from her desk. She was convinced that somewhere within the collected artifacts of a life lived small was the truth of her aunt's untimely death. She set the box on the bed and sat next to it before taking out the bundle of sketches from her first foray into the room.

She untied the string and contemplated the first image before slowly turning it over and staring at the next. As she progressed, she arranged the portraits in separate piles—children who belonged to the Greenwood family, named children she sometimes recognized, and those who were either identified by their initials or by nothing.

Halfway down the stack she found a charcoal drawing of herself sitting curled up in front of the nursery fire like an abandoned kitten. From the date she realized it must have been just after her mother had died. There was also a portrait of Susan as a baby in the arms of a nursery maid who looked remarkably like Mrs. Maddox.

"There," Caroline said softly, her fingers stalling on the picture of a scowling young boy who was only identified by the initials O and H. "Dr. Harris to the life."

There was no date on the portrait, but she guessed his age to be around ten, which would be about right according to what he had told her. She also noted how much better his clothing was than a lot of the children who arrived dressed in rags. He'd obviously come from a much better class of home, which also made sense as his parents had eventually managed to reclaim him.

She contemplated his mutinous expression for quite a while before setting him to one side. Just underneath his picture was one of the Price brothers, arms locked around each other's shoulders as they stood by the paddock fence. Had they met Dr. Harris? It was possible they would have been too young to remember him even if they had crossed paths. Joshua hadn't mentioned knowing the doctor in any of their encounters and he was a similar age to the Price brothers.

She placed the picture beside the one of Dr. Harris and continued on as the clock on the mantelpiece that had once belonged to her mother chimed the quarter hour. A piece of coal crackled to life in the fire, sending a shower of sparks onto the hearth. Caroline added more fuel and returned to her position on the bed. She was almost at the end of the stack of pictures and was hardly any the wiser.

She paused at the picture of a young girl, her head turned back toward the artist as she pegged out the washing. She was barely tall enough to reach the line and was standing on her tiptoes, her arms reaching high above her.

"R." Caroline read the name on the portrait. It wasn't someone she recognized so she set it to one side. Below it was another picture of the same girl, but this time she was sitting with another girl at the table in the nursery, the glass cabinet containing the Sunday toys behind her as they shared a book. "R and R." She frowned. "That isn't very helpful."

As she looked closer, she noted a faint date written on the edge of the picture.

"Whoever these girls are, they were there when Dr. Harris was living at the hall," Caroline murmured to herself. "I wonder if either of them is related to him?"

Both girls had dark hair like the doctor and appeared to be of similar age. Could she ask him? He certainly hadn't seemed inclined to discuss his sister with her and she had to respect that. But who else could she ask? Might Mrs. Maddox know? She had worked in the nursery when Susan was a baby before progressing to her current role of cook.

With a small heaving sigh, the clock gathered itself to strike the hour of twelve. Caroline waited until the ringing stopped before considering what to do next. Apart from her uncle and aunt, the only person left in the house who might remember the girls was the cook. Both Mr. Woodford and Great-Aunt Ines, who had certainly been around at that time, were dead.

Caroline stared at the line of portraits. Surely the fact that two of the people most deeply involved in the nursery when the Harris children were present were now dead was significant? If Dr. Harris was out for revenge on those who had mistreated him or his sister, then Joshua's protestations of innocence might be valid after all.

Chapter 16

"I don't have time to chat, miss."

Mrs. Maddox stirred something on the range and then walked through into the scullery to check on the progress of the washing up of the breakfast things. Caroline had woken early and headed down to the kitchen to get Mrs. Frogerton's breakfast tray so that she could deliver it in person.

"With all the guests needing feeding and watering I hardly have a chance to sit down all day."

"You do a marvelous job, Mrs. Maddox. I don't know what my aunt would do without you." Caroline followed her doggedly through the busy kitchen. "I won't disturb you for more than a minute."

Mrs. Maddox sighed heavily, wiped her hands on her apron, and shouted at Peggy, "Keep an eye on that stock, will you?"

She walked through into the large pantry and turned to face Caroline.

"Now what is it?"

Caroline hastily produced the two portraits from her pocket and showed the cook the first one. "Do you remember who this is?"

Mrs. Maddox squinted at the drawing. "That's Dr. Harris when he was here at the hall. I recognized that scowl the moment he sat down at my kitchen table to eat his dinner the night Mr. Woodford took ill."

"And how about these two?" Caroline held up the picture of the two girls.

The cook took the picture and scrutinized it for a long moment. "Hmm. I'm not sure. One of them might be the doctor's sister, Rose, but the other one? I can't say I remember her. She was only here for a while like the Harris children."

"Which one is which?" Caroline asked.

"I can't say. Must be at least twenty years since I've seen those faces. There were a lot of children in the nursery because times were bad for farmers and the workhouse and orphanages were bursting at the seams."

Mrs. Maddox handed the picture back to Caroline. "Why are you bothering about this now?"

Caroline shrugged. "I was just intrigued by the notion that Dr. Harris had lived here once. When I found these pictures in my great-aunt's possessions, I wondered whether it was him."

"Your aunt and uncle know who he is now and that's all I care about," Mrs. Maddox said abruptly. "And I'll give you the same piece of advice I gave them. Leave the past alone and let things be."

"That's excellent advice," Caroline agreed. "But sometimes when the past returns and interferes with the present it is hard to remain neutral."

"Keep your nose out of it, young lady," Mrs. Maddox said. "Or you'll suffer the consequences."

"Like you did?" Caroline asked. "Is that why someone destroyed all your hard work?"

The cook half turned away. "That was the cat, that was. And don't you be saying anything else." She walked back toward the main kitchen. "If you'll excuse me, miss."

Caroline remained where she was. Mrs. Maddox had confirmed that the picture was of Dr. Harris and revealed that one of the girls was probably his sister and her name was Rose. As she walked down to the butler's rooms, which were now vacant and undisturbed, her hand went to her pocket where she had concealed the diary. She'd pored over the account long enough to be able to flip instantly to the inside front cover page and reread the faint inscription.

"A rose for a rose," Caroline whispered.

Had Dr. Harris's sister written this heartrending account of her stay at Greenwood Hall? In retrospect perhaps Caroline should have recognized the author sooner. Very few of the children who came to live in the nursery had the ability to read and write so fluently at such a young age. The Harris children had come from a relatively wealthy background and would probably have had lessons from their mother.

But if the journal had been written by Rose, what had become of her?

Caroline headed back to the kitchen and picked up the breakfast tray. Mrs. Maddox didn't acknowledge her thanks or speak to her. She walked slowly up the stairs and entered Mrs. Frogerton's rooms. Peggy had already been in to lay the fire and open the curtains and Mrs. Frogerton was sitting up in bed.

"Good morning, lass. Why the sad face? You're not still worrying about your aunt, are you?"

"Not at all, ma'am. This is something far worse."

Caroline set the tray on her employer's knees and sat down beside the bed. She gathered her thoughts while Mrs. Frogerton poured herself some coffee and buttered her toast.

"Well, go on. Tell me the worst of it," Mrs. Frogerton encouraged her.

"Everything seems to point toward the time Dr. Harris was at Greenwood Hall."

"As in everything connected with the possibility of murder. How so?"

"Mrs. Maddox and Mr. Woodford were both working in the nursery when Dr. Harris and his sister were brought here against their parents' wishes. Great-Aunt Ines was also very involved in educating the girls at that time." Caroline looked up from contemplating her linked fingers. "Two of those people are now dead and the only one still alive had her kitchen ransacked."

"I can't disagree with any of that." Mrs. Frogerton chewed her toast and took another sip of coffee before continuing. "It sounds as if you are saying that Joshua had no reason to murder anyone whereas Dr. Harris might have."

"Yes, because of his treatment here and because of his sister, Rose." Caroline retrieved the pictures from her pocket and laid them out on the silk counterpane.

"That's her?" Mrs. Frogerton put on her spectacles and studied the two pictures. "Where did you get these from?"

"My aunt had a collection of portraits she'd done over the years in her desk. After finding out that Dr. Harris once lived here, I decided to go through them again and see if he had been drawn by my aunt. Mrs. Maddox identified Dr. Harris and said that one of these girls was his sister, Rose."

"Has Dr. Harris mentioned what became of his sister?"

"I tried to ask him that very thing yesterday. He changed the subject and walked away from me."

"Then we do not know if she is alive or dead? Did Mrs. Maddox have an opinion on the matter?"

"She told me to stop prying into things that didn't concern me."

"None of these answers are helpful. But if Rose Harris was mistreated here, then that would give Dr. Harris a very powerful incentive to punish those he deemed responsible."

"Yes, and as you mentioned before he is a very clever man."

"Would your aunt know anything about this?" Mrs. Frogerton finished her coffee and started on her second piece of toast.

"Even if she does, she's hardly likely to confide in me about it, is she?"

"Probably not." Her employer grimaced. "You are certainly not in favor at the moment. Would your uncle be more helpful?"

"He rarely gets involved in domestic issues and I doubt he'd remember something that happened twenty years ago unless it impacted him personally." Caroline sighed. "The thing is—I still cannot reconcile myself to the idea that Dr. Harris is a murderer."

"That's because you like him, lass. It's quite understandable. How is the weather this morning?"

"Slightly better, ma'am." Caroline blinked at the surprise question. "Do you wish to leave before the ball after all?"

"Didn't you say that Mr. Woodford's sister also worked in the house when she was younger?" Mrs. Frogerton asked.

"Yes, she did," Caroline said. "Do you think she might know something helpful?"

"If it's possible to get to the village and visit her, I can't see the harm in asking, can you, lass?"

"If her brother was implicated in whatever is going on, will she be willing to talk to us? She certainly wasn't before."

"We won't put it to her like that. Who does she dislike most in this house?"

"My aunt," Caroline immediately replied.

"Then we will think of a way to suggest that any information she provides will incriminate Lady Eleanor rather than her brother. Maybe that will persuade her to be honest with us."

"And what if it doesn't?"

"Then we will have neither gained nor lost anything."

"And we will be back where we started. I suppose if there is no other option, I will have to talk to Dr. Harris again."

"In truth, you could save us both a trip in the cold and drizzle if you did that first, my love," Mrs. Frogerton reminded her, as she flung the covers back. "Now, ring the bell, dear, and get Peggy to help me dress."

"Of course, ma'am." Caroline pulled on the bell rope. "Shall I go and see if one of the footmen can take a message around to the stables?"

"Yes, please. Tell them I'm willing to be most generous with my tips if they'll oblige me in this matter."

As Caroline awaited Mrs. Frogerton in the hall after being assured that a carriage would arrive momentarily, she noticed Joshua coming down the stairs. He didn't see her because his attention was focused on the door into the breakfast parlor.

"Dr. Harris?" Caroline eased even farther back into the shadows as Joshua called out to the doctor, who had just emerged from the room. "Might I have a word with you, sir?"

"If you must." Dr. Harris's strong voice carried easily across the expanse of the hall as he walked toward Joshua. "Although I don't know why you wish to speak to me. I haven't changed my opinion of you, and I doubt that I ever will."

"That's the thing, sir. I think you've misjudged me."

"I can't see how."

"Because we're on the same side."

"How in God's name did you come up with that notion?" Dr. Harris's voice became fainter as he walked away from Joshua.

"Because we both have our reasons for hating this place . . ."

Joshua had obviously pursued the doctor as Caroline could no longer hear either of them clearly enough to understand what they were saying. She remained where she was and considered what she had heard. If Joshua truly believed he had been mistreated in the nursery and had found out that Dr. Harris had been too, it wasn't surprising that he'd attempt to create a bond with the man who had accused him of a double murder.

"Caroline."

She startled as Mrs. Frogerton hissed in her ear.

"Did you hear that?"

"Dr. Harris and Joshua?"

"Yes! What if they are working together? They both have grievances against the Greenwood family."

"But Dr. Harris accused Joshua of murder."

"Maybe that was part of the plan, to lull our suspicions. Joshua's cruel pranks take the attention while Dr. Harris kills his victims with impunity."

Mrs. Frogerton's hushed tones were laced with a hint of excitement.

"Except that Mrs. Maddox is still very much alive," Caroline reminded her.

"Mayhap they decided she just needed a warning to remain quiet?" Mrs. Frogerton speculated. "She certainly isn't eager for you to investigate the matter further."

"With all due respect, your assumption does seem rather far-fetched, ma'am," Caroline said. "If my uncle had taken Dr. Harris's accusations seriously, Joshua could have ended up at the local assizes charged with murder."

"I suspect Dr. Harris knew his lordship would never take action about such a matter especially when his wife was against it." Mrs. Frogerton sighed. "It just seems to me that Joshua has to have something to do with it."

"Maybe I was wrong, and it is solely about Joshua stealing from the Greenwoods and blackmailing and murdering his coconspirators after all," Caroline offered. "Perhaps Dr. Harris and his sister have nothing to do with it."

"I think"—Mrs. Frogerton linked her arm through Caroline's and drew her inexorably toward the door—"that a nice carriage ride in the fresh air will help clear our minds. Come along, dear. Miss Woodford will appreciate our visit regardless."

Caroline wasn't so assured of their welcome but had to agree that getting out of the oppressive atmosphere in the house would be appreciated. She'd never attended a party where everyone was trapped within the walls for days on end and she was finding the experience unexpectedly trying. But she also hadn't anticipated two people being murdered, either. . . .

"Here we are!" Mrs. Frogerton said brightly as the carriage drew to a stop in front of Miss Woodford's front gate.

Caroline stepped down and immediately made certain her bonnet was tied firmly on her head as the wind coming off the marshy plains gusted around them. She offered Mrs. Frogerton her assistance to descend and then waited as her employer instructed the coach driver to await them at the nearby inn.

The curtains were drawn across the best parlor window and knocking loudly on the front door seemed to have no effect on those within.

"We shall go around the back," Mrs. Frogerton determined. She pointed to the left with the tip of her umbrella. "Come along."

Caroline followed her employer past the neat lines of foxgloves and delphiniums to the rear of the property. Mrs. Frogerton did pause to knock again, but on discovering that the door was unlocked, carried on into the house.

"Good morning, Miss Woodford," she said loudly. "I do apologize for being so informal, but the wind today probably makes hearing anyone seeking entry at the front door impossible. How are you?"

Even though Caroline came in behind Mrs. Frogerton, she saw the startled expression on Miss Woodford's face quite well.

"Who are you?" Miss Woodford asked. "Where is Ivy? She just stepped out a moment ago to fetch some bread from the bakery."

"Good morning, ma'am." Caroline smiled. "This lady is my employer, Mrs. Frogerton. You met her briefly a few days ago when we came to visit when your brother was unable to fulfill his obligations."

"My brother is dead." Vera Woodford produced a black lace handkerchief from her sleeve and dabbed gently at her eyes. "And no one from the hall has even bothered to come and offer their condolences to me."

"Obviously, I cannot speak for my uncle and aunt, ma'am, but I can assure you that Mr. Woodford will be greatly missed by the staff and the rest of the family," Caroline said gently. "And it has been almost impossible to leave the hall over the past few days since the river overflowed its banks."

"Yet you and Mrs. Frogerton somehow managed it twice," Miss Woodford said, twisting the handkerchief between her fingers. "Whereas your aunt, who has relied far too heavily on my brother's good nature for years, cannot even be bothered to write me a note of condolence."

"Perhaps that is because they were at odds before his death?" Mrs. Frogerton suggested as she took the seat opposite Miss Woodford. "You did mention that Lady Eleanor had consulted her solicitor about your brother stealing from the estate."

"*Stealing*? Is that what she's calling it now?"

"Well, removal of her possessions from the premises without her prior approval," Caroline hastened to add. "I assume that Mr. Woodford believed he had her consent?"

"He most certainly had approval from the family and what did it matter to Lady Eleanor if he made a little extra and saved her money in the long run?" Miss Woodford asked. "And they were hardly *her* property."

"That's right. She did marry *into* the family," Mrs. Frogerton said thoughtfully. "Therefore, everything in the house belongs to the generations of the Greenwood family who lived there before her."

"Exactly." Miss Woodford nodded. "Lady Ines said the same thing."

"Ah, of course. She was related directly to his lordship and thus a true member of the family," Mrs. Frogerton agreed. "Did Lady Ines also pay Joshua to remove the items for you?"

"I don't believe so."

"Did your brother engage his help, then?"

"Not at all." Miss Woodford raised her chin. "From what I understand, Joshua decided to involve himself in a most unseemly manner and actually threatened Thomas if he didn't pay him for his silence."

Caroline tried not to look at Mrs. Frogerton, who was tutting along with Miss Woodford.

"I wish you had mentioned your concerns last time we saw you, Miss Woodford, because we would have kept our eye on Joshua to make sure he stayed away from your brother."

Miss Woodford went still. "Are you suggesting that Joshua might have been involved in Thomas's death?" Her startled gaze encompassed Caroline. "I was informed by Mrs. Maddox that my brother died in his sleep."

"I cannot comment on that, ma'am, but I suggest you speak to Dr. Harris, who was with Mr. Woodford the night he died. As a medical practitioner he would be able to provide you with an accurate cause of death," Caroline said.

"If Joshua was involved, I can't say I would be surprised," Miss Woodford continued. "Thomas said he was becoming quite threatening as regards to his compensation."

"And by compensation you mean blackmail?" Mrs. Frogerton asked. "I wonder if he was blackmailing Lady Ines as well?"

"It wouldn't surprise me. Perhaps you should speak to her as well."

Caroline bit her lip. "I regret to inform you that Lady Ines is also dead."

Miss Woodford gasped and pressed her hand to her bosom. "Dear Lord. Perhaps someone should inform Lord Greenwood that his footman is a murderer!"

"We tried suggesting that to my uncle, ma'am, but he refuses to believe us." Caroline paused. "But if you were willing to write down your accusations it might help change his mind."

Miss Woodford shook her head. "Lady Eleanor will never allow him to pay any heed to me, Miss Caroline. She would rather see me lose this cottage and suffer than extend the hand of Christian charity to a woman who has wronged no one."

"I'm sure Caroline would be willing to write the letter if you were prepared to dictate it, ma'am?" Mrs. Frogerton suggested. "Lord Greenwood should know that one of his footmen is blackmailing members of his family and staff."

"And it might persuade my uncle and aunt to drop their case against you in return," Caroline suggested.

"I suppose it might." Miss Woodford looked thoughtful. "I mean if word got out about Joshua's deception it would not reflect well on the Greenwoods, would it?"

"Not at all." Mrs. Frogerton raised her eyebrows at Caroline. "Now, why don't you dictate your thoughts while I make us all a nice cup of tea."

An hour later, after they had returned to the carriage and been driven back to the house, Caroline was still pondering Miss Woodford's words. Everything came back to Joshua, who, according to Miss Woodford, had not actively participated in stealing items from the hall but had tried to blackmail those who had.

Could it really be that simple? That Lady Ines and Mr. Woodford had refused to pay Joshua any longer and he in return had tormented and murdered them both? Caroline considered the diary she now always carried on her person. Perhaps it had nothing to do with the matter at hand and had simply been given to her to read?

Which also made no sense.

She went into the nursery, which contained not only the

children but Mabel and Harry. Her cousin looked up with a smile as Caroline joined her at the table.

"Are you excited about the ball tomorrow? I was just describing my dress to Susan. I've promised to visit everyone here in the nursery before I go down to open the ball with Father."

"I'm sure you will look beautiful," Caroline said. "Aunt Eleanor said she had the dress made for you in London."

"It is very fine indeed." Mabel winked at Susan. "You won't recognize me."

"I will." Susan smiled up at her cousin. "Will you dance with Harry?"

"Of course I will. I've been teaching him to waltz."

"Aunt Eleanor is allowing waltzing?" Caroline asked.

"Indeed, she doesn't want to be thought provincial even though it is a country ball with a most peculiar guest list." Mabel grinned. "And, yes, I am aware that I need approval to waltz in London, but surely not in my own home?"

"Do you know the dance steps, Caroline?" Susan asked.

"Yes, indeed, but I doubt I will be dancing because I will be too occupied with Mrs. and Miss Frogerton."

"But if you were asked to dance? Would you do so?"

"If my employer agreed, then yes, but it is unlikely to happen."

"Mrs. Frogerton wouldn't stop you enjoying yourself, Cousin," Mabel said. "She is too kind."

"That is true."

"And mayhap Francis will ask you?" Susan looked so hopeful Caroline hated having to disillusion her. "Isn't it wonderful that he came here for the ball?"

"As I said before, Susan. Lord Francis and I have agreed that we do not suit, which means we are unlikely to be dancing together."

She'd first met him at a London ball and had been immediately smitten not only with his smile, but his ability to twirl her around the dance floor with great aplomb. She missed dancing more than she was prepared to admit to anyone—especially her sister. In retrospect perhaps Francis's dancing abilities and looks had blinded her youthful self to his lack of strength. What would he have done if they'd already been married when her father had died in such a huge scandal?

"Susan, it isn't fair of you to expect Caroline to dance with a gentleman who betrayed her trust," Mabel said gently.

"Francis wouldn't do that." Susan frowned. "Caroline released him from the engagement."

"Because she had no choice," Mabel continued, her voice as steady as her gaze. "She behaved honorably, and she is not to blame for his decision to abandon her."

Susan pressed her lips into a straight line that reminded Caroline forcibly of their father and shot to her feet. "I have to help Hetty with the little ones."

Mabel sighed as Susan stalked away. "I'm sorry. I was just trying to help."

"It's all right. Susan idolized Francis and was very angry with me for letting him walk away."

"Walk away?" Mabel snorted. "From all accounts he ran back to his father like a scared rabbit."

"He tried to tell me that I'd acted too hastily and that if I'd just kept faith with him, he would've found a way to make things work between us."

"I don't believe that for a second—do you? If Francis had tried to defy his father and he'd threatened to cut him off, he would've fallen back into line in an instant!"

"I suspect that's exactly what happened," Caroline agreed.

"He's weak, Cousin." Mabel held her gaze. "You deserve so much better."

"I am beginning to believe that is true." Caroline sighed. "But not all the blame can be laid at Francis's door. I thought I was in love with him, but it was a foolish girl's dream."

"You will find someone far superior," Mabel said. "And

Susan will forget all about Francis and learn to love her brother-in-law. In fact, when she confides in me about the matter, I will make sure she does that very thing."

"One can only hope." Caroline smiled at her cousin.

"Hope is an excellent emotion, Miss Morton." Harry Price slid into the seat beside Mabel and winked at her. "I hold on to it every day."

Caroline considered Harry's smiling countenance. Did he dream that he'd somehow defy society and marry Mabel? It was far less likely than Dorothy snaring her duke. But if the idea of it sustained him, then surely that was enough?

Mabel patted his hand and then rose to her feet. "Excuse me a moment, won't you? I need to make sure that Susan is all right."

Part of Caroline wanted to protest that it was her responsibility, but she was also aware that her cousin was far more likely to successfully persuade Susan out of her sullens.

"I hope Dan hasn't been bothering you again, miss?" Harry asked after a while.

"I haven't spoken to him recently."

"Good. He tends to run his mouth like a waterwheel, but he means nothing by it. He's very loyal to his family and friends and has a bit of a temper."

"Do you think if Joshua *had* erred, Dan would still choose to believe him?" Caroline asked.

"I suppose it would depend on what he did," Harry said.

"What if Joshua had been engaged in a spot of blackmail?"

Harry leaned back in his chair, folded his arms over his chest, and regarded her carefully. "It would depend on who he was blackmailing and why."

"It sounds as if you are already aware of this matter." Caroline decided she had nothing to lose by asking the question. Harry was hardly likely to murder her in the middle of the nursery.

He shrugged. "I might have heard something about it."

"And that the two people he 'might' have blackmailed both happen to have died in suspicious circumstances in the last week."

"With all due respect, Miss Morton, it seems to me that if I were blackmailing someone, I'd very much want to keep them alive so that I could keep collecting the money."

"One might think so," Caroline agreed. "But could there ever be circumstances that made the blackmailer believe he would get no more out of his victims and that they were better off dead?"

"His victims?" Harry frowned. "I'd hardly call them that."

"What if the scheme had been discovered and the income source was about to be cut off?" Caroline asked.

"How so?" Harry looked genuinely confused.

"By a lawsuit from another involved party."

His expression went blank. "You've lost me now, Miss Morton. I can't imagine anyone wanting to expose the real truth. Who told you that?"

It was Caroline's turn to sit back. "I am not at liberty to disclose that information, but rest assured that it is from an impeccable source."

"You don't trust me."

"I don't trust anyone in this house."

He nodded slowly and rose to his feet. "Good for you, miss. Now, if you'll excuse me, I promised Miss Mabel I'd accompany her on her ride this morning."

"Of course."

He headed out, his face rather grim, which didn't make Caroline feel terribly secure, but something had to give somewhere. If Harry had any influence with his brother or Joshua, perhaps it was time to encourage him to use it.

Chapter 17

"Miss Morton!"

Caroline had just escorted Mrs. Frogerton and Dorothy down to lunch when Dr. Harris hailed her from the doorway of the dining room. She pretended not to see him, but he stayed where he was with a frown on his face and continued to beckon to her.

"It's all right, dear. Go and see what he wants," Mrs. Frogerton said encouragingly. Caroline had told her about her conversation with Harry and Mrs. Frogerton believed she had done the right thing. "As we are now convinced that the good doctor has nothing to do with the murders, perhaps you might engage his assistance again?"

"I'm not convinced of anything, ma'am," Caroline murmured.

She hadn't told her employer about the strange diary someone had left in her room and was still reluctant to do so. If it had been written by Dr. Harris's sister, then should she ask him about it?

She went toward the door and Dr. Harris walked out into the hall. She followed him to the rear of the house and into a rarely used back parlor that suffered from a lack of light at the best of times and was currently quite dreary.

The window was open and the brackish smell of the rising flood waters permeated the air.

"Dr. Harris." Caroline curtsied.

"Miss Morton." He cleared his throat. "Yet again I somehow find myself in a difficult situation regarding my behavior toward you."

"It does seem to be something of a habit, sir."

He closed the door and went to stand by the window that looked out onto the side of the house facing the avenue of elm trees that lined the long drive.

"I am generally reluctant to talk about my sister. Her life has been somewhat difficult."

"I am sorry to hear that."

"Being taken away from her parents at such a vulnerable age was very damaging for her and the environment at Greenwood Hall in those days was not . . . helpful."

"So I understand." Caroline tried to keep her tone neutral.

Dr. Harris took a deep breath. "While she was here something terrible happened and it scarred her deeply."

Caroline went to speak, and Dr. Harris held up his hand. "You probably won't believe me, but she never told me exactly what occurred. I never inquired because she made me promise not to." He looked disgusted at himself. "She didn't want our parents to know in case they took the Greenwoods back to court and lost both of us forever."

"You never asked her about it after you left Greenwood Hall?"

"I think we were both desperate to put that episode of our lives behind us. She was older than me and I tended to do as she said. I wish I had asked her because she was never the same afterwards." He grimaced. "She became fearful of everything and began to refuse to leave the house and eventually her room. My parents were in despair and so angry at the Greenwoods—"

"Dr. Harris." Caroline interrupted him. "There's something important I would like to share with you, but I will need to fetch it from my room. Would you be so kind as to wait for me to return to you here?"

Her companion took out his pocket watch. "I can spare you the next ten minutes. After that I have to compose a note to Miss Woodford, who wrote to me concerning her brother. She said you suggested it."

"I simply thought she should hear your medical diagnosis rather than rely on local gossip. She said the Greenwoods hadn't even offered their condolences yet." Caroline was already at the door. "I'll be back in a moment."

She chose to go up the servants' staircase because it was closest and emerged on the nursery floor, panting for breath after the steep climb. She unlocked her bedroom door and went to find the sketches she had concealed under the mattress. The journal was already in her pocket. She was just relocking her door when she heard a scream from the nursery and the sound of breaking glass.

She immediately changed direction and went in to find Hetty hanging on to one of the small boys, who was doing his best to kick her in the shins. One pane of the glass cupboard containing the doll's house and Sunday toys had been shattered.

"Little rascal said he didn't like his boots, took one off, and threw it over his shoulder." Hetty gasped as she struggled to restrain the boy. "Lady Eleanor's going to be very angry with you, Liam, just you wait."

Caroline crouched in front of Liam and took his shoulders in a firm grip. "Stop hurting Hetty. She hasn't done anything wrong."

Liam scowled at her. "Don't want boots! They hurt my toes!"

"Then we'll find you a better pair. You can't go barefoot inside the house." Caroline signaled for Hetty to release Liam. "Now, which is your room? Let's go in there and see if we can discover what the problem is with your boots."

"Don't want to." Liam's lower lip came out.

Caroline pretended to sigh. "Then I'll have to call one of the footmen to take you to Lady Eleanor so that you can tell her why you broke the glass yourself."

"Not that snooty old cow."

Caroline fought a smile. "No, the lady of the house."

"The cook?"

"Liam, it's a very simple choice. Either you come with me or you'll face Lady Eleanor, who will undoubtably be very angry with you."

"I didn't mean to break it." Liam started to move toward his bedroom with Caroline and Hetty close behind him.

"Then perhaps you can sit on your bed and consider your sins while you miss your midday meal, young man." Hetty gave him a gentle push into the room. "I'll come and see you when I've cleaned up this mess."

Hetty locked the door and pocketed the key. "He can't do any harm in there for a little while."

The clock chimed the quarter hour and Caroline knew Dr. Harris had given up waiting for her return and was probably most displeased with her.

"Let me help you clear up." Caroline surveyed the cabinet door, which was swinging free. The dolls on the shelf above had been knocked over, and the front of the doll's house bore the imprint of Liam's boot heel.

"I'll clear the floor if you can start on the cupboard, miss," Hetty said as she used the empty coal scuttle and fireside set to sweep up the shards of glass. "I don't want the rest of the children to come back to this."

Caroline picked up each doll, shook out their skirts, and rearranged their hair before setting them back on the shelf. Most of the glass had fallen onto the floor, but there was still a fine sprinkling on the toys and the odd sharp piece to deal with. She used her handkerchief to clean off the shelves and turned her attention to the doll's house. The whole front piece had come adrift from the latch and was hanging askew.

She didn't want to open it up, but she had no choice if

she wanted to check the hinges. To her relief, someone had removed Great-Aunt Ines from the parlor and Mr. Woodford from his bed. She forced herself to count the other dolls and realized two were missing.

"Has anyone been playing with the house?" Caroline asked Hetty, who had succeeded in cleaning off the floor.

"We did find another key, so the children played with it last Sunday," Hetty said as she shoveled another load of glass into the coal scuttle.

"Two of the dolls are missing."

Hetty came over to look at the house. "The little rascals love to slip them into their pockets and play with them at night. I'll have to search their rooms again."

"I'm not sure I can latch the house shut," Caroline said. "I think the front panel is damaged."

"We'll have to ask Mr. Adams to come in and take a look both at the glass and at the house," Hetty said. "It won't be the first time he's had to replace that glass, I can tell you that."

She picked up the bucket. "I'll take this down to the kitchen and send a message to Mr. Adams. He's here at the house doing some work on the ballroom for Lady Eleanor."

"I'll wait here until you return and try to find a way to close these doors," Caroline said.

"Thank you, miss." Hetty paused. "Don't let Liam out yet, will you?"

"No, indeed."

They shared a smile and then Hetty went out, leaving Caroline alone. She studied the left side hinges of the doll's house door. One of the carpets had gotten stuck in the tiny gap between the interior wall and the front panel, which wasn't helping matters. She gently eased it back in place and immediately saw it wasn't sitting correctly. She eased her fingers underneath the woven cloth and felt something papery.

She slid it out and was just about to unfold it when her eye was caught by something dangling from the fireplace in the same room. She leaned into the house and was able to use her finger and thumb to pull the doll figure out of the chimney. It was one of the female dolls and had dark hair pulled back into a bun and a blue gown.

A thump on one of the doors made her jump and hastily put the doll back into one of the other rooms.

"Let me out!" Liam bellowed.

Caroline struggled to breathe as she approached the locked door.

"Be quiet, Liam. The sooner you regain your temper the quicker you will be released."

Silence greeted her words and she turned back to the doll's house just as Hetty reentered the nursery.

"I found one of the dolls," Caroline said.

"That's good news." Hetty came to stand next to her. "Miss Mabel was telling the children that when the dolls were made, they were dressed to resemble members of the household." Hetty chuckled. "You're probably in there somewhere, miss."

Caroline thought about the doll she'd just found stuffed up the chimney, which did rather resemble her, and shuddered. "I do hope not."

"Considering how the children treat those poor dolls I'd agree with you." Hetty took a look around the room. "Mr. Adams says he can come and fix the glass this afternoon. I'll ask him to take a look at the latch as well."

"Thank you, Hetty. I don't know what my aunt would do without you." Caroline used some string to temporarily close the doll's house front and then turned to the door. "Don't forget about Liam."

"Oh, I won't, miss," Hetty said. "And I'll certainly try and find him a thicker pair of socks to go with those boots because that's the only pair he's getting."

Caroline went back to her room, the piece of paper from the nursery still clenched in her fingers. It took her a few moments to calm herself before she dared unfold the parchment. She recognized the handwriting immediately.

Where has R gone? No one will tell me the truth. They said she'd been found a new position as a maid, but all her possessions are still here. She'd never leave without them. I am afraid. This isn't the first time someone has just left without a word of farewell. But who do I ask for help when they're all involved?

He says not to worry, that I'll be fine because he loves me, and I'll never have to leave, but R's my friend, and I'm not sure if I believe him anymore.

Caroline stared blindly out of the window. She wasn't sure if she'd been meant to find the note, but it was chilling to read. If Liam's boot hadn't gone through the glass, would she even have looked inside the doll's house unless forced to? She smoothed her fingers over the folds in the paper. Had she discovered what was going to happen before it occurred? She wished she knew which of the other dolls had gone missing.

If so, she needed to be wary, as her knowledge might encourage the murderer to make sure that she didn't share what she'd seen with anyone. After gathering up all the things, she left her room, and stood for a moment on the landing, her gaze on the nursery door where she could hear Hetty shouting at the children.

A shadow flitted across the end of the corridor by the servants' stairs, making her pause to reconsider her route. The secondary stairs were dark and narrow. If someone wished to accost her, there was little room to turn and flee or even stand and fight.

Caroline hurried down the main stairs to Mrs. Frogerton's rooms, where her employer was sitting by the fire knitting a sock intended for her son. Unlike poor Rose, Caroline did at least have someone she could turn to in her hour of need.

"Mrs. Frogerton?"

"What is it, lass? You look like you've seen a ghost. Not that it would surprise me in this house."

Caroline sank into the chair opposite Mrs. Frogerton and set the portraits and diary on the table between them.

"I want to tell you everything and ask for your help." She took a deep breath. "Someone left this journal in my room. . . ."

It was almost time for dinner by the time Caroline and Mrs. Frogerton had finished their conversation. As the weather had improved slightly, some new guests had arrived at the hall to spend the night before the ball and the house was full again. Caroline went down to the hall and found Bert just coming from the servants' entrance.

"Do you know where Dr. Harris is?"

"I haven't seen him around, miss." Bert frowned. "Do you need to speak to him?"

"Yes, please."

"Then I'll go and see if I can find him for you."

"Thank you." As she was already downstairs, Caroline poked her head into various rooms, but everything was deserted as the guests and family had retired to prepare for dinner.

Bert met her again at the bottom of the stairs.

"He's not in his room. Joshua said he thought he saw him heading toward the stables."

"Was he leaving the hall for good?" Caroline asked.

"I don't think so, miss. Maybe now that the weather has improved, he went to retrieve his evening coat for the ball from his house in the village?"

"That might be it." Caroline nodded as if she had no further interest in the matter at all. "Thank you."

"If I do see him, miss, I'll tell him you're looking for him," Bert said as he headed back toward the kitchen.

Caroline pelted back up the stairs and arrived at Mrs. Frogerton's door with one hand pressed to her stays, she was breathing so hard.

"He's not here."

"Dr. Harris?" Mrs. Frogerton was sitting at her dressing table while Peggy redid her hair.

"Bert thinks he went down to the village to retrieve his evening dress for the ball tomorrow night."

"He owns a decent coat?" Mrs. Frogerton asked. "I am surprised to hear it."

"Maybe as a medical man at university he had to present himself in polite company on occasion." Caroline bit her lip as she hovered uncertainly behind Mrs. Frogerton's shoulder.

"You should go and change," Peggy said. "I'll be done in a minute and you know how her ladyship doesn't like people to be late."

"Yes, of course." Caroline caught Mrs. Frogerton's eye in the mirror. "I'll be down directly."

It took her more time to decide where to hide the pictures and journal than it did to scramble into her second-best evening dress. Her hair was braided tightly to her head and didn't require any adjustment, and she didn't use any cosmetics to enhance her beauty. She changed out of her woolen stockings and boots into soft kid slippers and silk stockings and clasped her mother's pearls around her neck.

Her reflection looked serenely back at her, hiding her current state of unease. Mrs. Frogerton agreed with her that being open with Dr. Harris was now paramount. She still couldn't see how Joshua, Dan, and the Harris children were all connected to the murder victims. But Mrs. Frogerton had reminded her that someone had wanted her to know about Rose Harris and that had to be important.

She opened her door to leave her room and found Joshua leaning up against the wall opposite.

"What do you want?" Caroline asked.

"Just a quick word. If you want to tell lies about me, tell them to my face. Don't go and grass me out to my friends."

"I'm not aware that I told any lies."

"You said I was a blackmailer."

"And?"

"That's a bloody lie. I took their money, but it wasn't for myself."

"Which is why you were discovered with hundreds of pounds in your room."

"I was waiting for Dan to come home."

"He didn't mention that to me." Caroline eyed the distance to the stairwell and wondered how far she'd get before Joshua caught her.

"Why would he?" Joshua straightened up and Caroline tensed to run. "You don't know the ins and outs of this. Keep your nose clean and you won't get hurt."

"I suppose a man who likes to terrify old men and women and frighten the cook wouldn't balk at hurting a paid companion like me."

"If you shut your mouth, I won't need to do anything, will I? We'll all go our separate ways after the ball, and everything will settle back down to normal."

"Except that two people were murdered."

Joshua pushed off the wall and pointed his finger right in her face. "They deserved it."

"You decide who gets to live and who dies?"

His smile was as cold as the wind off the fells. "We all are. Someone has to stand up for the lost and the forgotten."

"*Tell* me," Caroline said urgently. "If I understood what was going on, maybe I would be prepared to let it be."

"Not my story to tell, miss." His faint smile quickly disappeared. "Leave well alone."

He moved away from her and went down the stairs, his footsteps fading far more quickly than the frantic beating of Caroline's heart. She leaned back against the wall, her knees barely supporting her, and took several deep, calming breaths.

She'd never wished for the comforting no-nonsense Dr. Harris to be by her side to tell her she was imagining things more. She still needed to speak to him and hoped to

God he wouldn't abandon her and would return to the house. She took a faltering step, and then another, and went down to Mrs. Frogerton's suite, where Dorothy and her employer awaited her.

"You're late," Dorothy informed her.

"I apologize." Caroline managed to smile. "I was detained by one of the staff."

"Yet you work for my mother."

"Dotty, stop being so disagreeable. It's hardly Caroline's fault that you are at odds with Lord Epping."

"She told me not to share his sister's wild imaginings with him." Dorothy glared at them both. "And, of course, his sister cried all over him and now he's upset with me."

"That's hardly my fault," Caroline rallied. "In truth, it indicates where his true loyalties lie. You wouldn't want to marry a man who put his sister before you, would you?"

"No, that's true." Dorothy nodded. "And I never intended to marry him anyway."

"So why be cross as crabs with Caroline?" Mrs. Frogerton headed for the door. "Let's go down. We are already tardy."

She waited until Dorothy went past her and then turned to Caroline. "Did something happen?"

"Joshua told me that I didn't know what was really going on, and that I should keep my nose out of it, or I might get hurt," Caroline said grimly. "I tried to get him to tell me the truth, but he refused."

Mrs. Frogerton sighed as they started down the stairs. "This is all remarkably complicated, isn't it? In my novels things are far less problematical."

"I do hope Dr. Harris comes back," Caroline confided. "I have a sense that he is key to understanding this matter."

"If he comes back. One cannot discount the notion that he is the murderer."

"That is hardly helpful, ma'am," Caroline said.

"Murderers are often very charming people," Mrs. Frogerton suggested.

"Then Dr. Harris is unlikely to be counted among their number. He is one of the rudest men I have ever met."

"I've always found him very personable." Mrs. Frogerton walked into the drawing room and smiled graciously at the assembled company.

Eleanor stood in front of the fireplace with her husband and Mabel at her side. She beckoned to Caroline, who was in no mood to approach her. Instead, she turned to Mrs. Frogerton and gently guided her toward a group of more elderly guests who had gathered by the bay window overlooking the garden.

"Good evening, Mrs. Ford, Mr. Ford. May I introduce you to Mrs. Frogerton, my employer? Her daughter will be embarking on her first London Season and I'm sure Mrs. Frogerton would love to hear how you managed to secure excellent alliances for all four of your daughters."

Several hours later, Caroline retired to her room and locked the door behind her. Dr. Harris had not reappeared, and Caroline was beginning to wonder if he ever would. Had he decided he wanted nothing more to do with her and Greenwood Hall? She could almost understand that, but surely as a man of science he would wish to review all the evidence and pursue the matter to the end?

Her gaze fell on her clothes chest and she walked over to open the lid and retrieve the bundle of letters she'd retrieved from Great-Aunt Ines's desk. She hadn't given them more than a cursory glance yet. If there was something nefarious going on, and in the absence of Dr. Harris, it might be her only chance to bring a murderer to justice.

She lit a new candle from the embers of the fire and untied the string around the letters. It took her a little while to sort them out by date because they spanned a number of decades, which made her wonder why her aunt had kept these specific letters. She laid them out on her bed and considered where to start. Instinct told her to look at the letters in the earliest time period, which was when Rose Harris and her brother had been in the nursery.

She picked up the oldest one, opened it up, and squinted at the tiny, crossed print. The limitations of only having the replies to her aunt's correspondence soon became evident but after an hour of reading she was able to understand that even all those years ago her aunt had been involved in several financial transactions.

Had she been selling off items from the house during her entire tenure at Greenwood Hall? And if so, why hadn't anyone noticed? From what Caroline could tell, at first the amounts had been trifling, but over time they grew from shillings and half crowns to guineas.

She rubbed her eyes and tended to the wick of the candle, which had a tendency to go out in the continuous draft coming down the chimney. Caroline undressed, wrapped her shawl around her shoulders, and climbed into bed to continue her reading. From the comments and complaints of her aunt's correspondents, whatever Ines was providing was not always acceptable or satisfactory.

She opened another letter, which was short and to the point, and everything suddenly fell into place.

The girl is not satisfactory. She cries incessantly, can barely speak a complete sentence, and refuses to work. We will be returning her at our earliest convenience and will expect to be reimbursed for her travel expenses as well as the full amount of our purchase agreement.

Caroline raised her head, aware of the silence of the house and her own harried breathing. This was the first direct reference she'd encountered of the commodity being a child, but there had been hints in previous letters that she'd allowed herself to ignore. She'd always assumed that the charity children her aunt had housed and fed were apprenticed to honorable trades or trained as house servants before being sent out into the world.

Had Eleanor accepted payment for the children? Even if

she had, and some might argue she had a right to be reimbursed for her charitable efforts, what did it have to do with Great-Aunt Ines?

Caroline set the letter to one side and continued reading. Now that she had a proper sense about exactly what was going on, the rest of the correspondence might yield further clues. One thing she did know was that ball or no ball she would be having a very difficult conversation with Eleanor in the morning that might get her banned from Greenwood Hall forever.

Chapter 18

"I do not have time or the desire to speak to you, Caroline." Eleanor shuffled the papers on her desk. "I have a ball to organize."

Caroline closed the door behind her and looked down at her aunt.

"I apologize for disturbing you, but this matter cannot wait."

Eleanor stood up. "I have had quite enough of your disrespect, Niece. I can only imagine that your employer's lack of class is beginning to wear off on you."

"Is it true that you were paid to provide children from the nursery to new employers?"

Eleanor frowned. "If you are referring to the fee paid for an apprenticeship, then of course not. In fact, we paid those fees for the children."

"What about those who went into service?"

"We never accepted money for them. Have you quite finished with your impertinent questions?" Eleanor advanced toward Caroline, who was still blocking the exit.

"Were you aware that Great-Aunt Ines was collecting fees for the children?"

"Where on earth did you get that ridiculous idea?" Eleanor snapped.

"From her correspondence?" Caroline held up a handful of letters. "From what I've read, it seems as if she was collecting money for them over several decades."

"Give those to me." Two spots of color appeared on Eleanor's cheeks as she snatched the letters out of Caroline's grasp and began to read. "There must be some mistake."

Caroline waited patiently as her aunt scanned the three or four sheets of parchment and then lifted her head.

"From what I can see, most of this is pure conjecture on your part."

"Did Ines deal with this matter for you, or did she offer to help with the arrangements?" Caroline asked. "I wondered if perhaps she was doing this without your permission."

"That is hardly relevant now, is it?" Eleanor said. "Ines is dead and whatever she was doing ended with her demise. I see no reason to blacken her reputation."

"But what about the children?"

"What about them? They all ended up in better situations because of our family's intervention in their lives. If anything, they should all be eternally grateful."

"Dan Price wasn't grateful, and neither was the Harris family. Do you remember when they took you to court to reclaim their children?"

Eleanor's mouth thinned. "I am not willing to discuss that with you. It was an . . . aberration and was cleared up well before any legal action was taken."

"What about the legal action you've recently taken against the Woodfords?"

"What action?" Eleanor asked. "I am not aware of any at this time."

"Miss Woodford told me that your solicitor sent them a letter ordering them to desist stealing from this house. Don't tell me you have forgotten?"

"I have no idea what you are talking about." Eleanor

raised her chin. "Now, get out of my way or I will call for one of the footmen to remove you."

Caroline stepped to one side. "I will not stop you leaving, but I can't say you have reassured me as to your innocence in these matters." She held her aunt's angry gaze. "Someone profited from those children. Are you quite certain it wasn't you?"

Eleanor yanked the door handle toward herself. "I will allow you to stay under my roof until after the ball and then you will leave. Do not expect another invitation to visit me here."

"As you wish." Caroline curtsied. "But I think that when you reflect on this conversation you will perhaps realize that both of us have been misled. I hope you will do everything in your power to rectify this intolerable situation."

"I doubt it. Once you are removed from my sight, I suspect my world will quickly revert to normal. I have obviously nourished a viper in my bosom." With a final glare, Eleanor wrenched open the door and stalked away.

Caroline turned in the other direction and went to the breakfast parlor, where her employer and daughter were enjoying a lavish breakfast. The weather had improved enough that the sun had broken through the sullen clouds to shine down over the house and estate. Dorothy, whose smile grew more complacent with every sidelong glance Lord Epping threw at her, departed quickly, proclaiming her intention to take a walk through the rose garden.

"How was Lady Eleanor this fine morning?" Mrs. Frogerton asked as she poured Caroline a cup of coffee. She'd decided to come down to eat so that she would be on hand after Caroline spoke to her aunt about her suspicions of Ines.

"She told me to leave after the ball and not come back." Caroline sat down and sighed. "She also said she had not set her solicitor on the Woodfords."

"How odd," Mrs. Frogerton said. "One might think that she would be interested in what was going on in her own house."

"She resents me bringing it to her attention and hates to be in the wrong. She was particularly annoyed when I suggested she was selling the charity children for money."

"Perhaps she wasn't aware of that part," Mrs. Frogerton suggested.

"I tried to give her the opportunity to say that, but my aunt would not entertain such a notion." Caroline eyed the line of silver warming dishes and considered whether she could eat anything with her stomach in such knots. "Did you inquire after Dr. Harris by any chance?"

"He hasn't been seen since last night." Mrs. Frogerton lowered her voice. "If he isn't the murderer, I do hope he is all right. He was rather outspoken about his opposition to the suspicious deaths being concealed."

What little appetite Caroline had left immediately died. "I hadn't thought of that. Perhaps I should check his room."

"You will do no such thing," Mrs. Frogerton said firmly. "It will not help your reputation one bit if you are seen coming out of an unmarried man's bedchamber."

"What reputation?" Caroline asked. "Who on earth would marry me anyway?"

"I will ask one of the footmen to ascertain Dr. Harris's whereabouts. Now, what are you going to eat?"

"I'll just drink my coffee." Caroline tried to smile.

"As you wish," Mrs. Frogerton said. "Do you want to try your new gown on? Peggy says that Martha has finished the alterations."

"I think I'll leave that until later." Caroline stood up. She'd just caught a glimpse of Joshua in the doorway. "Will you please excuse me for a moment?"

She followed Joshua out of the house and onto the path that led to the stables, where she was fairly certain he wasn't supposed to be at this time in the morning. Just before he reached the outbuildings he swung around and confronted her; his hands fisted at his sides, his breath coalescing in the still cold air.

"What do you want now, miss?"

"Is this all about Lady Ines making a profit from indenturing the children?"

He frowned. "Who told you that?"

Caroline shrugged. "I read some of her correspondence."

"You've always been a clever one, haven't you?" Joshua glanced around. "Got out of this place as well, which a lot of us never managed."

"Then you admit it?"

"That the old bitch was making money off us? I don't need to admit nothing. She's dead and may God have mercy on her soul because I have none to spare." He spat on the ground. "Good riddance."

"Was Mr. Woodford involved?" Caroline asked.

"In selling off the kids who were supposed to be in his care? Why would you think that?"

"Because he is also dead."

"And I don't care about that either, miss." He glanced toward the stables. "I need to get on."

"Without accepting any responsibility for what has happened?"

"Look, if I'd wanted to kill them, I've had plenty of opportunities over the years."

"But I still don't understand why you would want to."

"Making money off innocents isn't bad enough for you?" He shrugged. "You should talk to your friend Dr. Harris. Ask him what he'd like to do to the Greenwood family and why."

"When he comes back, I will certainly do so."

"Done a runner, has he?" Joshua grinned. "Can't say I'm surprised. Maybe that tells you everything you need to know about who has a good reason to murder someone, miss. Think on that."

He walked off whistling, leaving Caroline feeling more confused than ever. Joshua hadn't confirmed her suspicions about Great-Aunt Ines and Mr. Woodford, but he hadn't denied them, either. Joshua seemed to be suggesting Dr. Harris held the answers she needed, and she was beginning to fear he might be right. She turned back to the house and walked slowly along the sheltered path past the rose garden.

If something terrible had happened to Rose Harris and her friend when they resided in the house, Joshua and the Price brothers could hardly have been old enough to be involved in the matter. Which meant that Dr. Harris, who remembered the event very clearly, might have the biggest motive for revenge.

"No." Caroline said the word out loud. "I still can't believe that."

She opened the side door and went into the house, glad of the warmth that reached out and enfolded her. In the main hall the staff were busy cleaning and polishing for the ball later that evening. One of the gardeners was bringing in large arrangements for the ballroom and a string quartet had also been hired to provide the music. It seemed Eleanor had spared no expense in ensuring that her daughter's birthday ball would be a success.

It was odd not to be involved in the frantic preparations. Since their earlier altercation Eleanor had not reached out to Caroline to ask for assistance and Caroline had no intention of offering to help. As soon as she could provide for Susan, she would relieve her aunt of that burden and stay as far away from Greenwood Hall as possible.

She went up the stairs and paused on the landing to look down on the busy scene below. She would not miss the place, but she would never forget it. So many of her hopes and dreams had ended here—her mother's death during childbirth, her father's suicide, and more recently the painful realization that if she wanted to avoid her aunt's charity she would have to step back from society and take a job with a wage.

It seemed as if she wasn't the only person whose dreams had foundered in the flat wastelands of the Norfolk

Broads. Great-Aunt Ines had come here as an unwanted spinster and lived the rest of her life in a house she didn't own controlled by a family who didn't value her. Mr. Woodford had grown up here, too, and decided along with Ines that they deserved more.

The thought of them using the charity children as currency didn't sit well with Caroline. And the journal had hinted at worse. Caroline sighed as she turned to walk up to Mrs. Frogerton's suite. Would she ever know exactly what had happened and would Dr. Harris ever return?

If he didn't come back, perhaps she would have all the answer she needed.

Caroline knocked on the door and went in to find Mrs. Frogerton with Peggy and Martha.

"There you are, dear. Martha would like you to try the dress on now in case she needs to adjust anything as she won't have a moment to herself later."

"Of course." Caroline smiled at Eliza's dresser. "I can't wait to see what you've done."

"You must have curls with that gown," Peggy stated.

On Mrs. Frogerton's insistence, Peggy had come to Caroline's bedchamber before the grand dinner and ball to help her get dressed and do her hair.

"I'm not sure that's appropriate."

"You're still part of this family, miss." Peggy started brushing and soon had Caroline's dark hair gathered into her hand as she skillfully pinned it in place. "I've already got the curling iron heating up. Shame to waste it."

Caroline subsided into her seat and watched Peggy perform her magic.

"Where did you get those pins?" Caroline asked.

"Miss Frogerton said the sapphires would go well with your gown and your eyes, but she wants them back after the ball, mind."

"I'd expect nothing less. It's still very kind of her."

"She's pleasant enough." Peggy was nothing if not

diplomatic. "She asked if I'd consider leaving this place and coming to work for her in London as her personal maid."

"It would be a great opportunity," Caroline said.

"I don't have any family around here to speak of, so I'm not averse to going," Peggy said. "But she can be quite sharp when something isn't to her liking."

"She's definitely outspoken, but that isn't necessarily a bad thing." Caroline tried to be fair. "I don't think she'd be deliberately unkind."

"I don't mind a bit of plain speaking myself." Peggy slid another pin into Caroline's hair. "There, I think that will stay put even if you dance a jig on the table."

"I don't expect to be dancing at all." Caroline admired the bunches of curls over her ears and the way the light caught the brilliance of the pins. "It's not really my place."

"I reckon some of the gentlemen will try to change your mind when they see you looking so fine, miss."

"Thank you, Peggy."

"I'll go and see if Mrs. Frogerton needs any more help and tell her you're as fine as fivepence!"

Caroline stood and shook out the ice blue satin skirts of her new gown. She hadn't felt quite so fashionably impractical for a long time and wasn't sure whether to smile or cry at the reflection in the mirror of the girl she'd left behind. The hopes and dreams she'd nurtured had been dashed but she'd also learned, and survived, and refused to be discounted. She wasn't weak like her father and that gave her immense satisfaction.

She had two hundred pounds tucked away in her stocking drawer, a decent yearly wage, and was employed by a woman she not only respected but had come to like. Once she had Susan by her side again her life would be complete.

With a brisk nod at her serene reflection, she picked up her shawl, fan, and reticule, and went to the door. The dinner started in less than an hour and would be followed by the grand ball. Tomorrow morning, she would leave Greenwood Hall with no regrets. It was galling to accept that all the evidence she had against Joshua would never be used in a court of law. There was no way of proving that he, Dan Price, or Dr. Harris had murdered anyone.

Caroline walked slowly down the stairs to Mrs. Frogerton's suite, quietly admiring the rustling of her new skirts. Denying herself the opportunity to purchase new or refurbished gowns suddenly seemed ridiculous, something she would remedy when they returned to London.

She knocked on Mrs. Frogerton's door and went in to find her employer resplendent in purple satin with a red trim and an elaborate turban on her head. Dorothy wore pale pink with heavily embroidered puffed sleeves and a matching deep hem of riotous flowers.

"You look lovely!" Mrs. Frogerton beamed at Caroline.

"So do you, ma'am." Caroline turned to Dorothy. "And Miss Frogerton looks beautiful."

"I do, but you are certainly more elegant," Dorothy said as she smoothed down her skirts. "We all look very fine."

"Then shall we go down?" Mrs. Frogerton gathered her possessions and headed for the door. "I understand that now the weather has improved sufficiently there will be several new guests at dinner and even more for the actual ball."

"How nice for Mabel to have all her friends and family gathered for her birthday," Dorothy commented. "She is certainly looking forward to it."

"You will have an equally fine ball of your own in London, Dotty," Mrs. Frogerton promised as they descended the wide staircase to the hall below. "And you will now have a few special friends to invite."

"That has certainly been useful," Dorothy agreed with a glance at Caroline. "I suppose I should thank you."

"Thank my aunt for the invitation."

Caroline scanned the groups of guests, but she couldn't

see the tall figure of Dr. Harris amongst them. The Price brothers were present as well as Tina Brownworth, and Joshua was currently circulating with a tray of drinks. Mabel stood in front of the fireplace accepting congratulations and compliments from the arriving guests. She wore a new ruby necklace and matching earrings Caroline assumed had been given to her as a birthday gift and her smile was radiant.

The Frogerton ladies and Caroline joined the procession of guests to wish Mabel well and were greeted with great exuberance and gratitude. There was no sign of Eleanor or Lord Greenwood, which meant that Caroline could enjoy the moment with her cousin.

"Is Nick coming?" Caroline asked.

Mabel made a face. "He said he would, but he and Father are at odds about his gambling debts and his expensive mistress again. I suspect he'll use that as an excuse not to attend."

"I'm sorry."

"I'm not. I hardly know him and from all accounts he's as bad as Father."

"At least George and Eliza are in attendance." Caroline was still slightly worried Eliza would recognize her madeover dress and call her to task over it.

"Yes, although Eliza is already complaining about her placement at the dinner table and Mother's lack of sympathy for her 'condition.'" Mabel looked over at the bay windows, where George was entertaining a group of young men. "George is a dear, though."

"Indeed, he is," Caroline agreed.

"There is something I want to tell you, Caroline, but I am afraid you will be angry with me," Mabel said.

"I can't be angry with you on your birthday, Cousin."

"It's my fault Lord Francis was invited to the ball." Mabel spoke in a rush. "Susan was convinced that if he saw you again, he would instantly change his mind, and everything would be as it had been. I allowed myself to believe her, and I wanted to do something nice for you both. I invited Nora knowing her father was away on a diplomatic mission, and that her uncle would probably be called upon to act in his stead."

Caroline simply looked at her cousin, who appeared close to tears.

"I am *so* sorry, Caroline. I just wanted you to be as happy as I am."

"It's all right." Caroline patted Mabel's shoulder. "It wasn't pleasant to see him here at first, but we've at least had the opportunity to acknowledge that we wouldn't have suited and to forgive each other."

Mabel blinked hard. "You are far too kind and forgiving of me *and* of Francis."

Caroline smiled at her cousin and moved on, her thoughts in turmoil. She had wondered how Francis ended up on the guest list and had initially assumed it was her aunt's doing. Mabel's well-intentioned intervention made much more sense. After all, she'd been allowed to pick half the guests with her mother's reluctant approval.

Even as she nodded serenely at various faces she recognized, Caroline made sure she was aware of where her employer and her daughter were in the room. Mrs. Frogerton moved through the crowd conversing easily with anyone who deigned to make conversation with her. Dorothy went to stand by the Price brothers and some of Mabel's other young guests.

"Lady Caroline. How well you look tonight." Francis came toward her.

"Thank you, my lord." Caroline curtsied.

"I believe you were wearing that particular shade of blue the first time I asked you to dance." He smiled. "It will always remain a favorite of mine."

After her recent conversation with Mabel, Caroline wasn't quite sure how to reply to him. She decided to smile and started to turn away.

"Will you save a dance for me later?" Francis asked.

"Why would you wish to draw attention to yourself like that?" Caroline glanced over her shoulder at him. "No one expects you to acknowledge the woman who broke off her engagement to you."

"I'd simply like to dance with you." He hesitated. "I want everyone to see that I bear you no ill will and that we have remained friends."

"Have we?"

"I don't see why not," Francis countered. "Perhaps it is time we refused to allow our fathers to define us."

Caroline held his gaze. "If I do agree to dance with you, it will be for the last time."

"As you wish." He bowed. "Save me a waltz."

Needing a moment to compose herself, Caroline headed toward the far end of the drawing room to the large bay window looking out over the formal gardens behind the house.

"Caroline." Eleanor spoke from behind her.

"Good evening, Aunt." Caroline curtsied.

"You look very fine for a woman who earns her own living." Eleanor raised an eyebrow. Her anger with Caroline had obviously not diminished in the slightest. "Another lavish gift from your employer, perhaps?"

"No, merely a made-over gown."

"It draws attention."

"And what is wrong with that?"

"I noticed you speaking to Lord Francis. Everyone here knows your current financial situation, Niece. The only kind of offers you are likely to receive are not those involving marriage."

"Is that a warning or a threat?" Caroline asked.

"Merely an observation."

"Then one has to wonder at the caliber of guests who would consider it appropriate to proposition a single lady in the home of her relatives. One might 'think' a woman would be safe in such a house, but as we have established recently, ma'am, not everything in this house is quite as it seems."

"You are impertinent." Eleanor raised her chin.

"No, I am tired of being blamed for the sins of my father. I have done nothing wrong. My reputation is my own and your insinuation that I would be willing to accept such a proposition even if it was offered to me is insulting."

"I did not say that."

"You implied that I was dressing to attract the attention of 'gentlemen' who might be willing to support me financially in return for certain favors."

"Your behavior reflects on your family and I cannot have Mabel's reputation besmirched before she even makes her London debut," Eleanor retorted. "And you have shown no loyalty to me, miss."

Caroline took a hasty breath. "I am very grateful for everything you have done for me, Aunt, I truly am. But I can't sit by and allow someone to get away with murder."

Eleanor pressed her fingers to her forehead. "Please stop. I simply wish to celebrate my youngest daughter's birthday with my family and friends."

"Then I hope you enjoy it," Caroline said. "I wish Mabel every happiness."

For a moment they simply stared at each other as the gulf between them grew ever wider before Eleanor gave a brisk nod.

"I must go and speak to Joshua about dinner."

"Yes, of course."

Within a few moments, Joshua was announcing that dinner would be served. Because it was quite a large party, Eleanor had stationed herself by the door to gently assign the correct guests to appropriate partners. When Caroline approached with the Frogertons, Eleanor called out to them.

"Mrs. Frogerton, here is the vicar waiting to take you in, and Miss Frogerton? My son George is ready and willing to escort you."

Caroline waited as the Frogertons met their dining partners before looking inquiringly at her aunt.

"What are you waiting for, Caroline?" Eleanor asked.
"Paid companions eat in the nursery or the kitchen."

"I say . . ." Her cousin George, who was still in earshot,
stared at his mother aghast. "That seems rather harsh,
Mother. Caroline's *family*."

"It's quite all right, George." Caroline smiled at her cousin. "I understand that your mother has a limited amount
of space on such a grand occasion."

"I still don't like it." George scowled at his mother. "It's
not on."

Unwilling to involve herself in another Greenwood family argument, Caroline walked back into the hall. A year
ago, such a social humiliation would have devastated her
but now she didn't really care. Sitting at a table full of people who simply wanted to enjoy her misfortune was no
longer something to be wished for. She'd be far happier
eating with Susan in the nursery anyway.

"Miss Morton!"

She turned to see Dr. Harris at the entrance to the servants' wing. He still wore his greatcoat and had his hat in
his hand. She was not in the mood to be summoned and
considered ignoring him and proceeding up the stairs.

"Miss Morton!"

Unfortunately, curiosity had always been her besetting
sin. With a resigned sigh, she walked over to him. He
looked her up and down.

"You look . . . different."

"I'm wearing a new dress."

"And you've done your hair in curls." He held the door
open and gestured for her to go along the corridor toward
the butler's apartment.

"One tries to make an effort when attending a ball,
Dr. Harris."

"Of course—it's Miss Mabel's birthday." He nodded.

"Then why aren't you in there eating dinner with the rest of the guests?"

"Because my aunt relegated me to the servants' table."

"She's still annoyed with you?" Dr. Harris snorted. "I've never met a woman so reluctant to admit she's in the wrong."

Caroline swung round to confront him. "Where have you been?"

His brow creased as he slowed to a halt. "Why does it matter?"

"Because some people might think that your disappearing without a word of explanation might indicate that you have a guilty conscience!"

He studied her intently for a long moment. "You missed me."

"I most certainly did not. Why would I be concerned when a gentleman I wanted to share some information with absconds without an explanation or an apology?"

"You were the one who didn't come back, Miss Morton. I waited a full fifteen minutes before I decided to take matters into my own hands."

"There was an accident in the nursery, and I went to help out," Caroline said stiffly.

"Ah. That explains that then."

"It doesn't explain where you've been for the last day or so."

"I can remedy that." He grabbed her hand and towed her along the corridor with him. "Come along, there's someone I want you to meet."

He opened the door into the butler's sitting room and a woman who was sitting by the blazing fire rose to her feet and turned toward them. She had dark hair, brown eyes, and a rather anxious expression.

"This is my sister, Rose, Miss Morton. I thought it was time you met her and that between us we could sort this muddle out."

"You went to find your sister?" Caroline asked.

"Yes, he did." Rose Harris spoke for the first time. "He insisted it was time for me to face what had happened to me here and to assist you in proving that Mr. Woodford and Lady Ines had been murdered."

"You forced your sister to come here without a moment's notice?" Caroline stared at Dr. Harris. "Where does she reside?"

"Norwich." His brow creased. "It's not that far. I hired a carriage."

Caroline simply stared at him. "Have you even offered her some tea or something to eat yet?"

"I thought you could do that. When I went into the kitchen Mrs. Maddox shooed me away because she was too busy with the grand dinner before the ball." He studied her gown. "Why are you all dressed up if you aren't allowed to dine with your family?"

"I didn't know that when I chose this dress," Caroline said. "And it's quite unimportant when compared to your sister's current needs and your neglect of her after dragging her from her home."

"I was more than willing to come when Oliver explained the circumstances to me, Miss Morton." Rose hesitated. "I fear that my silence might have cost others their lives."

Caroline turned to the door. "Let me just make certain that someone brings us tea and something to eat before we begin." She glanced over at Dr. Harris. "I also have something to show you both. I will fetch it from my room."

By the time she returned to the butler's pantry, Rose was drinking her tea and sharing a plate of leftover food from the grand dinner with her brother. Dr. Harris pointed at the tray.

"Mrs. Maddox sent food for you as well. Apparently, she'd heard about your banishment from the dining party and was anxious to make amends."

Caroline stared at the delicate salmon mousse, roasted

asparagus, and fresh bread rolls. Ladies were never supposed to acknowledge they were hungry, but as she'd been relegated to the serving class perhaps it didn't matter anymore. She sat down opposite Rose, spread a napkin carefully over the skirts of her new gown, and ate everything on her plate.

Rose, who had eaten far less, was still regarding Caroline rather anxiously as she sipped her second cup of tea. Caroline remembered Dr. Harris had told her that his sister's experiences at Greenwood Hall had shaped and damaged her life. She couldn't imagine how Rose had forced herself to come back.

"I am sorry that you had to return to this place, Miss Harris. It is very brave of you."

"When Oliver told me about the deaths I didn't feel as if I had any choice." She grimaced. "I'm not quite sure whether what I know will help, Miss Morton, but I felt I should at least try."

Caroline took the battered journal and folded note from her reticule.

"Someone left this in my room last week." She handed the book over to Rose. "It bears an inscription on the inside cover. I thought it might have belonged to you."

Rose opened the cover and glanced down at the faded words. "Where on earth did you get this from?"

"I don't know. I have to assume someone wanted me to have it because they felt it was important." Caroline paused. "Was it your journal?"

Rose was busy flipping through the pages and reading the scrawled notes.

"No, it's not mine."

"I don't understand. I *assumed*—"

"Never assume, Miss Morton. It leads to terrible outcomes," Dr. Harris said.

"It belonged to someone with the initial R." Caroline ignored him and continued to speak to his sister.

"I suspect it belonged to my friend Rosemary. We were often mistaken for each other."

Caroline delved into her reticule again and took out the sketches. She handed the one of the two girls to Rose, who smiled.

"That's me and Rosemary. Where did you get that from?"

"Lady Ines had a large collection of sketches of the nursery children."

Rose's smile faded. "I suppose she used them to advertise the merchandise."

"Is it true that she sold the nursery children into servitude?"

Rose took a deep breath, and her brother came to stand behind her, his hand on her shoulder.

"Yes, but it was much worse than that." She looked down at her clasped hands. "She and the Woodfords pretended that all of us would be going to good Christian homes and would end up with secure, paid employment for life."

"Is that what happened to you?" Caroline asked, and gestured to the journal. "In the book Rosemary writes that her friend has gone and that no one will tell her anything. She was obviously worried."

"The irony is that Rosemary was supposed to be the one leaving because at that point my parents had returned and were trying to get us back from the Greenwoods. I originally believed Lady Eleanor deliberately sent me away to make it more difficult for the authorities to find me."

"That's cruel."

"Very few people involved in our care and housing back in those days weren't cruel, Miss Morton. Mr. Woodford was a bully, Lady Ines had a horrible temper, and Ruth Maddox terrified and humiliated the little ones in the nursery."

"I can attest to that," Dr. Harris spoke up.

"Where did they send you?" Caroline was almost afraid to ask.

Rose looked up at her brother, who nodded. "You can tell her. She's not like the rest of them."

"I was told I would be trained as a nursery maid at a house in Wroxham run by a Mrs. Wilson." A slight shudder ran through her frame. "It was not quite as I'd imagined. Mrs. Wilson wasn't the matriarch of a good Christian family at all. In truth she wasn't even married and her house . . ." Rose paused. "Was full of unwanted children."

"She ran a charitable foundation?" Caroline asked.

"No, she sold unwanted babies and children to anyone who was willing to pay for them, no questions asked." Rose met Caroline's gaze. "There were dark unheated rooms full of cradles and screaming babies. My job was to keep them alive just long enough for her to make a profit out of them."

Caroline pressed her fingers to her lips to stem the desire to scream.

"Were there . . . any good people who took the babies?"

"Occasionally a well-intentioned couple came in, but it was rare in the month I lived there."

"Do you think the Woodfords and Lady Ines knew what they'd sent you to?"

"Of course they did." Rose Harris raised an eyebrow, which made her resemble her brother even more. "How do you think they got rid of the majority of the charity children who lived at the hall?"

Caroline shot to her feet and turned away from the Harrises. The flat certainty in Rose's voice was impossible to deny.

"They made money from innocent children," Caroline whispered. "I can quite understand why you dislike my family so much, Dr. Harris."

"Not enough to kill them, if that's what you're asking. I promised Rose I wouldn't do that." He glanced down at his sister. "And despite some immense provocation I have kept my word."

"How did you escape?" Caroline returned to her chair opposite Rose.

"My parents succeeded in their threatened lawsuit against the Greenwoods. I was collected by Mr. Woodford and returned to the hall. On the way back he said that if I told anyone where I'd been, he'd have me killed." Her smile was slight. "By that point I was so broken from everything I'd seen that the last thing I wanted to do was talk about it. I regret that now."

"I can quite understand why you felt like that," Caroline said. "I always try to repress the worst memories I have of my father. It was the only way I could still allow myself to love him as a daughter should."

Rose's gaze turned toward the journal that lay on the table between them.

"When I returned to the hall, Rosemary had disappeared, and no one would tell me where she'd gone. I assumed at first that she'd been sent to replace me at Mrs. Wilson's, but the Woodfords had stopped sending any of the children there in case I told my parents the truth." She sighed. "And all her carefully acquired possessions had been redistributed to the other children, which she would not have appreciated, having grown up with nothing."

"Then what do you think happened to her?" Caroline had to ask.

"I have my suspicions. She was . . . in love with someone. I suspect that person was instrumental in her remaining at the hall when I was sent in her stead. I fear she overestimated her importance to this man and perhaps suffered the consequences. As far as I know she was never heard of again."

Caroline had a sudden horrible image of the dark-haired doll from the doll's house.

"What is it?" Dr. Harris was studying her intently.

"Nothing in particular," Caroline said hurriedly. "I cannot believe—"

"What?"

"I found a page of the journal folded under one of the carpets in the doll's house and in the same room, one of the dolls had been stuffed up the chimney."

Silence greeted her remark as the brother and sister exchanged glances.

"Oliver told me about the doll's house," Rose said.

"Everything comes back to the nursery, doesn't it?" Caroline looked at her companions. "The children, the house, the staff and family who used to work there. Everything comes from there."

"It is hard to ignore all the connections," Rose agreed.

Caroline sat forward. "Excuse me for being blunt, but if your brother isn't a murderer—and I can quite understand why he might choose to be one now—then who else could it be?"

Rose set her hand on the journal. "Why, Rosemary's younger brothers, of course. You did say they were present at the house party, didn't you, Oliver?"

Caroline's breath hitched. "Rosemary is related to the Price brothers?"

"Yes, Dan and Harry. I doubt they were aware of exactly what was going on at the time because they were quite young, but if they received her personal items and the diary was amongst them, I'm fairly sure they'd be able to piece things together."

"And exact their revenge," Caroline added faintly. "It all makes a horrible kind of sense now." She took a much-needed breath. "The problem is, how do we prove it?"

"Do we even want to?" Dr. Harris frowned. "We all agree that what the Woodfords and Lady Ines did was inexcusable. Perhaps Joshua was right all along, and we should let things be."

"But what about Rosemary Price?" Caroline asked.

"Don't her brothers deserve some answers if she was killed by a member of this household?"

"It's possible that murdering Mr. Woodford took care of that matter," Rose said quietly. "Someone was influential enough to promise Rosemary a permanent job at the hall and send me away in her stead. Mr. Woodford had just been promoted to first footman."

"Perhaps Joshua agreed to help his friends so that he could take over as butler, although extorting money by blackmail was probably far more lucrative." Caroline sighed. "He'd probably see it as justice being served."

"And he'd be right," Dr. Harris argued.

"Except there is still no justice for Rosemary," his sister reminded him. "One does have to wonder why the Price brothers, having achieved their aim, haven't already departed this place."

"I think they promised Mabel they would stay for her ball." Caroline sat up straight. "I could talk to them."

"Aren't you banned from the ballroom?" Dr. Harris asked.

"Not yet. I still have my duties as companion to Mrs. Frogerton and her daughter to perform. My aunt won't want to create a scene at her daughter's birthday ball."

"I've still got an invitation. We can go together," Dr. Harris said. "If you don't mind being left alone for a while, Sister?"

"I'm quite comfortable here by the fire," Rose reassured them. "And I would very much like to know what happened to my old friend Rosemary. I couldn't have survived my first weeks here without her."

"Then we will do our best to find out for you." Caroline stood and moved toward the door. "Perhaps we will discover some good news for a change."

Dr. Harris was careful to shut the door before answering her. "I doubt it."

Caroline turned her gaze resolutely forward. "Aren't you going to change your coat?"

"I suppose I should—what with you looking so splendid." He caught hold of her hand and brought it to his lips. "You really are quite beautiful."

"Don't sound so surprised."

"I'm not. All it means is that you received good bones from your parents and an interesting hair and eye color combination. You hardly did anything yourself."

"I am aware of that." She frowned at him. "I will wait in the hall for ten minutes. If you do not return in time, I will go in without you."

"Understood." He offered her a salute and turned smartly on his heel. "It will be my pleasure to demonstrate how men understand the value of punctuality as opposed to most women."

She took up a position in the shadow of the main staircase where she could observe the comings and goings of the guests, staff, and family. The men were still at the dining table enjoying their port, cigars, and political talk while the ladies had migrated to the drawing room for tea.

There was still the occasional guest arriving, so the staff were busy dealing with carriages, coats, and directing the ladies up the stairs to refresh themselves after sitting in cramped conditions on the way to the ball. Caroline saw Bert heading toward the drawing room with a plate of macarons and waved at him.

"Will you please inform Mrs. Frogerton that I will meet her in the ballroom and apologize for my being unavoidably detained?"

"Yes, of course." Bert nodded and then hesitated. "Lady Eleanor not letting you sit down to have your dinner with the rest of them wasn't fair, miss."

"She is the mistress of the house and she is entitled to make her own decisions."

Bert didn't look impressed. "Still wasn't nice of her, was it?"

He went toward the drawing room and Caroline checked

the time. Just as the clock struck the hour and both the gentlemen and the ladies emerged from their respective rooms, Dr. Harris came down the stairs.

He'd done more than simply replace his coat and had on a clean starched shirt, new cravat, blue waistcoat, and pressed black trousers.

"You look very nice, Dr. Harris," Caroline said.

"As my sister says, I do scrub up well." He bowed and offered her his arm. "Shall we go in? The sooner we sort out this matter with the Price boys, the sooner I can ask you to dance."

Chapter 19

"I don't intend to dance," Caroline said even as the string quartet started playing quietly in the background while the guests filtered in from various places. "I'm not an invited guest, merely a paid companion."

Dr. Harris snorted as his gaze swept the room. "Don't be ridiculous. You're just as entitled to enjoy yourself as anyone else."

"My aunt wouldn't agree with you."

"Well, we both know my opinion of your aunt." He touched her shoulder. "I see the Price brothers over by the window. Come on."

She allowed herself to be taken over to where Dan and Harry were standing. They both looked very smart in their evening clothes.

"Dr. Harris, Miss Morton." Harry offered them a pleasant smile while Dan frowned. "Something we can help you with?"

"I sincerely hope so," Dr. Harris said. "Go ahead, Miss Morton."

"I understand that your sister Rosemary lived at the hall." Harry's smile disappeared. "What about it?"

"There is no way of asking this politely but is she still living?"

"That's an interesting question, Miss Morton. One I'd quite like the answer to myself," Harry said. "Is there something you want to tell me?"

"We know about the scheme to make a profit out of the nursery children. We know Lady Ines and the Woodfords were involved, and that Joshua somehow found out."

"Originally, Joshua was asked to help them steal things from the hall and resell them," Harry said. "He soon realized they were doing much worse."

There was a slight disruption at the door as Mabel came into the ballroom with her parents, George, and Eliza. Mabel wore a simple white gown overlaid with a shimmering net of pearls which set off the rubies at her throat and in her ears to perfection.

Caroline turned back to Harry Price, whose appreciative gaze had stayed on Mabel.

"Did you leave Rosemary's diary in my room?"

He frowned. "No. We only have fragments of what she wrote, and with respect, miss, I certainly wouldn't have left them with you."

"Someone wanted me to know about your sister's time here."

"I suppose they did. And what conclusions have you and the good doctor drawn from that?"

Caroline took a deep breath, glad that Dr. Harris was standing at her side. "That Rosemary never left this house and that someone—probably Mr. Woodford—made sure of that."

"You think Mr. Woodford murdered her?" Dan joined the conversation.

"It would explain why you and Joshua taunted and murdered him," Dr. Harris said. "And why Lady Ines died."

"I suspect Rosemary is buried somewhere in or near this house," Caroline said. "Someone knows."

"I think you're right about that, miss."

Harry's gaze returned to Mabel, who was opening the

ball with her father. A slight ripple of applause followed them as they circled the dance floor.

"But wrong about some other things."

As soon as the music ended, Mabel went on tiptoe to whisper something into her father's ear, one hand on his shoulder. She was still smiling sweetly when he stepped away from her, his expression horrified, and backed toward the door.

Caroline's view of the couple was obscured by the arrival on the floor of the couples for the next dance and she turned back to Harry.

"If I am incorrect, will you tell me where I erred?"

"Lady Ines and the Woodfords profited from innocent children for years. If they suffered a fraction of the fear they inflicted on others in their last moments, then they damn well deserved it."

"So, you admit you murdered them?"

"I'm not that stupid, miss." Harry smiled at her. "And neither is my brother. Not that anyone will believe you, anyway."

"That might be true, but it doesn't mean that what you did was right."

"The Bible might disagree with you there. As Lady Ines taught us, God is a great one for vengeance and justice being served."

Caroline went to speak, and Dr. Harris touched her shoulder. "I don't think you will change Harry's opinion on this, Miss Morton. Perhaps we should return to discussing what happened to Rosemary."

Dan nodded. "I'd like to know where she's buried."

"Then perhaps you shouldn't have murdered Mr. Woodford," Caroline said.

"You think I didn't ask him about that very thing before he died? He swore he didn't know anything about it."

"But I thought he and Rosemary . . ." Caroline didn't finish the sentence, as someone appeared at her side and everyone else went quiet.

"Good evening, gentlemen." Francis bowed to the assembled company. "Lady Caroline. You promised me a dance."

Aware that Dr. Harris was frowning at her and that there was no polite way of telling Francis to go away without causing gossip, she curtsied and placed her gloved hand on her ex-fiancé's arm.

"Of course." She smiled up at Dr. Harris. "Perhaps we can continue this fascinating discussion later."

"You seem distracted," Francis murmured on the third occasion when she stepped on his foot.

"I can only apologize."

"You need not fear social condemnation for your decision to dance with me. I will defend you to the last."

"To be honest, I hadn't even thought about that," Caroline confessed.

She'd been too busy trying to puzzle out why there still seemed to be a piece missing from her understanding of Rosemary's disappearance and death and why the Price brothers seemed so uninterested in what Mr. Woodford had done to their sister. Perhaps having killed him they were satisfied. But it hadn't felt like that. It was almost as if they too were still waiting for the last piece to fall into place. . . .

"Caroline?"

She smiled up at Francis. "I'm so sorry. I'm being a terrible dance partner. Are you looking forward to returning to London for the new Season? I'm afraid that you might have to tolerate my occasional appearance when I accompany Mrs. Frogerton to balls and such."

"Tolerate? You know I always liked you for yourself and not just because you are beautiful."

"Not enough to defy your father, though," Caroline reminded him.

"I realized I can't . . . live without my allowance and his patronage."

She looked up into his eyes. "Thank you."

"For what?"

"Being honest for the first time about why you obeyed him."

He sighed. "It seems such a weak and paltry reason. I suspect I was too ashamed to admit it at the time."

"It doesn't matter now." Caroline focused on remembering the steps of the dance, aware of the guests, particularly the appalled face of her cousin Eliza. "Perhaps we both learned something about ourselves and will do better next time."

The music ended and she stepped back and curtsied. "Thank you, Francis. I wish you nothing but happiness from now on."

He bowed low as if to royalty. "And I wish the same for you. Please, consider me your friend and do not hesitate to ask for my help should the occasion ever arise."

He walked her over to where Mrs. Frogerton sat at one of the tables and smiled at Dorothy.

"Good evening, ma'am, Miss Frogerton. Would you care to dance?"

Dorothy winked at Caroline as they exchanged places, and she set off for the dance floor, leaving Caroline with her employer.

"I don't care what he says, my dear, but that man is still quite smitten with you." Mrs. Frogerton waved her fan gently in front of her face.

"He is not," Caroline said calmly. "We have simply agreed to be friends."

"And Dr. Harris over there glowering at the two of you as you danced." Mrs. Frogerton laughed heartily.

"He's annoyed because Lord Francis interrupted a very important conversation we were having with the Price brothers about their sister Rosemary, who also lived here and who disappeared."

"The other R in that portrait?"

"Yes, indeed." Caroline appreciated Mrs. Frogerton's

excellent memory. "Dr. Harris brought his sister here to meet me."

"Right to the hall? That's where he's been?" Her employer shook her head. "Then at least we know she's not dead."

"But her friend is." Caroline told Mrs. Frogerton what had happened to Rose as succinctly as possible.

"The poor girl. Those places sell children to brothels and worse, you know." Mrs. Frogerton shuddered. "I've a charity set up in Bradford to offer women a place to have their babies. It's properly run with every family vetted before they're allowed to take a child away with them."

"Rose said that her friend thought she was in love with someone at the hall. But when she returned, Rosemary had disappeared, and no one would tell her where she'd gone. Rose thought it might have been Mr. Woodford."

"But you said he'd only just been promoted to first footman." Mrs. Frogerton frowned. "He had very little influence about whether Rosemary would get a job at the house."

"Maybe he boasted that he could do so, and when she realized he was lying she broke things off and he killed her."

"That seems rather extreme when all he had to do was sell her services off to one of his dubious contacts and never have to see her again." Mrs. Frogerton paused. "That's far more likely, isn't it? Maybe Rosemary discovered what he and Lady Ines were really doing with the nursery children and threatened to turn him in to Lady Eleanor."

Caroline considered her employer's words. "That's probably what happened, although Dan Price implied that Mr. Woodford had nothing to say about the matter when asked."

"And one might assume that Dan 'asked' when Mr. Woodford was at his mercy."

Caroline gazed at the crowded dance floor, where Mabel

was now dancing with Harry, and Dan with Tina. Both couples looked remarkably pleased with themselves, and why wouldn't they?

"I meant to ask you what your cousin said to Lord Greenwood to make him rush off like that after their dance together," Mrs. Frogerton said.

Caroline blinked and turned to her employer. "I beg your pardon?"

"Lord Greenwood left the ballroom after the first dance. He looked rather unwell."

" 'A rose for a rose, love from N,' " Caroline whispered as she abruptly rose to her feet. "Please excuse me, ma'am."

She didn't wait for permission as she skirted the dancers until she was directly in her cousin's path. When the music ended, Mabel caught her eye and waved.

"Caroline! Isn't this delightful?"

Ignoring everyone around them, Caroline took her cousin's hand and drew her out into the hallway. "What did you say to your father?"

"Oh, *good.*" Mabel's smile widened. "Harry said you'd worked most of it out."

"What did you say to him?"

"Only that we knew what he'd done and that he was next." Mabel met her gaze. "I can hardly let my own father get away with murder, can I?"

"He was involved with Rosemary?"

"Involved in that he ruined her, promised her everything, and then when she became pregnant disposed of her?" Mabel's smile was gone. "You read her journal. I left it for you when I realized you were the only person who understood that Mr. Woodford and Aunt Ines had been deliberately murdered."

"You orchestrated this whole thing?"

"Yes, indeed. I insisted that my birthday ball happened here in front of all my friends. I told Father I'd reveal the lawsuit he'd stupidly started against the Woodfords to

Mother if he didn't make her agree to my request. I felt it would be fitting to bring those who deserved justice to see it being carried out."

"But who appointed you judge, jury, and executioner?"

Mabel shrugged. "Who else had the power to kill those despicable people? There is rarely justice in the courts for those of inferior status—look at how the Harris parents almost lost their own children. No one would even listen to you."

"But—"

"Caroline, my father needed to know that I knew what he had done and that I intended to bring him to justice. He *needed* to experience how it felt to be powerless." Mabel's gaze was absolutely clear. "I told him tonight I was going to marry Harry and that meant he'd murdered my sister-in-law."

"What did he say?"

"Nothing, of course. Why would he?" Mabel's words dripped with contempt. "He turned and ran away like the coward he is."

"Do you intend to pursue him in the courts?" Caroline asked.

"I certainly want him to believe that I will while I negotiate a financial settlement to ensure my marriage to Harry can go ahead."

Caroline stared at her cousin for a long moment. "Blackmail? I thought this was all about justice for the dead."

"It is!" Mabel stamped her foot.

"I'm not sure I believe you, Cousin." Caroline stepped back.

Mabel grabbed hold of her arm in a tight grip. "You won't tell anyone, will you?"

"As you already said, no one would believe me even if I did. Enjoy the rest of your ball, Mabel."

She wrenched free of her cousin's fingers and walked down the connecting corridor, back into the main hall, and onward to the servants' quarters. Rose looked up as she came in and took the seat opposite.

"Miss Morton. Are you quite well?"

Caroline swallowed hard. "I thought you should know Lord Greenwood was Rosemary's lover. She was apparently pregnant when she . . . disappeared."

"When he killed her, you mean?"

Caroline could only nod into the silence. "That is what I believe, yes."

"And will his bloody lordship stand trial for that?" Rose snorted. "Of course he won't. He'll get away with it just like his wife nearly stole us from our parents."

"I understand that he is aware that his guilt is known."

"Much good that will do," Rose muttered. "And her with no resting place for us to remember her by."

"If anyone would listen to me, I would—"

Rose interrupted her. "It's all right, miss. Oliver already told me how hard you've tried to make things right."

"I need to go and tell him what has happened." Caroline rose to her feet. "I just wanted you to know first."

"I appreciate that." Rose sighed. "At least I can give up hoping and start mourning her properly. Thank you for trying, Miss Morton."

Caroline left the butler's rooms and made her way back through to the main hall. Most of the kitchen staff had been given the evening off and would only return to serve a late supper at midnight just before the ball ended.

Dr. Harris was standing at the bottom of the stairs looking upward when she joined him.

"I was wondering where you'd gone."

"I spoke to Mrs. Frogerton, then to my cousin Mabel, and lastly to your sister."

"Don't forget dancing with the charming Lord Francis Chatham, when you swore to me that you didn't intend to dance at all."

"That hardly matters, Dr. Harris. When there are much weightier issues to discuss."

"Such as what?"

"I realized that the journal was inscribed to R from N,

not T for Thomas Woodford. That's my uncle's name—
Nicholas. When I asked Mabel about it, she admitted that
she'd orchestrated the whole thing."

Dr. Harris frowned. "As in the murders?"

"The birthday ball when she insisted all her waifs and
strays were included, the guest list, the pranks, probably
the notes to her own sister, and the manner of how the of-
fenders were to be killed." Caroline gestured wildly. "She
did it and she enjoyed every second."

"I doubt she actually killed anyone herself when she
had so many willing partners in crime." Dr. Harris observed as he took Caroline's shaking hand and walked her
out into the gardens.

"She sees herself as an avenging angel, righting wrongs
that those below her cannot."

"Why does that make you angry?" he asked.

"Because . . ." Caroline shook her head. "It comes
clothed in a threat to reveal her father's past if he won't
give her money to start her life with Harry."

"Hmm." He moved away from her to light a cigar and
leaned back against the stone parapet to observe her. "So,
less an angel of justice and more of a means to an end."

"Exactly."

"And that offends you?" He shrugged. "It seems remarkably pragmatic to me."

"It would."

"Not everyone is as morally correct as you are, Miss
Morton."

"I am hardly that. I removed a two-hundred-pound
note from my great-aunt Ines's possessions and didn't turn
it over to my aunt."

"That reminds me." He dug into his coat pocket. "Here."

She instinctively caught the bag of gold coins he tossed
at her.

"I'm certainly not giving them back to Joshua. I thought
you would be the best person to decide what to do with
them." He raised an eyebrow.

"Mayhap I'll keep them for myself." Caroline defiantly met his gaze. "The sooner I can get Susan out of this house, the better."

His slow smile was worth waiting for. "Good for you, Miss Morton."

"Perhaps I shouldn't be judging Mabel so harshly when I am not so innocent myself."

"Mabel condoned murder. I don't think that is quite your style." He held out his hand. "Now that we have discovered the worst of it, and that no one will listen to either of us even if we presented them with the evidence, will you come and dance with me?"

"What about Rosemary's body?" Caroline asked even as she took his hand. "Doesn't she deserve a Christian burial?"

He looked down at her and sighed. "Then shall we postpone our dance, find Lord Greenwood, and have the matter out with him?"

"Yes, please."

"That's my girl."

They went back into the house and through to the door of Lord Greenwood's study. Caroline knocked but there was no answer. When she peered inside, the room was dark apart from the red glow of the fire.

"Shall I go and see if he has retired for the night?" Caroline asked.

Dr. Harris frowned. "Let's go into the kitchen and ask the staff."

Mrs. Maddox wasn't present, and all the footmen were busy. Nathaniel, the kitchen boy who was keeping the range fires alight, raised his hand at Dr. Harris's inquiry.

"I saw his lordship going down to the stables, sir. He said there was something wrong with one of his prize mares."

"That's exactly the kind of thing that would make him abandon his own daughter's birthday ball," Caroline murmured to Dr. Harris. "He is remarkably selfish."

It was a clear night without a hint of rain, so they decided to venture forth without bothering to change. The light from the ballroom lit up the path as did the full moon. For some reason, Caroline allowed Dr. Harris to hold her hand again, but as he didn't mention it, neither did she.

The stable block was well lit and well maintained. There were few staff around when there were visiting coachmen and footmen to be entertained until the ball ended. Dr. Harris stopped in the middle of the stable yard and raised his head like a hunting dog.

"I hear howling."

"It's probably one of Uncle Nicholas's dogs."

"He has a pack?" Dr. Harris set off toward the corner of the yard.

"Yes, but they're housed in the opposite direction," Caroline said as she followed after him. "Maybe this is one of the house dogs."

She shivered as they approached the closed door. Dr. Harris stopped in front of it and met her anxious gaze. He spoke over the hound's desolate howls.

"May I suggest you stay out here?"

"Why?"

"I think something is amiss." He turned back to the door. "Please wait."

She knew as soon as he opened the door, and the dog ran out still barking frantically. The smell of gunfire, copper, and blood was unmistakable. She turned away with her hand to her mouth.

Eventually, Dr. Harris appeared at the door, his face grim and a splash of blood marking his immaculate linen.

"Miss Morton, could you alert the head coachman? There appears to have been a terrible accident."

Chapter 20

They waited until after the ball to inform Lady Eleanor about her husband's demise. She immediately collapsed and was taken to bed, unaware that Mabel had departed the house with Harry Price for parts unknown. Joshua, Dan, and Tina had disappeared, too. Caroline and the Frogertons stayed because there was no one else to help stabilize the distraught household.

Mrs. Frogerton proved particularly useful in organizing new staff and finding a nurse to care for Lady Eleanor, who appeared to have suffered some kind of stroke, while Caroline focused on the legal necessities with the family solicitor. Nick was recalled from London and arrived promptly, but with little appetite for his new role as head of the family or any idea of how he wished to proceed.

Eliza retired to her home to rest for the sake of her unborn child, leaving George to help Caroline navigate the choppy waters of his father's estate. He'd proven to be an excellent supporter and her respect for him increased tenfold. Dr. Harris had left with his sister without speaking further to Caroline, but Rose had at least written to provide her address at the girls' boarding school in Norwich where she was a teacher.

"You have been very helpful to your family, my dear,"

Mrs. Frogerton said to Caroline as they shared breakfast in the vast and now almost deserted parlor. "Lady Eleanor's condition is improving, and your cousins will be quite capable of managing the estate with a little guidance from Mr. Jones, his land agent."

"You have been very patient with me, ma'am." Caroline managed a smile. "Especially when I am aware that you should be in London with your daughter enjoying her first Season."

"Never mind that." Mrs. Frogerton waved a dismissive hand. "Think of the scandal we bring with us. We will be in high demand."

The news of what had happened at the house party— Lord Greenwood's death and Mabel's elopement—had leaked almost immediately. Even the London papers had gotten hold of the story, and speculation was rife as to both the sequence of events and the notion that Mabel's lover had shot her father before escaping to the Continent.

The fresh scandal had also resurrected all the old stories about the suspicious circumstances surrounding the death of Caroline's father in a similar "shooting accident," which had been remarkably unpleasant for her. In truth she wasn't sure whether she preferred to remain at a house where she wasn't wanted or return to a social circle where she would be ignored or ogled.

"What is keeping you here?" Mrs. Frogerton asked gently. "Are you worried about your sister? I don't think your aunt is in any state to insist that Susan must leave. Even if she was, you must know that there will always be a place for her with me."

"That is beyond kind of you, ma'am. I could not expect—"

Mrs. Frogerton covered Caroline's hand with her own. "She is your family. Where else should she go? I was thinking there might be a school she could attend nearby."

"That is certainly something to consider." Caroline hesitated. "If she wants to live with me, that is. She is still upset about Mabel leaving so abruptly."

Susan had been inconsolable at the loss of her cousin and insisted that Mabel would soon send for her as promised. Persuading Susan to leave Greenwood Hall before she lost hope of that happening seemed unlikely. Caroline was reluctant to force her distraught sister to do anything in case she lost her good will entirely.

"It's not only Susan," Caroline said. "It's Rosemary."

"You wish you knew what had happened to her." Mrs. Frogerton nodded. "It is unfortunate that all the people who could've provided you with an answer to that question are dead."

"Yesterday, George and I were going through some of my uncle's correspondence that he kept in a locked drawer of his desk. We found details of the court case he intended to pursue against the Woodfords," Caroline said. "I wonder if Mabel started her threats of blackmail earlier than we realized and her father tried to prevent a scandal by threatening the Woodfords with the charge of stealing to shut them up?"

"I wouldn't put it past young Mabel. She was remarkably focused for a seventeen-year-old. They so often see everything in black and white and allow for no middle ground," Mrs. Frogerton commented. "Lord Greenwood was probably worried that if the Woodfords spoke up, they might inadvertently reveal what happened to Rosemary Price." She sighed. "It's even possible that he had no knowledge of their more nefarious schemes and just wanted to protect himself. It also explains why Lady Eleanor knew nothing about it."

"There was also a bill for building work that was not in the usual household accounts book my aunt oversaw." Caroline hesitated. "I checked the date, and it is of a similar time period to when Rosemary disappeared."

Mrs. Frogerton considered her carefully. "Then perhaps you should investigate further."

"I must admit that I am almost afraid of what I might find," Caroline confessed.

"Sometimes it's better to face those fears rather than leave them unresolved so they'll haunt you for the rest of your life. If something needs doing, lass, do it now, and then we'll be able to leave for London with a clear conscience."

"Yes, ma'am." Caroline stood. "I'll go and speak to Mr. Jones."

Three hours later she stood with Mr. Jones and the estate carpenter in front of the chimney breast in the back parlor where Great-Aunt Ines had liked to do her needlework. A small pile of rubble lay on the covered hearth along with a bird's nest and a smattering of soot.

She'd made herself return to the nursery to work out which room in the real house would relate to the one in the doll's house where she'd found the note and the doll. While she was there, Hetty had remarked that she'd found the other doll tossed in with the farm and stable animals, which had made Caroline's stomach roll.

"There's something blocking the chimney." The carpenter's voice echoed back down to them. "Looks like someone narrowed the chimney at some point leaving a ledge on the inside just above the mantelpiece. Whatever they left there has shifted over slightly and blocked the flue."

Mr. Jones frowned and shouted up the chimney, "Can you remove the obstruction?"

"I'll try, sir."

There was silence for a moment and then the carpenter spoke again.

"Bloody hell."

He emerged from the chimney, his face ashen against the streaks of soot on his skin.

"I think someone stuffed a body up there." He crossed himself and shuddered. "Gave me a horrible start, that did." He stepped back to stare up at the chimney. "There were always stories about bricked-up nuns haunting this place—maybe they were true after all."

Mr. Jones, who already knew what Caroline suspected, nodded. "Thank you for your efforts, Fred. If it is indeed a body, I will contact the local authorities to determine how to proceed. All I ask is that you keep this matter to yourself until we can determine the identity of the remains."

"I'll keep quiet about it, sir." Fred shuddered. "Don't you worry about that."

He gathered up his tools and left as quickly as he could, leaving Caroline staring at the land agent.

"It seems you might have been right, Miss Morton." He cleared his throat. "Do you have any idea who it might be?"

"I suspect it is Rosemary Price, sir."

"Ah . . ." The land agent paused. "I believe my father might have mentioned that name to me in a private conversation just before he retired. He told me Lord Greenwood had paid her off, and sent her away because she was with child, and that I was never to mention it to her ladyship."

"I don't think he paid her off, Mr. Jones," Caroline said. "I believe he killed her and concealed her body here."

Her companion grimaced. "If your suspicions are correct, one has to wonder whether the old ghost stories gave his lordship the idea of where to hide the body. I'll get the doctor in to take a look before I notify the magistrate in the next county. Does this woman have kin in the village?"

"She has two younger brothers, Harry and Dan, who used to live at the hall as well."

"The men who were here for the ball who have since disappeared. I am beginning to see why they might have feared apprehension if this story had come out. Their connection with Lord Greenwood through their sister would surely have been discovered. It makes one wonder whether his lordship's death was really an accident." He sighed. "I should imagine there will have to be an inquiry."

"I would assume so." Caroline took one last look at the open fireplace. "I am quite certain I can leave this matter in your capable hands, sir. I am due to leave for London tomorrow with my employer."

"I'll be sad to see you go, miss. You've a level head on your shoulders and your help has been invaluable over the past two weeks."

"Thank you." Caroline smiled at him. "Please write and let me know if anything comes out of the inquiry, or if I am needed to give evidence."

"I will certainly do that." He opened the door for her. "Lady Eleanor will be sorry to lose you. I believe even before the ball she was hoping you would stay."

Caroline repressed a shudder and drew her shawl more tightly around her shoulders.

"Unfortunately, my time is no longer my own as I am bound by the terms of my contract with Mrs. Frogerton. I'm sure the new Lord Greenwood will manage everything admirably once he settles in."

Mr. Jones's dubious expression said otherwise, but Caroline didn't need to worry about what happened after her departure. As long as Susan remained safely at the house until she lost hope of Mabel returning and was willing to listen to her sister again, Caroline was content.

She went up the stairs into Mrs. Frogerton's suite, where a lugubrious Peggy was busy packing the trunks for their departure early in the morning. Caroline had already packed her own trunk. She'd left the altered ball gown hanging in the wardrobe as she didn't need a reminder of the ghastly night of the ball and Mabel's unexpectedly frank confession.

Had justice been served in its own twisted way, or had her cousin and her coconspirators gotten away with murder? Caroline could only hope that the discovery of Rosemary's body would allow the Price family, which now presumably included Mabel, to grieve for their sister. Even if the right connections were made between her uncle Nicholas and Rosemary Price, she doubted anything would come of it. She could only hope that those who had conceived of the scheme to wreak havoc on the Greenwood family would live with that guilt forevermore.

And, if that wasn't enough, she was more than willing to offer up her own testimony to try to convict all of them. Mabel might think she was above the law, but the death of her father, and her marriage to a commoner, made her position far more precarious than she perhaps realized. Her brother Nick, like most reformed rakes, was unlikely to bow to her demands for money, which might make the prospect of turning in the Price brothers and Joshua for murder far more palatable.

Caroline was no longer sure whether Mabel's thirst for justice had been genuine or completely self-serving all along. But if her cousin hadn't put the diary in Caroline's room and played around with the dolls in the nursery, Caroline would not have known about Rose and Rosemary, or been able to locate the body. Had someone gossiped about the work done on the chimney at some point, or had one of the nursery children actually seen it happen? Mabel had always been good at getting people to confide in her.

Caroline picked up a stray lace cap that had fallen behind a chair and passed it over to Peggy.

"Thank you, miss." Peggy took the cap. "I've decided to take up Miss Frogerton's offer. I'll be traveling up to London with you all."

"That's wonderful news," Caroline said. "I think you will be a great success."

"We'll see about that." Peggy curtsied, her cheeks flushed with excitement. "I won't sleep a wink!"

Peggy left and Mrs. Frogerton turned to Caroline.

"Did they find anything?"

"Yes. Mr. Jones is alerting the coroner, the magistrate, and the local doctor."

"God rest her soul, and may she finally be at peace," Mrs. Frogerton murmured. "Tell your aunt when you see her that I'll pay for the burial in the local churchyard so she can rest with her kin."

"I wasn't planning on seeing my aunt." Caroline went over to the dressing table and started sorting out the contents of Mrs. Frogerton's extensive jewelry box. "What could I possibly say to her now?"

"You'll think of something," Mrs. Frogerton said bracingly. "Go and do it now so you'll be ready to leave in the morning with a pure conscience."

"I've failed to bring a single person to justice, ma'am. I feel only guilt."

"You solved an old mystery, lass. Whether or not you think you've been successful isn't important. You've done your best and now you'll move on." Mrs. Frogerton gestured at the door. "Now go and speak to your aunt and when you come back, we can go down to dinner together."

"Yes, ma'am."

Caroline did as she was told. After her week in the country, returning to the rigors of a social Season suddenly seemed far less daunting. She'd dealt with her ex-fiancé, bested her aunt, grown to appreciate her employer, and survived to tell the tale. What more could life possibly have in store for her?

She knocked on her aunt's door and went in. The nurse who was sitting by the fire reading a book glanced up and smiled.

"She's awake if you wish to speak to her, miss. She had a comfortable night."

Caroline turned to face her aunt, who was propped up against her pillows. The right side of her face appeared distorted and her hand was curled into a tight fist like a claw.

"I came to say goodbye. As soon as I am settled, I will contact you about Susan coming to live with me."

"I . . . didn't know," Eleanor whispered, her words slightly slurred. "I refuse to be blamed for anything."

Caroline simply looked at her.

"Dr. Harris told me what had occurred. I was unaware of the lawsuit your uncle filed, and of what was going on with the children in my care." A tear slid down Eleanor's cheek. "I would *never* . . ."

"I am sorry for your loss, Aunt, and regret that I won't be able to attend my uncle's funeral." Caroline continued steadily, unwilling to allow her aunt's sudden remorse to sway her. "I'm leaving for London tomorrow morning. I'm sure George will keep me informed as to your progress."

"I see you are as unforgiving as your father."

"Perhaps it is a family trait." Caroline curtsied. "Thank you for everything you did for us. I will never forget that or cease to be grateful."

Eleanor turned her face to the wall and Caroline walked out of the bedroom without a backward glance.

As she returned to Mrs. Frogerton's suite, she took the time to notice the sun shining through the salt-hazed windows, the slight smell of the marshes beyond, and the overwhelming quiet. She might not return to Greenwood Hall, but she would never forget it. She wasn't sure if it was her imagination, but the house seemed lighter now, the bad memories cleansed, the wrongs brought into the light and righted.

There had been no sign of Mabel or the rest of her conspirators since they'd fled on the night of the ball. Caroline doubted her cousin Nick would bestir himself to pursue them while he was still busy attempting to learn how to manage the estates. He might change his mind if Mabel started demanding money, but that would have nothing to do with Caroline, which was remarkably freeing.

She paused for one last time to look out of the window that faced the lake and beyond that the narrow straits of the Broads and the flat landscape surrounding them. All was serene and comfortingly familiar. Caroline took a deep breath and slowly let it out.

Life would go on; the tragedies and echoes of the past would always linger, but she had a new life to live and she intended to pursue it without remorse.

"Caroline?" She turned to see Mrs. Frogerton standing at her door. "Are you almost ready to go down to dinner?"

"Yes, indeed, ma'am." She smiled. "I am coming right now."